None there are to believe how long I have lived, or how long I have waited, while uncounted millions of little mortal men have strutted the earth, and bred like the pigs they are, and slew and slew. So much of the Old Knowledge was lost that what remains—in the hands of these "Druids"—is but the ghost of the shadow of the shadow of what *I* know!

But I have *lived;* I have remained on this earth in this dimension, whilst others have died and returned scores of times. And now . . . at last I will have my vengeance, after a hundred and eighty centuries . . .

THE UNDYING WIZARD

More Swords-and-Sorcery from
Ace Science Fiction. . . .

The CORMAC MAC ART series, based on the legendary Irish hero created by Robert E. Howard, written by Andrew J. Offutt, the popular author of heroic fantasy.

#1. THE MISTS OF DOOM—*Cormac's boyhood, and why he fled Ireland.*

#2. THE TOWER OF DEATH—Available in August, 1982—*Cormac and Wulfhere grounded in Spain.*

#3. WHEN DEATH BIRDS FLY—Written with Keith Taylor—*The sequel to TOWER OF DEATH.*

#4. SWORD OF THE GAEL—*REH's old villain Thulsa Doom makes a comeback.*

#5. THE UNDYING WIZARD—*The fight against Thulsa Doom continues!*

#6. SIGN OF THE MOONBOW—*Sequel to THE UNDYING WIZARD.*

Also by Andrew J. Offutt:

KING DRAGON (Illustrated)
CONAN THE SORCERER (Illustrated)
CONAN THE MERCENARY (Illustrated)
And don't miss Andy Offutt's tales in Robert Asprin's wildly popular swords-and-sorcery anthology series: Thieves' World, Tales From the Vulgar Unicorn, and Shadows of Sanctuary.

THE UNDYING WIZARD

BY **ANDREW J. OFFUTT**

SF

ace books

A Division of Charter Communications Inc.
A GROSSET & DUNLAP COMPANY
51 Madison Avenue
New York, New York 10010

THE UNDYING WIZARD
Copyright © 1976 by Andrew J. Offutt and Glenn Lord, agent
for the Estate of Robert E. Howard

An ACE Book

First Ace printing: February 1982
Published Simultaneously in Canada

4 6 8 0 9 7 5 3
Manufactured in the United States of America

Acknowledgments

The author wishes to express thanks to Robert Adams and Chuck Holst and others who helped with information and books (including the authors of 131 books and encyclopedic articles); and Kirby; and, for letting him see and feel what it's *really* like:

HRM Albert Von Dreckenveldt,
Baron Würm Wald, MK, KSCA, OL

Sir Polidor Haraldsson, KSCA, OL, OGW

—and others of the Middle Kingdom

to
Jodie of the Erin-born
until further notice

CONTENTS

Prologue

The enormous reptile lay in a cavern passage, eerily lit by some means surely preternatural; sorcerous, perhaps. Walls and ceiling *glowed*. The strange illumination was dim, pearly, hardly akin to that of torch or lamp, much less the sun—which could not pierce the cavern's ceil of earth and rock beneath the man-made pile of masonry that capped the thick natural layer. The pale light emanated from the very walls of the world-old tunnel itself.

In this weird luminous emanation from a source not visible the great reptile lay, a green monster twisted as a vine on rocky soil.

Several times the length of a man the creature was, and nigh as thick. It lay motionless in a great lake of red-brown cruor. The blood had thickened and crusted over in coagulation, so that it shone as if glowing, reflecting the wall-light. The serpent was still. Its eyes, the colour of new flax and large as a man's eyes, were filmed over.

Yet it gave off no stench, nor was it bloated. There was no sign of putrefaction. Nevertheless, the monster was dead. Its great twisted tree-trunk of a body bore the many wounds that had ended its life. It had been stabbed and hacked, sliced and chopped.

1

No juices remained in that prodigious corpse; the number of wounds and its own volcanically violent death throes had seen to that.

It was fearsome, even in death. No ordinary man had brought red death upon this haunter of subterrene passageways.

In a somber cavern beneath the earth beneath a towering castle of extraordinary antiquity, the reptile that appeared to be the father of all snakes lay dead.

And . . . it moved.

Only the hint of a shudder was that movement— but no, it was a *shimmer,* giving but the weird illusion of motion. A Something stirred within the corpse. Some . . . *thing* was struggling to gain freedom from its prison of death.

In the whelming silence of a tomb, the air stirred about the great snout. Slowly, above the moribund shell of the reptile, a haze formed. It spread, lengthened, billowed only slightly, and rose. Tenuous, wavering creepers of mist shuddered on the stale air of the cavern. Luminous walls were clearly visible through the gossamer floating haze. It was blue-grey, that ever-shifting amorphous cloudlet; the colour of human death.

Yet about it there was nothing human.

For just a moment among the fleeting motes of time, the necrotic haze seemed to coalesce, as if attempting to form a shape: rounded at the top, pierced below by two holes, narrow and latticed below—a death's-head.

But that was gone in an instant, nor were there living eyes present to have seen.

The mist floated up, free of the serpentine corpse that had spawned it. It moved, and surely there was *purpose* in the flowing movement of that faint cloud of haze along the subterranean corridor.

The passage bent and twisted again and again, as though formed by a restless reptile—or by long-dead men who had sought to confuse and slow possible pursuit. For though the mist-thing moved away from it, the tunnel gave off a concealed passage in the centuries-old castle above.

The mist-thing drifted along above a dusty, ever-descending floor of packed earth. Around convoluted turnings and twistings writhed the wraithy haze, and it touched nothing but air, this form of life from death that trailed in eerie silence through the soundless channel beneath the earth.

Then it paused, writhing in air. It hovered above . . . another corpse.

The body was that of a man. Old he had been, aged enough to have died of natural causes. But there was visible evidence to the contrary. He who had been tall and unusually thin wore a cowled robe, dark as night. Cloth covered his reed-thin body from head to instep. He lay belly down, and in the center of the robe's back a darker stain spread. Dried trails of it led over the fabric to the corridor's floor of packed, dust-piled earth. The splotch and its coagulated runnels were a reddish brown, like old rust. The robed man had been stabbed from behind and had got his death thereby.

Grey and white, forming silver, were his beard and the hair that straggled limp as corn tassels from his head over his cheek. Grey too were his eyes, nearly white in the paleness. Though open, they saw nothing. Bony hands with fingers like claws had not even torn at the tunnel floor; he had been dead even as he fell. Open too was his mouth in a rictus that had been a gasp or cry.

The hovering mist lowered. Wraithy tendrils of transparent blue-grey touched the corpse, as though the amorphous haze-thing was putting forth exploratory pseudopods.

One of them entered the open mouth of the dead man.

Swiftly then, like smoke somehow filtering *into* a bottle, the haze entered the corpse.

Then all was quiet and still, and none was there to measure the passage of time. Minutes, or hours, or days, or weeks or months . . . they were as nothing to the dead—and to the mist-thing.

The seagreen serpent lay dead, and it began to rot. Well away along the twisting corridor beneath the earth, the robed man lay dead. And the mist had vanished, as silently and hazily as it had appeared, from one corpse and into another.

The body of the robed man did not swell, or rot.

Then, in that silence and motionlessness of death, there was movement.

It was fingers that twitched; the fingers of the right hand of the dead man.

They curled, clawing inward and leaving trails in the dust of the ancient cavern. Hardly more than bone, these fingers straightened again. And curled once more.

A ripple flowed through night-dark fabric as the dead man's left leg moved, only a twitch like the rigour after death—but he had been dead far too long for that.

Both arms bent. Both bone-lean hands moved back toward the body. They planted themselves, palms down, at the shoulders. The head moved. Lank silver hair stirred. The hands pressed down. Buskin-shod feet scraped.

The corpse pushed itself up from the dusty floor.

On its feet, the dead man who was not dead wavered, tottered on long-still legs. A hand swung out to slap the earthen wall, as a brace for a body that had long lain prone. A long moaning sound issued from the thin slash of a mouth. All through the tall form, a great shudder ran. Then, as though just remembering, the mouth closed.

The head turned on its thin neck with another stirring of shoulder-length hair like lifeless silver thread. One hand, the right, rose before the face. It turned there, like a specimen the dead eyes studied, while the robe's dolmen sleeve slid down. Revealed was a wrist that was only skin drawn over bone like hide tedded for its tanning.

The skin was not tan, but nearly white, like new linen.

The hand slapped the chest, moved over the face. It traced out the high forehead, the deep crag-surmounted sockets of the pale, pale eyes, that thin nose with its porcelain-like nostrils, the gaunt cheeks, the mouth that was little more than a horizontal gash between mustache and ashy beard.

The resurrected corpse, alone beneath the earth . . . spoke.

"*Thin,* O Great Serpent, this body—merely skin over bone like the fine parchment of Vanara stretched over stone to dry!" The voice that issued from the corpse was soft, almost a whisper. "A lean body, far from young. A priest, a seer, a mage—a *Druid,* it is called. From a land called Norge, where the ice remains long and snow falls and lies ever atop the craggy peaks, and wind howls cold to cut like a chariot-wheel's scythe."

Up leaped robe-swathed arms, to raise clenched fists on high.

"ALIVE! Alive and in the form of a man once more, with *hands,* aye and feet to walk the earth again! *Cutha Atheldane.* That was the name of the life-force that quickened this body before mine animated it anew."

The Undead man laughed aloud and turned quite around in its jubilation.

"ALIVE! One is grateful for having been snatched from eternal exile in that other dimension that would have been like mortal death, from the life-sucking sword. Yet . . . to have lain here, waiting, handless and voiceless in the body of a son of the Great Serpent . . . for *eighteen thousand years!* Ah!"

Again he turned about, he who had been Cutha Atheldane, Druid of Norway and was now . . . some-one else, someThing else. His movements were quick and more sure now, animated by one of the strongest life-forces that had ever existed, one that had lived and trod the earth before Atlantis *rose* from the deeps, let alone sank.

"Cutha Atheldane am I, then!" And he laughed. Exultant, was the new Cutha Atheldane. He moved, he cried out his joy.

But he did not breathe.

"One hundred eighty centuries! Ah, Chaos that existed before all and will reign again, a hundred and eighty times a hundred years! But a moment in eternity, aye—but what an eternity to have been held here by both stone and spell . . . and in a body with neither voice nor hands! And liberated . . ."

Cutha Atheldane, who was not Cutha Atheldane, broke off in a short laugh that would have raised the hackles of a dog and sent birds aflying.

"Ah I knew him, I recognized him at once, ere even he came floundering like a barbarian puppet down into my prison . . . to release me by slaying the serpent's body that incarcerated me! I know ye for who ye *were,* not who ye are *now!* In any incarnation would I know thee, ancient enemy, barbarian king on a throne of fiery gems—a throne you *usurped* after slaying the noble lord who sat it!"

The voice trailed off like whispering leaves when the wind dies. When it commenced anew it was much lower, quiet now, and full of menace and deadly purpose.

"None there are to believe how long I have lived, or how long I have waited, while uncounted millions of little mortal men have strutted the earth, and bred like the pigs they are, and slew and slew, and so much of the Old Knowledge was lost that what remains—in the hands of these 'Druids'—is but the ghost of the shadow of the shadow of what *I* know! But I have LIVED, I have remained on this earth in this dimension, whilst others died and returned scores of times. And now . . . at last I will have my vengeance, after a hundred and eighty centuries."

The risen dead man looked about, ruminating. "First I must be *invited* to leave this isle, for still I am bound here by the old spell. But . . . I shall come to thee, you who men know now as Cormac mac Art of Connacht in Eirrin! I . . . will . . . have . . . my . . . VENGEANCE!"

And as the tall and cadaverous figure in the night-dark robe hurled aloft both arms amid a flapping of full tapering sleeves, the eyes and lips of his visage seemed to waver and vanish, to be replaced for an instant by a ghastly, grinning, chalk-white skull!

The most powerful and dedicatedly evil sorcerer in the world's history was loose again on the face of the earth.

Chapter One:
Eight-and-twenty Picts

Sped by strong hands at its ten banks of oars, the hide-covered ship—or long boat—clove the water as though with good wind behind. Yet its blue sail was furled, for no air stirred the sea that basked so lazily in the sun betwixt Britain and Eirrin. Only where the ship passed was the bluegreen water disturbed; it foamed cloud-white along the little ship and for a short distance in its wake.

The men at the oars had set aside their helmets, some of which sprouted horns, while one was decorated with feathers and still another trailed a horsehair plume after the Roman fashion. Long was the hair of these men, plaited or caught back by a thong, and there was but one among the crew of that lone vessel whose locks were more dark than the colour of new copper. Some of the oarsmen were daubed on face and arms with blue paint or dye. Others wore no such paint, though the face of one huge-armed fellow was etched with a scar so fierce it might have been mistaken for a red dye, only slightly faded.

Three men were aboard who rowed not.

One stood well forward; another manned the tiller. Wargirt they both were, and brawny.

He at the prow wore no helm, but he had chosen to crown his dark yellow hair with a cap made of catskins. From that barred cap sprouted a little plume of seven eagle feathers. Bronze were the bracers on his arms, one blade-etched from some past time when it had saved his shield-hand. His tunic was blue; over it he wore an excellent leathern jerkin that covered him from collarbones to his thighs just below his genitals. The cordwain belt slung at his hips supported a dagger on either side. He wore no sword. This man's weapon, with a broad thong forming a loop where it had been stoutly wet-tied in a groove ringing the haft, was an ax. Its head was invisible, covered with an oiled cowhide bag against the salt spray.

The ax-man's feet and ankles were laced into what were unmistakably *caligulae,* the short boots of the Roman legionaries who had for so long ruled his land . . . and protected it from those many who now came from oversea to carve it up among themselves; Saxons and Angles, Jutes and Frisians, Irish and Danes; aye, and from the north over the old wall, Picts and the Scoti of Alba that the Romans had called Caledonia.

The blond ax-man at the prow looked asea.

The man at the stern wore a sword, long at his left hip and down his leg. Though he stood the deck of a hide-covered longboat and with his light auburn hair plaited behind each ear to fall down his back, the sword had surely belonged to a darker man more at home astride a horse; it was a *spatha,* a Roman cavalryman's sword. No adornment relieved his helmet, which was composed of four bands of dull grey metal laid onto a soft leathern caul. He too wore a jerkin of boiled leather, over a tunic of grey wool. The score or more steel rings fixed to the front of that plain lorica were as much reinforcing protection as decoration. This man's full drooping mustachioes contained more bronze-red than his braids.

Oars creaked and thumped. Men grunted; water gurgled and swished, and the twenty-oared boat seemed to scud on the very surface of the sea as it swept forward, with unusual smoothness. Its heading was southerly.

The man at the bow was gazing southwestward, ahead and to starboard. Gazing that way as well were the auburn-haired man at the tiller and the third of those who did not row.

The blond ax-man at the prow moved his left arm out from his side, almost stiffly. It was fisted but for the forefinger, which pointed. With a nod, though no eyes were turned his way, the man at the stern changed the pressure of his tanned hands on the tiller. The ship, which was little more than fifty feet in length, did not veer, but angled to port; eastward, on its southerly bearing.

The blond at the bow glanced back. His nose had once been broken and was askew, nor did he quite close his mouth, ever.

"Irish," he grunted, just loud enough to be heard by three-and-twenty men.

An oarsman to port asked, "Reavers?"

"I think not. Cynwas?"

"I think not," the steersman said, just as quietly. "They'd be fighting else, Bedwyr, not suffering that . . . harassment."

"Leaguered about by wolves," Bedwyr the blond ax-man said, and there was amusement in his voice. "They'll not see this sun set, though it's soon crimson they'll see!"

"Wolves?" This from another oar-plier, a man with a break in his beard from an old slash of sword or knife; surely no ax could have sliced him so without wrecking his jaw.

Bedwyr said, "Aye."

"Picts," Cynwas said from the stern.

"This far south? What be *Picts* doing this far south of their damned heather?"

"Or this far east," Bedwyr said. "Mayhap they be Picts from far side Hibernia."

Silent had been the third man who was not rowing, and him nigh-naked. Now he spoke.

"*Eirrin*, ye corn-headed ass. Eirrin! Ye talk like a Roman . . . miss ye your masters so much, ye Briton molester of ewes?"

The blond at the prow turned to stare at the speaker. He was a great burly giant of a man with a red mane and full bushy beard.

"Ye talk foolishly free for a man bound to a ship's mast, Dane! Be ye so anxious to be oped up for the sun to bake your drunkard's gizzard?"

The bound man grinned. He wore only a dirty tunic that had been red before its dyes succumbed to wear and sun and salt water and sweat. Now, but for the soil, it was lighter in colour than his full beard.

"It were better than having to list to your stupidity, Briton."

Bedwyr of Britain cheated his captive, who was bound so that he must remain standing and stare straight ahead, like a stronge bow ornament moved back amidships. The blond Briton only grinned, and turned away.

"Row. An they see us, they all be far too busy— and about to be busier still—to trouble us. Nor need we have worry of them."

The oarsmen rowed. The ship of Britons—and captive Dane—swept on to the south and east, well east of the Eirrinish craft "leaguered about by wolves."

Aboard that beleaguered ship from the land of Eirrin, caught by the same calm and now by the swift boats of its harriers, a man watched the vessel from Britain. A tall, rangily built man he was, deepchested and manifestly strong, his eyes deeply planted and slitted, grey as steel or ice. The distance was too great for faces to be seen; had there been aught of the crew of the other craft he knew, he'd not have recognized him. The hair of the ax-man at the prow seemed sun-white from this vantage.

"They go on."

The words came from the warrior beside the tall and rangy man; this one was both short and slight, and wearing a bronze-studded leathern cap that covered brow and cheeks, ears and nape.

"Aye. Ours be no business of theirs. It's a broad sea, and it bears up many peoples. Those be neither Gaul nor Pict, and if it's Celts they are—not likely—it's not from Eirrin but Britain they sail."

"Britain!" called up one of the men at the oars. "The Britons be no seafarers!"

"Some fare asea."

The small beardless warrior spoke nervously: "Could . . . might their destination be . . . the same as ours?"

"No no, dairlin' girl," the tall man said. He too was beardless, his narrow-slitted eyes giving him a peculiarly sinister aspect. Though he was of Eirrin, his squarecut hair was black as the shaggy mops of the men in their hideboats round about them. He wore neither beard nor jewellery.

He went on, "How could they be knowing of it? Samaire-heim be not known in their land—nor any other, save wherever it is Wulfhere may be. Nay, they be reavers as I was, though Crom and Manannan only know what they do so far south—HA!"

His shout was elicited by the arcing up of an arrow from one of the little hideboats that sought to encircle his vessel of fourteen oars; the flint tipped shaft fell short.

"HA!" the tall man barked out again. "Try on, Picts—once one of ye comes close enough to bounce one of your puny sticks off this ship, I'll huff and puff until I blow over your snailshell!"

A cry of rage was the reply from the archer; the dark, squat men of Pictdom were not known for sense of humour.

In the Irish craft, a man called. "A fine threat, Cormac. But . . . what do we *do?* There be fourteen of these 'snail-shells' as ye're after styling them, and us between them like a man running the Behlfires!"

The dark man named Cormac looked about.

Two Pictish boats trailed the little ship he commanded. Six paced it on either side. They might have been an escort, save that the Picts were friend to none in the world but themselves. Cormac knew that an ancestor of his had been friend and fighting companion to the last great Pictish king, Bran Mak Morn, years ago. That meant nothing now, either to the squat swarthy men or to the current bearer of the name Cormac mac Art of Connacht in Eirrin.

Small were the Pictish boats, of well-scraped hide rubbed with butter so that they were as if faced with glass that sparkled in the sun flashing on the placid waters. In each were two Picts, armed with spear and knife—and oar. A few had bows and arrows. The two-man craft were light and swift-gliding. Full a hand's breadth had the sun moved in the sky since the little flotilla had intersected the ship's course. Nor did the barrel-chested rowers seem in the least winded, nor minded to abandon their odd, paralleling chase.

"Ah for a wind," Cormac said with anger and longing, "a *wind,* that we might leave behind these apish scum from Time's dawn who seek our very hearts!"

He glowered ferociously about at the ringing skin-boats, *de curucis* or *curraghs:* caracks. All remained just outside the distance to which any sensible man would seek to speed a spear. And few used the bow, which was a hunting tool, rather than a weapon of war.

Cormac snapped, "A-port!"

The steersman responded at once. Swiftly his craft began to move away from the caracks on their right. Nearly as swiftly, the Pictish boats to port swung away, nimble little craft rowed by experts.

In his anger and desperation Cormac himself snatched up arrow and bow of yew and sent a shaft at that skinboat which seemed nearest. The Picts howled in derision; Cormac mac Art was an indifferent archer at best.

"What do we *do?*"

Cormac looked at the short, leather-capped warrior at his side. "Row," he said, in a snarl. "Go on. And hope for *wind!*" He glanced half the length of the ship at the druid.

The man in the robe of forest green either did not notice, or affected not to feel the accusing gaze. But he made answer, staring straight before him as though talking to himself.

"Behl and Crom," he said, "cede power asea to Manannan mac Lyr and the Morrigu of the waves. And Manannan, as all seafarers know, is deaf from the roar of the surf."

Cormac blinked. "In all my years asea," he muttered, "I never heard *that.*"

The warrior beside him smiled, but wisely kept silent.

"CORMAC!"

The Gael spun at the alarmed shout of his name. Seeing the pointing finger, he wheeled. The Pictish boats to starboard, all six, were closing on his ship. Cormac's reaction was not understood by those possessed of more patience and less experience and warlike joy than this Gael among Celts: Cormac grinned.

"Lugh!" he snapped. "Ferdiad!"

With grunts Lugh and Ferdiad shipped their oars, Ferdiad the first to starboard, Lugh the last. So had Cormac placed them, after giving both careful instructions and some small rehearsal. These two were better archers than their comrades along that side, and they knew their duties. Each man snatched up bow and clapped on helmet; each wore a jerkin of well-boiled leather, and long bracers on both arms.

Lugh and Ferdiad moved quickly into position at the starboard hull's bulwark, looked, ducked, nocked, pulled string, rose, released, ducked again. The shafts may perhaps have taught some small respect; otherwise they were ineffective.

Cormac's grin faltered not. He'd trained these two hunters well. No sooner were they again hunkered below the top of the bulwark than four arrows whished over their heads. The Pictish shafts passed completely over the ship. One persuaded a portside oarsman to helmet himself.

"HARD A-PORT!" Cormac bawled.

At the same time, he pounced like a panther to Ferdiad's oar. A mighty pull he gave that foremost oar, so that the men behind him felt the sudden ease in their own pulling. Their lean captain's strength was astonishing. The steersman had responded, and Cormac's impulsive move added to the ship's sharp swerve. Ferdiad sprawled; Lugh again straightened and launched an arrow. Like all others thus far, it found no fleshy home.

The ship's stern was more effective. It crushed a carack in its swing. With a cry, one nearly naked Pict went flying to splash, thrown twice the length of his own body. The other man of that boat was surely more fortunate than brilliant; with a warrior's reflexes he was able to grasp the tiller even as his boat, spear, oar and bow were lost to him.

Like most of his kind he was a short, dark man with long arms slung from prodigiously broad, meaty shoulders. He clung fast to the tiller. The ship lurched. The steersman cursed. Cormac's voice rose too, cursing magnificently in two, then three languages.

"The fatherless dog clings to the tiller!" the steersman cried.

"Shake him off!" Cormac wrestled with his oar. "Up oars and sweep: One . . . Two . . . Ferdiad! No!"

"It's shaking him off I'll be," the hunter had muttered, and he rose to hurry sternward and put an arrow into the clinging enemy.

Even as Cormac shouted his warning, Ferdiad's right cheek sprouted a gout of blood and a flint arrowhead. The shaft had entered his other cheek to smash through his mouth and pass completely through his face. Ferdiad was choking on his own blood even as he fell—onto the third starboard oar. Both that oarsman's curse and his look of horror were purely reflexive. Again Cormac too cursed; already chaos threatened, rising and shaking its shoulders like a grim spectre over his ship.

Shouts arose both within the Irish vessel and on both sides now, and the ship wheeled insanely. Its oars whipped back and forth less than a meter above water level.

To a god looking down from the dual vantage points of height and immortal lack of concern, the scene might have been amusing.

The Irish ship was like a mighty horse, beset by a swarm of rabid cats. Already it had kicked one—and been scratched. Those to port had started to close just after their comrades on the far side, and then suddenly their prey had swung about, like a mindlessly bucking stallion. It bore down upon them to divide their number yet again or crush one of them under its hard hooves. Next it was bucking like an unbroken colt under its first rider, swinging this way and that, oars lashing out like flying deadly hooves, while one tenacious attacker clung to the hoof that was its tiller.

And now the ship lost momentum. Pictish yells rose triumphant on both sides. They howled like wolves now, not cats.

"Stupid," Cormac muttered, to none save himself. "Had I known these men to be seasoned competents, and Samaire not aboard, I'd have ordered all oars shipped and *allowed* this attack, long ago!"

Now battle had been forced upon him, nor was he unhappy.

Jerking in his oar, he bellowed the order for the other rowers to do the same. Then the mail-coated Gael was on his feet and snatching up spear and buckler. The sword at his side was a fine weapon— once the enemy had pressed in too close for good spear-work.

"The mad-dogs want to board!" he bawled. "The worse for them . . . EIR-R-R-R-RIN-N-N-N-NNNN!"

It was merely the first rallying shout that sprang into his mind; long a weapon man and a sea-roving reaver as well, Cormac well knew the value to men of a battle cry—any battle cry. It was one more aid to the heating of the blood.

Naturally the shout was instantly taken up by those about him, as would have been any but the most ridiculous. The fire-eyed screamers included the short warrior in the studded leathern cap and strange high boots who'd stood beside him . . . Samaire that warrior's name. Samaire of Leinster of Eirrin.

Weighted ropes flew. Some ended in grappling hooks. Others were knotted about stones, one of which sent a son of Eirrin to his knees, clutching his arm. Then Cormac was beside him, his eyes terrible. Without releasing either spear or buckler, the Gael boosted the jagged stone up with his bronze-bossed shield, lifted, and hurled it back over the side.

And ten more came over the bulwarks of the hull, on either side.

The Picts kept up their awful wolf-howling as they attacked, for this was their battle cry both to spur and excite themselves and to shake the enemy. Frail skin-boats rocked as squat men stood in them, tugging at their grapple-ropes. Men from time's dawn they were, avatars out of place in this age—and knowing it.

Deagad mac Damain, who'd kissed his plump Dairine farewell and vowed they'd *demand* her hand of her father on his return, a hero, thrust with his good spear at a burly dark man who stood below, in his boat. The nearly naked Pict deflected the spearpoint with a twisting movement of his shield that turned the jab into a scraping carom accompanied by a grating ear-assaulting noise. At the same time, he miraculously kept his footing in the rocking carack. Without pause the black-haired man drove the tip of his own spear, a jagged wedge of flint the length of his hand, straight up into young Deagad's eye. It ran deep, destroying eye and pricking brain. Deagad lurched backward with a moan rather than a cry. The Pict, whipping back his spear, cocked his arm and launched the death-tipped stave at another man who leaned over his ship's bulwark fifteen feet away, engaged in a thrust-and-parry spear-duel with another attacker.

Deagad's killer looked astonished when a dark, scarred son of Eirrin appeared and, swifter than any man should have moved, bashed the spear away, only inches from its intended victim.

"Take MY spear, Pict!" Cormac yelled.

His hurled spear burst into the chest of Deagad's slayer with such force that it tore out of his back to the length of a tall man's foot. Pict and boat went over; only the shining skinboat remained on the surface of the water. Its surface darkened suddenly as with red dye.

Cormac's crew were not seasoned seamen, nor had any save one so much as seen a Pict before. While they howled like the dread wolves of the forests they loved, the little apelike men the Romans had called

Pictii—the very old ones, or aborigines—fought like bulls. They *charged*, heedless of defense against them. Mothers of Eirrin frightened their children with tales of the awful Picts, with long greasy black hair and woad-daubed faces. It was said too, and often, that a Pict was harder to reduce to that final twitchless death than a cat.

With a battle-mad, blood-loving ferocity and overwhelming momentum, several had gained the ship. It was not that those who should have kept them away were terrified; they were worse: disconcerted, and caught up in memories of old and horrid tales.

Nevertheless Cormac brought death of wound or water on three, and one pouncing man of Pictdom drove his head straight onto the point of Samaire's spear, which was wrenched from her hands as he dropped into the water. Her arm whipped across her belly under her loose mailcoat and dragged out her sword; Picts were aboard and sons of Eirrin were down.

Hand in hand with the grim god of war, red chaos, the oldest god of all, seized the rocking ship.

Steel flashed in the sunlight like behlfire.

Men—and a woman—shouted and screamed and iron clangour rose loudly. Spears jabbed, knives and swords and two axes flashed and swept. Men reeled on hard-braced feet. Blood spattered and flowed.

A slashing sword taken from the corpse of a slain Irish struck blue sparks from the helm of another son of Eirrin. Beside him another sword struck through hide-armour and flesh and muscle and into bone, and whipped back trailing a flying wake of blood that spattered and smeared ship and woundless men.

Dark eyes blazed with animal blood-lust while whistling blades clanged on shields, skittered skirling over mail byrnies, found vulnerable flesh. Even though the short-hafted ax that struck his shield nigh broke that arm against his own body, Ros mac Dairb of far Dun Dalgan remembered their captain's counsel to *thrust*, not slash. He thrust, and was rather surprised at feel of resistance at his point, then a lessening as it went on, as though into a good haunch of meat. Surprising too was the sudden flare of the dark eyes of the stock man before him, and his guttural gasp. Ros of Dun Dalgan remembered to yank back his blade, and saw the bubble of blood over the Pict's lips even as he stuck him again, though it were unnecessary.

A Pictish head with a gaping mouth flew from one side of the ship to the other in a shower of blood. The man who had swung that decapitating blow so dear to the heart of a weapon-man set his lips and teeth in a grim, ugly grin. For beside him was the former exile from Eirrin's shores, the former reaver of several coasts, the reigning Champion of Eirrin, Cormac mac Art an Cliuin—and Cormac said "Beautifully done, Connla!" and Connla glowed, and struck with sword and parried with buckler, and he died not that day but emerged scatheless as though god-protected.

There were few duels in that howling, clangourous melee. A man parrying the stroke of a second while slashing or stabbing at a third was often wounded or given his death by a fourth, and sometimes by accident. Bright red dotted the air and gleamed on helm and mailcoat, jerkin and blade and skin. And on the deck, where footing grew precarious with flowing scarlet and moveless corpses.

"Och, I love to fight!" Brian of Killevy enthused, and hewed away an arm.

Men died, or were sore wounded, or were wounded and got their deaths from another's hand, almost negligently, or took wounds that slew them later rather than at once. A hacked calf guaranteed a Pict a limp the rest of his days—had not the boss of Cormac mac Art's shield smashed his face and, in crushing his nose, driven splinters of its bone into his brain.

Some who fell or reeled had eyes of blue or grey; others' were black as the bracelets of polished coal they wore on their thick dark arms.

It was a princess of Eirrin's Leinster who took a swordcut on the helm that made her head ring and formless grey dance before her eyes, and who drove a booted foot into the crotch of him who had landed that blow turned by her bronze-bossed helmet, then spitted the enemy's mouth and nose and most of his chin on her sword. The Pict died without even knowing it was a woman had sped his soul. Samaire took a cut on the hand too, and was pinked in the right forearm, but managed to crush that attacker's face with her buckler's boss even as his sword dropped.

Sons of Eirrin fought the better for her presence among them, for she was like unto Agron goddess of slaughter that day, or Scathach, the war goddess whose tutoring had made invincible the hero Cuchulain of Muirthemne.

It was she who ferociously out-shouted the Picts, and was hoarse three days after, while limping from the thwack of a shield-edge against her leathershod shin.

And then the ship was clear of living Picts.

So too was the sea all about, save for one. He had plunged overside and, gaining a carack, began paddling madly away. A hard-flung spear missed him but brast through the bottom of his boat, so that he was forced to leave it there, a strange sail-less mast, lest by withdrawing the point he was reduced to floating while he baled.

Yet there could be no immediate rest for the victors, each of whom was ghoulishly blood-spattered, for it had fountained on that weltering ship this day and those without scathe were bloody as their wounded comrades.

There was the gory, twice-unpleasant business of pitching overside Pictish corpses—and pieces, including three limbs, a grimacing head, and a ghastly long coil of pink sausage from a sundered belly.

Even then none could sink down gasping to rest; there were the wounded to see to, and the dying to comfort, and the dead to be buried in the only available grave, that great endless tomb of the sea. Too, the tyrant who commanded them insisted that every inch of blade and mail be wiped of blood and gore, then greased against salt spray.

"Ye fought well," he told them, "and these weapons served us well. It may be we'll be having need of them another day—and rust, lads, is the weapon-man's worst enemy!" He grinned. "Aye, and were some of ye hardly weapon-men this morning—so ye be all now!"

The final words assured willing compliance with the unwelcome command.

Then the sun died, as bloody-red on the horizon as the many battles it had witnessed, and eleven men and a woman sank down to the sleep of exhaustion, while the ship wallowed.

Chapter Two:
Warrior and Priest

The wind was hardly worthy of the name. A gentle breeze, it was just enough to fill the sails. Laeg mac Senain was well chosen, and Cormac was grateful to have the man aboard. Laeg the navigator made the most of even this pallid stir of air, with hardly a limp nor complaint whatever of the cut he'd taken in his right thigh. It was as much Laeg's skill that made the vessel skim over the water, oarless, as the breeze that others might have thought too little.

The Cormacanacht—so were the men happy to. call themselves, men of the Champion of Eirrin who'd bested even Bress Long-hand of Leinster at the great Feis of Tara—took their ease. They lounged, or exercised, or talked idly and looked about, though there was only water to see. Not so glassily flat as on the battle-day afore, Manannan mac Lyr's bluegreen demesne was nevertheless quiet. The breeze turned only little ripples that gleamed in the sun like twinkling gems.

At the prow, Cormac son of Art of Connacht leaned on the bulwark, gazing ahead.

Beside him was the short, slight warrior. The strange high boots still sheathed her legs above mid-thigh. Overlarge for those slim firm thighs, the rare

boots she loved were held up by thongs she'd fastened
to the belt of her tunic, under her coat of good mail.
The yellow tunic covered her legs to the knees. Of
linked steel in the Irish fashion, her mailcoat fell
almost as far, and covered her upper body to the
throat.

Discarded this day was her bronze-studded cap of
leather. Her hair, which was of a light golden red that
might be called orange, blew this way and that,
caught by the wind of their passage and by the wind
that pushed them so gently.

They'd launched the light Irish longboat with its
single sail from the baile or town called Atha Cliath,
which some called Darkpool, or Dubh-linn. The
vessel skimmed along east by south. Well behind
them now was the Pictish attack, and the bodies of
good sons of Eirrin that nurtured the ever-hungry
sea. They were mourned, though none aboard
Quester was of the New Faith, whose adherents believed in an eerie bodily afterlife not of this earth, but
cluttered all together in a sky-place called *coelis* or
heaven. There they lived eternally, with their god Iosa
Chriost. They did naught, so far as Cormac mac Art
had been able to ascertain; he held no discourse with
the dark-robed priests that had followed Padraigh to
Eirrin.

A venerated Druid rode this ship of men of the old
beliefs. None had failed to note that he lifted no
weapon against the Picts, nor was he menaced by
them . . . which would hardly have been the case, had
he been a priest of the new god from the East—and
Rome. The Druid's robe remained green. All aboard
were of his belief, for Cormac mac Art had no Christians about him. These men knew that their slain
comrades would return to tread *this* earth, though with
different visages and names.

"Cormac," the orange-haired warrior said, "is't
true what that man of Baile Atha Cliath said, that
once he sailed with you?"

"Aye. Tiobraide lost his arm with me, Samaire, in a battle with the men of Norge up north of Britain."

"He called you Wolf."

"So did they all. It was Cormac an-cliuin I was then; Captain Wolf."

"How came you by that name?"

"Men are fanciful, Samaire."

"And ye be evasive, dairlin' boy. Come—how came you by that fierce name?"

Cormac continued to look ahead, on the sea. "I earned it."

Samaire daughter of Ulad Ceannselaigh heard, and heard more than his spare words. She queried no further into that matter.

"He said too that it was your wont ever to counsel that one should kill only when necessary."

Staring ahead, the one-time wolf of the sea said nothing.

"Cormac?"

"Aye."

"Be it true?"

"Aye. Often I said it," he said, with a catch in his voice that was not quite a sigh.

"And . . . but . . . was it *meaning* that, ye were?"

He nodded, without turning his face toward hers. He was aware of her bright green eyes—and of nine other men.

"Aye. I meant it. Ye'll be asking further, and I'll make answer first. It's true, Samaire: I believe that one should kill only when necessary. Unfortunately it is more often necessary than not."

The daughter of Leinster's murdered king was silent for a space, whilst Cormac stared ahead and the sea furrowed past *Quester's* prow to ripple all along her length.

"I know not whether to laugh or sigh," she said at last.

"Nor do I, Samaire. It's a world of killing we habit, and it's good at it I am." His tone and mien were matter-of-fact, and without pride.

"I want to hug you."

A crease deepened at the edge of his mouth, in the slightest of smiles. "I hear you, dairlin girl. And it's the hug I'd like to be feeling . . . but I salute you for the saying of it, rather than the doing."

"Had I known there'd be so much discomfort for all, I might not have come."

" 'Twas you insisted, Samaire," he said, noting that she'd said "might" not. A princess asea, among weapon men!

"I remember, dairlin boy."

"None dare call me boy, save you, woman."

"Think you I'd suffer being called 'dairlin girl' by any other than yourself, man?"

Cormac chuckled. "Likely not. And *discomfort* is the word. It's why I insisted that ye dress as ye have, and keep on that mailcoat ungirt. No man asea should have a woman's form flaunted to his eyes."

Samaire heaved a sigh and tucked back her nether lip. "It's not that I meant by discomfort, though I understand it, too."

"Oh. Well . . . methinks it hardly inconveniences these men to look away now and again, whiles you do that which is necessary. It's knowing they all are, too, that on yester day you were a warrior among warriors."

"It inconveniences them to worry about whether *I* be looking away!" Samaire assured him, and they chuckled together. "I try, Cormac. And . . . I miss your touch, your arm around me, and mine about you."

"Not aboard this ship."

"I know," she said, with a hint of exasperation; she need not, Samaire of Leinster was saying, be told that again.

"I have a question of my own," he told her, turning his face at last toward hers.

The lift of her brows was invitation enough to the asking of it.

"Our . . . benefactor," Cormac said. "He who provided money for this boat and crew, your cousin Aine's husb—"

Samaire was laughing, though not in amusement. *"Benefactor!* Dealing with Cumal Uais was worse than bargaining in the marketplace of Tara! The tenth portion of what we bring back we must give him, for financing our quest—and that after bargaining him down from the third he demanded! And him the husband of my own cousin . . . and his coffers full already with the price of five hundreds of cattle won by his wagers on you in the championship games! *Benefactor!"*

Cormac was smiling. "Well, he did a bit of losing that day, too . . . sith he also placed wagers on Bress."

Samaire looked at him in shock, her green eyes huge and indignant. "No!"

"Aye. He did risk more on my prowess, though—fortunately for him. Besides, it were a better return: the odds were against me."

She shook her head. "Oh gods defend us, why is it thus? Cumal was *born* wealthy, Cormac! And all his life he's spent adding to that wealth."

"And counting it," Cormac said. "And *eating,"* he added, for Cumal's girth was nigh as fulsome as his tally sheets. "At any rate . . . it's his name I wanted to question, Samaire. How could parents nobly born and with wealth, and them residents of royal Tara as well, name a son Cumal Uais . . . 'Slavegirl the Noble'?"

For a moment Samaire stared at him. Then she was laughing.

His cool stare stopped her. "Oh, Cormac! It's not his *name* . . . he's but *called* that. His *name* is Tuathal, though he likes not being called after a High-king of

four centuries agone, a king whom Cumal considers
to have been no good man. He welcomes being called
Cumal, ye see, though in truth it began as but a bit of
waggery, poking fun at him for his love of gains!"

Cormac understood now. And to think he'd not
asked before out of . . . manners. Until a few months
agone it was long and long he was out of Eirrin, an
exile for the old "crime" of which he was now
absolved by Council, High-king, and druids alike, after his testing. He'd forgot. "Cumal" meant slavegirl,
aye. It also meant a unit of exchange, as the Romans
used their coins stamped with the faces of rulers with
bird-of-prey beaks. A *cumal* was a unit of exchange
worth the value of three cattle; it was by cows, *boru,*
that those of Eirrin had long measured value and
wealth.

Not often was Cormac mac Art embarrassed.

Samaire was still a-chuckle. "Hush," she was bade,
and she gave him a look that invited him to force her,
even as she ceased.

Cormac was rescued; sensing movement, he turned
to see that Bas the Druid had come to join them.

"It's a god's blessing ye have on ye, Druid," the
Gael said, "for of all aboard I see no drop of blood
on ye." Then, lest the man think he was being deni-
grated for having had no part in the battle with the
Picts, Cormac added more. "It's glad I am to have ye
aboard, beloved of the gods."

Bas nodded acknowledgment. "There be two of us,
Champion of Eirrin, for as ye proved when ye un-
derwent the Trials of the Fian and had sorcery done
upon ye as well, all saw that Behl and Crom do love
their staunch defender, Cormac mac Art."

"I hope it's right we both are, Druid, and that we
live to count many grey hairs. Being a staunch defender, as ye put it, be easier now, and all a true man
can do, with the priests of the Dead God upon our
land like a plague."

Art's son of Connacht was ever wont to call the
god of Rome and the bishops "the Dead God," since
all knew he'd been executed on a Roman cross by
some forgotten procurator enforcing the sedition
laws.

Bas sighed. "Say not 'No true man,' mac Art, with
so many in high places converted from the ways of
Eirrin to the new faith."

"Perverted," Samaire corrected.

"There'll come a time for the dealing with that
problem, Lord Bas, and none will find my blade
averse to being wetted through black robes!"

"They are holy men, Cormac mac Art—or think
themselves so. But I came to ask ye of our destination. How much farther?"

Cormac looked upon the priest of Behl and the an-
cient god of the Gaels of older Eirrin, Crom Cruach.
He did not smile as he said, "I cannot tell you,
Druid."

Bas lifted his brows. "Cannot? Still, this far on our
way—and you will not tell *me?*"

Cormac gave his head a jerk. "No no, Lord Bas of
Tara. Cannot, I said, and it's cannot I meant; Druid
or no, be assured that had I meant 'will not' I'd have
spoke it so. It's enough years I've spent asea that I
have an animal's sense of direction. Though there
were *changes* in the seascape . . . land rose even as we
sailed, and—"

"Land rose?"

Samaire shuddered in memory. "Aye. In fire and
thunder! Rock and ash mingled with flame vomited
up to slash the clouds and rain down upon us. The
winds from that eruption of angry gods drove us far
to the south and west, and we missed by mere fin-
gerlengths smashing into a new isle *even as it rose*
from the sea bottom!"

"So that," Cormac said, "we returned by a some-
what different route, from far off our course. What I

know is how we *came* to the isle that Wulfhere named Samaire-heim. Even so we cannot approach it as we did afore . . ."

The Gael trailed off. The face of the druid showed thorough confusion; Samaire was smiling.

"Wulfhere Skullsplitter," she told the druid, "is a Dane. A huge great towering oak of a man with hair and a beard—oh, a great full beard, Bas—like uncarded wool dyed red. He and Cormac are . . . were . . ."

"Companions asea," Cormac swiftly interjected. Most knew he'd been a reaver, a pirate, and he saw no reason to remind Bas, whose sister was the wife of Eirrin's High-king. "When first we see land ahead, we must swing well to the west. For full ahead lies a combination of horror and death, a whirlpool called the Ire of Manannan, and then the Wind Among the Isles. We discovered them not ere they discovered us, to our dismay. Many jagged little rock-isles cluster there, and the wind that howls among them is insane. First we were whirled and spun and dunked and hurled helpless as a child's boat when he tires and tosses stones at it. Three-and-twenty of us there were aboard *Wolfsail;* when we awoke on the beach of a tiny, rocky isle on no maps, we were but nine. The sea ate the rest, and our ship.

"We found a *castle* on that island, Druid, a prodigious towering pile of superbly-stacked stones more thousands of years old than I'd care to say—or than ye'd believe."

Bas was staring, with more than interest now in his expression, in his entire attitude. His fingers toyed idly with the sprig of dried mistletoe he wore about his neck.

"Think ye so, descendant of Gaels?"

The two descendants of Gaels stared at each other, warrior and priest.

"What . . . found you there, Cormac mac Art?"

"Booty! A treasure-trove. The castle had been found afore us, and was the lair of a band of Norse reavers. We awaited them. When they came, they had as captive the Princess Samaire and her brother Prince Ceann. Their murdering, throne-thieving brother had *arranged* for these his younger siblings to fall into the hands of those men of Norge."

"Ah—it was thus you and Samaire met and linked destinies."

"We knew each other long before, twelve years and more agone, when she was but a girl and I a boy, a weapon-man in the employ of her father."

Bas nodded. He had heard the tale. First, because of the plotting of a fearful High-king, Cormac's father had been slain. The boy, well trained and big for his age, had fled his native Connacht, to serve in Leinster under an assumed name. Later discovered there, he'd been forced to flee that kingdom too . . . and then Eirrin. For twelve long years he'd been an exile. There was a story that he had crossed the King of DalRiada, too, up in Alba. A man to rouse the fickleness of men and gods, was Cormac of Connacht.

He was speaking on: "None of the Vikings survived. Of us, only Wulfhere and I did—and Samaire and Ceann. And the Norsemen's ship. It was no easy matter, but the four of us reached Eirrin aboard that ship."

"When last we saw it," Samaire said, with a reminiscent sadness in voice and face, "Wulfhere plied it alone, on a northerly bearing, 'twixt Eirrin and Britain."

Bas was shaking his head. "What lifetimes of adventure and horror ye've crowded into your short term in this body, son of Crom Cruach! Oh . . . and sith I note how ye call my lord and lady the prince and princess of Leinster by their given names, Cormac, call me Bas."

"It's Lord Bas ye be, or should. Ye gave up much

to don druidic robes, man!"

"I gained much, Cormac."

Again they gazed upon each other in silence for a time, and not without admiration and respect. Then Bas spoke.

"And so this voyage is to take ye back to this isle your Danish friend named Samaire-heim, and carry off the rest of the Norsemen's sword-gains."

"It is, Lor—Bas. That be the reason we few sail on a ship large enough to bear twice our number. Were the Lord Cumal Uais not so . . . cautious, we'd have two ships and more armed escort. The pr—Samaire and Ceann, ye see, need the wealth."

"It's no comment I'd be making on what seems implicit in that, Cormac, my lady—"

"Samaire," she corrected, the orange-haired warrior. "No comment is necessary, Bas. My brother Ceann and I are what we are. When our father died, Leinster's throne passed to his eldest. Within the year he was dead—slain, we know, by our brother Feredach's scheming. Next it was us Feredach the Dark did treachery upon. Mayhap it's grateful we should be that he did not have us slain. He *is* our older brother, and so Ceann and I have no claim on the throne."

"While Feredach lives," Cormac added.

Bas nodded, taking no note of Cormac's sinister addition to Samaire's words. "All this I know, sweet lady; I was present during the drama of accusation at the Council of Kings on Tara Hill but a month agone. Nor still will I comment, nor on Cormac's dark remark. But . . . Cormac. Why am I along on this quest?"

"Why—ye asked to come!" Samaire blurted.

Cormac almost smiled. "Nay, so I told you, and it's apology I make, dairl—Samaire. It was I asked my lord Bas the Druid to accompany us. There is sorcery on that isle, or was, and any who believe druids know naught but such as oak and mistletoe and the rites of Behltain and Samain be a fool before the gods."

Bas neither smiled, nor affirmed nor denied; that was affirmation enow.

"The castle, Cormac," he said, after a time of silence. "It is older than old?"

"Men of Atlantis builded it, Bas."

"Ye know this."

"I know it."

Bas looked at neither of them, but straight ahead, and he spoke as if to himself.

"A castle of Atlantis . . . . There is a story, a story passed down through thousands and thousands of generations of druids. It speaks of Kull, King of Valusia and an Atlantean born, and another man, a mage. Through some means Kull was able to best this wizard, who is variously said to have been a servant of the serpent god far more ancient than Atlantis . . . and to be immortal . . . and to be already dead but not dead, alive yet not alive, a man stronger than the grave, whose true face was that of death itself: a fleshless skull. There is a story . . . It is to these climes Kull is said to have sailed, where again he met that dread sorcerer. With the latter now was a legion of allies: *serpents*. Perhaps the serpent-god himself, who ruled the earth before we men came up from the seas . . . or, as some say it, down from the trees! Thus man met serpent again in a last great battle, and King Kull prevailed . . . ."

"Gods of my ancestors," Samaire murmured, "against such a foe—*how?*"

The closing of Cormac's fingers on her arm deeply indented the flesh, and made her flinch. *Hush*, that sudden squeeze and grip bade her, without a spoken word.

"Kull had his own mage by then," the druid spoke on, "and besides Kull was of the mightiest of men

ever to walk the ridge of the world. By sword and
sorcery he and his prevailed, and raised a great castle
over the ensorceled mage of evil. Some say those men
ranged on, even to Eirrin where there were then no
men, and that terrible war upon the Great Serpent's
last servant is the reason our green fens and blue hills
are marred even today by no slithering serpent."

Bas came to a halt in his murmurous narrative—
which was more like unto a remembrance, or a day-
dreaming recall of the tiniest part of the lore that
belonged to the druids. As though lost still within
himself, he looked not at Cormac or Samaire. The
grey eyes of the High-king's brother-in-law stared
ahead as though seeing only things that lay behind his
eyes, not before.

Dully Cormac said, "It is more than story, O
Druid. It *is* Kull's isle, and his castle. I . . . *know.* And
beneath it . . . I like to have ended my days in this
form. To a *serpent,* Lord Druid . . . a serpent several
times the length of my body. And once I'd slain him
. . . he bled scarlet, like a man."

"O Behl," the druid murmured, "I am your servant. Lord of Sun and Oak, accept poor thanks and
promise of restoration. That I should be the one who
sees the castle of my father's father's fathers half a
million times removed!"

The trio at *Quester's* prow fell silent.

Samaire, herself no mewling girl nor yet a small
souled person, but a woman of will and determination even among the free women of Eirrin, looked
from one of those men to the other. Gaels both, dark
of hair and pale of eye. The weapon-man and the
druid; the eternal twain: warrior and priest. Samaire
could not help but feel that she stood in the presence
of giants, and of the eerie. These were men sure who
stood above other men, whose lines ran back into the
mists of time out of mind, and were likely to continue
into the far mistier future, even as far.

These two had been here again and again, and would tread this earth again and again still.

And she knew too, with an absolute though never explicable certitude, that she had known at least one of them before.

She was a princess born, and had been wed as a King's daughter must be, to a prince now dead in his youth. But their relationship had been a tiny and tenuous thing in the immensity of time, even in the limited sweep of this lifetime. He could not have been the man Cormac mac Art was, that prince of Osraige whose loveless wife she had been; nay, not even in his dreams.

And now she was certain too that there was no way she and Cormac could have failed to meet—again—or could part, not ever. She had known him before this life, she now realized, and she would know him again, and again in the unwoven tapestry of the sprawling time-to-come.

Then she looked out before their gliding ship, and what she saw interrupted her reverie and drove it from her mind.

"Cormac—land! Islands!"

And he looked, and gave the orders to swing *Quester* sharply to starboard, and hold that westward course until they dared turn south again, safely around the Ire of Manannan and the Wind Among the Isles.

Chapter Three:
Death-tide

The man had been roped to the great rounded spire of sea-rooted rock for hours.

From the sea that tall chunk of granite rose, at the very edge of a rocky isle, before which it stood like a sentinel. With the sun shining down, men had walked to it from shore in no more than a foot of water. At high tide, only its upper two feet were visible.

The monument of water-smoothed white stone rose twice the height of a man.

The man bound to it was tall, taller than tall. Nevertheless, both he and those who had bound him here knew that he was not tall enough. The salt sea was coming for him. The water had lapped about his ankles when his captors had left him, well tied. Now it quivered just below his nipples, and crept ever upward. High tide was but a little over an hour away. Sooner than that, he knew, was death.

First there would be the desperate tipping back of his bearded head, the desperate straining to remain above the salt water that lapped at his lips . . . into his mouth . . . until it at last rose to his moustache . . . and above his nostrils. And then he would see the one-eyed All-father, Odin . . . if the Valkyries could find him, at the time of tide's ebb.

Behind the mighty rock and the giant with the fiery beard bound to it, another man sat. Well back up the beach was he, with a goatskin bag to hand. It gurgled with the thin, sour wine of Briton grapes. He had situated himself so that he could see the rockbound man, to whom from time to time he called taunting words.

The seated sentry's shield lay beside him, upturned, and at his other hand was his spear. Between his outstretched legs, though he expected no trouble, lay his ax, a thin broad blade with a hook at its top edge. Down his back fell a thick straw-coloured braid from just behind his right ear; the left braid lay on his shoulder. Both were wound about with two plaited strips of leather, brown and red and tightly bound.

"I'm having another fine sip of wine, now, son of a Danish dog and a piggish slut; can ye hear its gurgle as it goes down to quench my thirst? Or . . . can ye hear only the gurgle of . . . *water?*" He laughed. "Well, drunken dog of Dane-mark, it's soon your own thirst will be quenched . . . *with salt water!*"

Chuckling, the man drank.

Awaiting death, the Dane made no answer. He was a big man, and many heads had fallen to his ax, and making answer to such a one as his Briton ghoulguard was beneath him. He'd plead with Odin and Thor, Woden and Thunor, until the end of time itself, to be allowed to come back and meet this taunting midden rat as men should meet, and to end his days . . . slowly.

"Ahhhhhhh," the man from Britain sighed, with much exaggeration. First licking his lips, he wiped them with the back of his hand and set the goatskin bag aside.

"Tide," he called out, "come! Bledyn of Gwent grows weary of watching this ugly Danish body swallowed by the sea!"

"Then rise, Bledyn, pig of Gwent, and let me aid you in the shortening of your vigil."

For a moment Bledyn froze at that cold voice that came from behind, where no man should be. Then he hurled himself to roll sidewise, snatching at both spear and buckler even as, backing like a crab, he drove himself to his feet by main will.

Brooding dark and menacing before him, a tall man stood, lean and chainmailed. Deepset eyes were only just visible in a scarred grim face set like death itself. Though this challenger was helmeted, Bledyn saw that he was dark of hair. On his left arm the man wore a small buckler, a targe, with a ferocious boar emblazoned on its face. The shield was seemingly negligently held, nor did the man from the night have a spear. He held a goodly sword whose double-edged blade was nigh straight, and slimmer than Bledyn's own glaive.

"Who . . . be you?" Bledyn demanded, speaking with care to keep the quiver from out his voice.

"Kull of Atlantis. You Britons profane my castle and raise a stench therein, by your piggish presence."

The accent was none Bledyn knew, and thus was barbarous. And . . . *Atlantis?*

"What . . . do you want here of me, outlander?"

"It's yourself's the outlander, man; ye be not now on your own piteous isle, which you first gave to the Romans and now suffer to be taken by all who come from oversea with a few spears! As to what I want . . . the man on yon rock. It's a better man than you he is, and I like not your taunting of him. He dies not this night."

Bledyn's fingers tightened sweatily about his spear. From out the haunted dark of this unknown bit of rocky land came this strange dark man, calling himself by no name known to Bledyn of Gwent, and calling that fantastic inland keep *his*. Holding lips and teeth tight, the Briton spoke.

"Be ye man or shade, the Dane dies. So be the decision of us all, and so be the decree of Bedwyr son of Ingcel, and so it's to be. Begone, man of night, an ye value your hide."

"I do not."

That flat stark statement sent Bledyn's short hairs astriving against the pressure of his helm. Best to move swiftly and end this menace, this insanity, ere the other made the first move. Spear against sword, the Briton of Gwent was sure, were no contest—particularly when he struck first.

Bledyn of Gwent drove his spear with its long leaf-shaped blade at the man's belly. At the last moment he twitched it upward, to skewer the face of this "Kull of Atlantis" whilst he strove to protect his vitals.

The other man's shield was a blur. There was a clang accompanied by Bledyn's grunt as his spear-point struck that small buckler which, twisted slightly in a hand both expert and signally swift, sent his weapon aside. Then in another blurring motion that was silvery in the moonlight, the stranger's sword swept. Again Bledyn grunted; the blow of the blade not only sheared away two feet of his spear, but slammed its haft into his side with its terrible force.

Rather than follow up the advantage that so shocked his opponent, the stranger was still, staring, hardly so much as crouched in combative stance.

"Quarterstaff against sword be no good match, Bledyn of Gwent. Best pick up that ax, or yield yourself. Yield and live."

Still feeling as though he were a wanderer in some weird dream, Bledyn stared at his decapitated spear a few seconds more. Then he dropped it even as he bent and snatched up his good ax all in one swift motion. Nor had it ended; in a continuation of the same movement, he lunged. The ax-head rushed straight upward. One step backward the dark man took, and then with a frightful clang ax rang off the very boss of the stranger's shield. It was sped so swiftly aside that Bledyn thought his arm would come off.

"The same tactic twice? Pitiful, Bledyn. Best ye yield, man; I kill only when I must, and there are few enough Britons on the ridge of the world to face off the invaders of your land."

Bledyn yielded not. Grim, back-prickling fear lent strength to his body and skill to his attack. His great swinging slice was aimed at the other man's sword-arm.

Somehow that seemingly magic shield was there again, the stranger turning partway aside—and then completely around, to crash his buckler against Bledyn's with such force that he groaned and felt his shield-arm strike his mouth with a splitting of lip. Desperately he tried to chop. Upward whipping shield-edge struck his arm, his fingers flew open, and his ax went sailing.

At the same time the other man used his sword against the Briton for the first time. He drove it with jolting power into Bledyn's belly, through leathern jerkin and blue-dyed tunic. A strong arm gave the imbedded blade a half-twist before whipping it free.

The tall slender man stepped back while the Briton, in his eyes a startled look, stretched his length on the sand.

"Ye were warned, Briton," the man from the night said with a sigh. He half-bent to thrust his sword into the sand. "Unfortunately, killing is usually necessary, though one does try . . . ."

With care, he returned his sand-cleaned blade to the sheath he had slung across his back. Bledyn made no reply, nor did he see aught, for all that his eyes were wide. His feet kicked the sand in spastic jerks.

First looking all about, straining his eyes against the moon-shot dark, Bledyn's slayer nodded; the Gwentish Briton had been alone. The tall man walked down the strand to water's edge, behind the rock to which was bound the red-bearded captive. There he left his targe, and waded out through the tidewaters.

Coming around the huge rock rising up from the sea, he looked into the face of the outsized man bound there. The latter's eyes widened.

"Cormac! Thunor singe my beard—it's COR-MAC!"

Cormac shook his head. "For shame, Wulfhere, leading total strangers to *our* island. Ah, Samaire'll not be liking this, after it was you your self named this isle for her! And man, man, the *vanity* in ye . . . bathing your ugly self at this hour!"

Wulfhere Hausakliufr's fiery beard twitched as the giant's mouth writhed. He was able to curb hot rejoinder: "It's shame upon me on both counts in truth, Wolf. But meseems to've got entangled . . . might ye be prevailed upon to lend a poor shame-filled son of Woden a sharp blade?"

Cormac showed his old comrade his dagger, a Saxon's sax-knife the length of his forearm. "Why o'course, old friend. Where would he like it best: across the throat, or the belly, or straight into the heart?"

After a moment, Wulfhere made reply, "The heart were best; I'd prefer death to come all at once."

"Aye."

Unsmiling, Cormac put up his left hand to the Dane's massive chest, which even in naught but sodden tunic looked as if he wore one of those moulded cuirasses that gleamed on the high officers of the Romans.

"And whiles I be finding the exact spot—so as to be sure to miss it first time, old friend—suppose ye occupy your gross self with the telling me of how it is ye came here in company with *Britons*. When I last saw ye it was crew ye were going in quest of—and naturally methought they'd be Danes, sith ye could not afford the best—Eirrin's sons. But . . . *Britons!* And to *our* island!"

"*Cormac!*" Hurt broidered Wulfhere's tone.

Cormac lifted his brows. "This grows more difficult. Your nipples are already under water." He glanced about, then up at the moon. "Well, ye probably have time for the telling of your tale, ere the tide silences ye."

"Cormac! Ye . . . ye demand explanation of ME, battle brother?"

"Humour me."

"Use your reason, man! Those Britons tethered me here to die as the tide came in. Now no great brain be needed to know we are not allies, they and I! Nor to know that the man ye've just come through had an ax, which is my weapon. Now if it's Britonish blood ye'd be seeing and *our* booty ye'd prevent their taking, it's much worse ye could do than to have with you a man in search of the same goal—vengeance sped!"

"A good argument," Cormac said in the same flat, emotionless tone that was all Wulfhere had heard this night. "And unsullied by statements of old friendship and the like. But Wulfhere . . . how came ye here in their company?"

Wulfhere sighed. When Cormac the Wolf had a point to make or to hear, he was tenacious as the jaws of his namesake. Nevertheless, Wulfhere tried still again. "How know ye I did?"

"This water grows chill, Wulfhere. Saw you a ship of Eirrin a day or two agone, and it ringed about by Picts?"

"Aye—was you, then!"

"We were too far to recognize, but I know now who was the big fellow standing so close against the mast of the ship I saw."

"Then ye know I was their prisoner," Wulfhere

said in his chesty rumbling voice, "and *roped* to that mast. That, Cormac who sore injures me with his doubts, is how I came here 'in their company.' "

Cormac nodded. He said nothing.

Wulfhere waited, hopefully. Still the Gael spoke not, and the Dane realized that Cormac, too, was waiting. At last the huge man heaved a sigh and gave it up. Looking straight ahead into the darkness so as not to meet the other's eyes, he told his tale in a swift-running string of words that were quietly spoken indeed.

"I left ye, with Ceann and Samaire, on Eirrin's shore, nor will I ask aught of what befell ye after. As for me, Odin smiled. I had crew before I reached Dane-mark. Next we found an easy, ah, prey, and soon we were as happy as men can be, with a good ship and no wounds and the wherewithal to buy the best ale. That we did—unwisely, though, for one of my company told me this townlet of Britain, at the Demetian point, was open and there we'd be welcome. Too, he spake of a fine inn, and a great thirst was upon us. There we put in, and went to the ratty inn of that mud-heim, and whilst I wet my throat I let it be known I was alook for more seamen. None came forward, though there were friendly spirits there—"

"Meaning you bought the ale."

"—and, to my eternal shame, a tavern-wench, an exotic Romish looking girl with shield-broad hips— and may she be accursed with lice, piles, and phlegmy throat all her days! I . . . she . . ."

"Ye got drunk with her and your lip flapped like a loose sail in the wind."

The massive chest rose and fell in another great dolorous sigh that rippled the waters. "Aye, old comrade. When I awoke, my men were gone and I was captive. The wench had two brothers and she brought them fast enow, once I was asleep."

"Blood of the gods," Cormac said, his wondering

tone not all feigned. "You, drunk unto sleep! Why ye must've drunk the land dry as far inland as Powys and Gwent!"

"The place *was* . . . well stocked," Wulfhere admitted. "Naturally it was only denials I made, despite some small pain . . . I be missing a fingernail now. But these fellows had a ship, and plenty there were about who sought any sort of hope other than being pushed into the sea by the Saxons—ye know how goes it with the Britonish."

"Ye denied what ye drunkenly blabbed to the wench, but they elected to come and look for themselves."

"Ah, that brain—how I've missed ye and your wise counsel, Cormac!"

Cormac said nothing. Wulfhere, waiting, realized then that so was his fellow-pirate of old. He went on, dully.

"Aye, they decided to sail down here anyhow. With me bound to the mast, stiff and baking by day and shivering by night."

Such things Wulfhere Skull-splitter was not wont to admit, Cormac knew; how anxious the giant was becoming, with the water approaching his collarbones!

"Were there no such isle they said, or no such castle upon it, they avowed it was back they'd take me, and mayhap even aid me in seeking out my crew and the ship they stole from me. An it were here, I'd die though, for having lied that it wasn't. They claim to set great store by the truth, these lying Britons!"

"It's considerable regard for it I've always been having myself," Cormac said musingly.

He ruminated. He believed most of the woeful story, and decided to press no further into the matter of a few points he believed not, and some few details he was sure had been left unmentioned. He knew Wulfhere. He understood.

Cormac was sure that the Dane's shame was unfeigned. Mayhap he had foolishly made alliance with the wrong men, who'd turned on him when he spoke too much of their destination and what it held—though he'd split many skulls indeed, Wulfhere might too have been surnamed "the Impetuous." Or mayhap he had indeed fallen deep into his cups and blabbed to some Roman-descended Briton temptress who knew how to love a man and bring his secrets from out him—particularly when they were bragging matters. And mayhap there was another explanation altogether.

It did not matter. Cormac knew he'd been told the greater part of the truth, and that assured him Wulfhere remained the same, and his friend. The Dane had ever been too much given to the moment's call and too little to thinking a bit. It was a fortunate good pairing they'd made, after they'd met in that foul prison years ago; the Dane had always bent ear to his Gaelic comrade's counsel, and nearly always abided by it.

With a few swift movements of his knife, Cormac cut Wulfhere loose. He waded back onto the beach while the giant stood flexing his great arms and sucking up vasty breaths.

Following, Wulfhere picked up the Briton ax. He hefted it, plucked up the buckler, with its large protruding boss—which Bledyn had failed to use as he should have done. Wulfhere rushed the ax through the air, swung the shield in a blow that would have sent a foeman flying.

"Nice of ye not to carve up his shield, old Wolf!"

"It was on you my mind was, o'course. I fear his armour won't be fitting you, though."

Wulfhere chuckled. "Well, it seems to be leaky in the area of the stomach, anyhow. Mayhap this." But no, the helmet would not encompass his head. He tossed it aside. "Where be your ship?"

"You know. Down below the spur of rock that cuts down to sea's edge and ends this pretty beach."

"Umm. How many men have we, Cormac?"

"*I* have ten, not counting Samaire—and I do. The Picts robbed me of a few."

"Samaire!" But Wulfhere said no more. If he refrained from asking aught of mac Art—such as what he was doing traveling asea *from* Eirrin with the princess he'd taken so much trouble to convey there— perhaps Cormac would ask no more questions either.

"There be two-and-twenty with Bedwyr—oh." Wulfhere looked down at his former death-watcher, and his big strong teeth flashed in a grin. "*One*-and-twenty, and Bedwyr. Good odds, surely: one for each of your men and seven for me. Ye *can* handle five, Crom's own son?"

"Four is what your accounting left for me, ye rapacious barbarian."

Wulfhere shrugged. "Four, then. Whatever. Saw you their ship?"

"Hours ago." Cormac pointed; Wulfhere nodded.

The beached longship of the Britons, so painstakingly hide-covered, lay ten tens of paces up the strand. Cormac had come along the beach from the opposite direction. It was the ship he'd had as goal in his reconnoitering; his discovery of Wulfhere and Bledyn had been accidental.

Wulfhere nodded. "Bedwyr left two men aboard." The Dane scratched under his beard.

"Two. Apparently they be earless!"

Wulfhere made a foul noise. "You know how it is with men fit for naught but crewing, when their chief's not at hand to bid them scratch their itches. They were drunk hours ago." Having recalled that sore subject to his mind and his friend's, Wulfhere looked away. "That leaves a score for us to brace. Tonight, or by ambush on the morrow, when they return from the castle."

"Mmm. Ye recall how we hid the Norsemen's ship, when last we bode here?"

Wulfhere's teeth flashed. "Aye! Your men are with your ship?"

"Aye."

The Dane hefted his new ax. "Do you fetch them then, old friend, whilst I stroll up the beach and discuss possession of yon ship with its present occupants."

"Ye've no armour man, and no helmet, and ye be wet and muscle-tight from long strain, and . . ."

Cormac's voice trailed off. Wulfhere had turned to look at him.

The Gael read what was in those blue eyes, and he understood. Wulfhere had lost much face, and nearly his life. Helpless as a hare in a Dumnonion snare, he'd had to be rescued from death, and that rescuer had not so much as left him Bledyn for the venting of his spleen and the betterment of his sore-wounded pride. Wulfhere wanted atonement, and needed it. Those two Britons on the beached ship would be only a beginning, but his bracing them alone, Cormac knew, would help. Too, he knew that this giant Dane with his prodigious reach and mighty thews was a match for any five men . . . and probably eight of Britain.

Besides, Wulfhere had said the two men were drunk.

With a nod, Cormac turned without a word. He set off back along the moon-sparkled strand, to bring his crew for the floating and concealing of the Briton ship.

Chapter Four:
The Castle of Atlantis

The ship of the Britons, its two guardians afloat facedown, was concealed near the Irish vessel. The latter, just in case, was hidden even more thoroughly.

This island south of Britain was a bare and inhospitable one, despite the incredible structure inland. There was only one slender strip of sandy, sparkling beach that split a coast otherwise stony and high and forbidding, and . . . of rock. Brooding granite rose like a bulwark just back of the beach, and the darker stone too of basalt, igneous rock that was like petrified sponge.

Their visit here before had established it: Samaireheim was one great wall of stone like a giant's castle. Even its coast consisted mainly of precipitous stony faces, totally without promise. It seemed minded to wear an attractive face, like an aged and tired tavern-doxy: the dark, high coastline gleamed jewel-like here and there with veins of lipartite and studs of twinkling quartz.

They were a lie, as the sandy beach was a lie. There was no life on this island of stone, no hint of green.

Into the wall of rock ran a slim declivity, like an unceiled tunnel that was braced on either side by nature's high-looming walls. So narrow was the passageway in places that two men could not walk abreast, while elsewhere it widened to accommodate five. In addition it wound about, as though some whimsical god had raised walls on either side of a path laid out by a meandering cow, time out of mind.

Well back within the grim shadow of the barren cliff-walls, that natural corridor widened to become a canyon, which debouched into a valley carelessly strewn with pebbles and boulders ranging up to the size of houses in Eirrin.

Save for the winding natural "hallway," the canyon was bounded about by rocky cliffs, more often sheer and unscalable than not. Yet at its far end, *against* that rearward cliff that dropped sheer to the sea, rose other walls: man-made walls. The castle of Atlantis. There last night had slept the Britons; from there today they must come.

Cormac and his nine men, with Wulfhere and Samaire and Bas the Druid, awaited them. Their vigil had been taken up before dawn. When the men of Britain came along the narrow, twisting defile, doubtless bearing booty, half their number would be down ere they could draw steel. Ambush was the only sensible course when twelve men sought to best a score; the druid, of course, would not take up arms.

But the sun was high, and the Britons had not come.

Long and too frequently had Cormac stayed his companions. Now he, too, was beyond curbing his natural impatience. The sun's light should have brought the foe happily along the natural hallway walled with sombre basalt and roofed with naught but cloud-strewn sky. Surely they were anxious to see Wulfhere's corpse . . . and to load their ship with what Cormac and Wulfhere had found here months before, at summer's beginning: the sword-won spoils Norse reavers had stored in a castle whose origin and existence they doubtless never questioned.

But the Britons came not.

At last Cormac took Lugh and Bas, and scaled a talus formed by the slippage of rock over thousands of years. Up they climbed, onto the nigh-flat mesa that was the island's main surface. Over one shoulder Cormac bore many loops of stout rope.

The others had to stay and maintain the ambuscade, lest the Britons come forth. There'd be noise aplenty then, Cormac had pointed out, and he and Lugh would be terribly effective against the men of Britain from above! Wulfhere was troublesome. Him Cormac persuaded to remain with the others only by reminding, quietly, that the Dane was the most experienced fighting man among them, and worth any five others as well.

Any seven others, Wulfhere corrected, and stayed, scratching under his beard.

With Bas and the archer, Cormac moved inland, well above the level of the beach, the valley of the castle, and his own men.

"Like walking the roof of the world it is!" Lugh commented.

Above them the golden eye of Behl moved steadily and unconcernedly toward its zenith. It was by that watchful god Lugh swore when they caught sight of their goal: soaring, straight stone walls raised by the hands of men skilled beyond any now alive.

"Behl's eye!"

Cormac half-smiled at the man's astonishment and awe, though he felt it, too. Towered and columned, builded of stone laid upon stone by master builders, the thrice-ancient keep was of spectacular proportion. The whole was no less than awe-inspiring, topped off by flashing rays of bronze standing out from the towers near their tops, like sun-rays.

"Ah," Bas the Druid whispered. "No Roman hands raised this magnificence. See the carving—see the Behl-rays on the towers!"

Cormac nodded. "It's from the Celtish ancestors of Lugh that we Gaels sprang, Druid," he said in a fervidly quiet voice, "and from those fierce men of forgotten Cimmeria came the Celts, and in the oldest land of all, the Sunken Land, that the Cimmerians had their birth."

"World-spanning Atlantis," Bas breathed.

Lugh ignored the Gaels; he was content to stare in silence.

"It came upon me when first I set eyes to it, Bas, that which affrights other men around me. My . . . remembering. I saw it, and I *knew*." Then Cormac laid a hand on Lugh's shoulder, which he found a-quiver. "See you the two pillars and the deep shadow between, Lugh mac Cellach, like a black gaping mouth?"

"Aye."

"That be the doorway . . . the only doorway. No door binds it now; it hangs by one hinge-strap and the entry gapes full the length of a man. Just within is a blank wall . . . to enter the keep itself, one must turn to the upper level. It is a defensive hall: see ye its windows, like slitted dark eyes? Archers' windows! Behind the rear wall of that defense-hall is a gallery, and below that . . . a vasty room into which fifty, a hundred longships might be piled."

"Gods of my ancestors, a half-score men could defend it against an army!"

"Exactly. Hunter or no, Lugh, it's a fighting man's instincts ye have. Our few then, would never win past our own number, were they inside, much less a score of men!"

"Even Britons, aye. Then . . . but we've seen them not, and heard naught of them . . . must we wait forever, then, for them to come forth to us?"

"Why no, Lugh," Cormac told the archer with the hair like corn and the knotty, bandy legs. "You are our hope, man."

While Lugh stared at him, Cormac peeled from his shoulder the coils of rope. It was of two sizes, one less thick than the little finger of a thin man.

"See how those projections stand out from the castle's towers like slim straight horns or the sun-king's rayed crown?"

"And so they are," Bas said quietly. His thin face remained turned toward the awesome castle. "They knew Behl, those men of that land so long ago swallowed up by sea and time."

"By whatever name, aye," Cormac agreed. "Now first, see you how this 'roof of the world' as ye put it runs so closely alongside the castle. There go we first, where man-built walls cast gloom between them and these natural ones. Then . . . we climb down. And then, Lugh, it's you who will gain us safe entry!"

Neither Lugh nor Bas fathomed that plan, but both saw now the reason for the rope, or so they thought: on it they would climb down, *beside* the castle in the gloom, rather than risk being seen in a frontal approach—and be dropped by arrows with them powerless as fish flopping on land.

Along the mesa they went, and beside the castle, until its pillar-flanked entry was invisible to them— and thus they to it. Cormac gazed with longing across at the stone wall, from which they were separated by a chasm more than three man-lengths across.

"Had we brought a grappling iron . . ." Bas murmured, gazing fixedly at slitted windows so near —and too far.

"We'd have made noise," Cormac finished for him, "steel on stone. No. First I secure this rope, thus and thus. Then I bid ye both farewell, and hold on here whilst you climb down and await me."

The druid looked at him a moment, thinking perhaps to challenge that which resembled an order. Then, with a glance back at the castle, he sighed. Its walls tugged like the eyes of an enchantress. Without a word, he followed Lugh down on the dangling rope —bordering on the ludicrous, with the skirts of his robe hitched up to bare that which a druid seemed not to have: legs. His leggings, his companions saw, were the same deep, foresty green of his robe.

At their tug on the rope, Cormac loosed it and let it slide over the edge, into the deep shadow where they waited. Then he followed.

The Gael went slowly, testing each little ledge or rocky projection before giving it his weight. His feet were sea-sure, and he had done more than his share of scaling. Down he went, with but one slip that fingers like cables turned into no more than a delay. A few feet above the upturned faces of the other two men, he dropped and alit like a cat on bent legs. His hands slapped the earth a second after his feet.

"Crom's eyes," Lugh said in a gasp, "an I dropped that distance I'd be wearing my stones around my knees!"

"An ever-active man learns to keep them bound up tight to his body," Cormac assured him. "And learns how to fold up when he drops so. Now, Lugh. It's your bow and skill we depend upon, all. Pluck you forth a good straight shaft with a wicked heavy head, and let us tie this little cord to it."

Three times Lugh assayed to arc an arrow up and up and over one of the bronze poles standing out like sun's rays from the castle. On the third try, three delighted men watched the cord-trailing shaft sail up and over its target. It dropped; the cord caught, lying across the pole: the arrow dangled well above their heads.

First Cormac gave the hunter's shoulder a squeeze of congratulations and thanks. Then he began working the cord up, shaking it, lifting, coaxing . . .

Jerking and swaying like an erratic pendulum, the arrow descended. Cormac flashed one of his tight almost-smiles as he caught hold of it. He began pulling. Up went the slender cord, followed by the stout ship's rope knotted to its tail. And over the projection, and down. And then the thick rope was in Cormac's hand. There was just enough cordage; only one end touched the ground now, and with little to spare.

"Another man's length and we'd have failed for my lack of planning!" he snapped, while his companions silently wondered at his excellence of forethought. "Now, we haven't enough rope to tie off. But if you will wind yourself with it, Lugh, and brace your feet against the castle wall, I can climb up—without, hopefully, breaking either of our backs."

Lugh gazed at him, amazed at the ingeniousness, and he smiled at the joke his leader made, between comrades.

"My back will hold, mac Art!"

The cleverer Bas bobbed his head in one nod, and stepped forward.

"Mac Art would not ask a druid to hold the rope's end, as he would any other man. I will. Come, Lugh. An we stand side by side, facing the castle, we can draw the rope across our backs and brace it well. It's a brave man we're to support and keep safe . . . and him no boy whose weight might be measured against feathers!"

The two men braced themselves.

By all the gods, Cormac thought, *that I should see the day! I entrust my very life to an army composed of a farm-born hunter of hare and boar, and a robed druid whose strength I know not . . . but would hardly make wager on!*

First he tugged at the dangling rope with all his strength. Then he gave it his weight. With no word of apology, he hung from it—and set himself a-swinging. Lugh gasped and Bas grunted openly. The rope held.

"Rest," Cormac bade them, and prepared for his climb.

His buskins he hung by their laces around his neck. Buckler he fastened to his belt behind, its curve hugging that of his backside. By a thong, he made his sword-scabbard immobile against his thigh.

He looked at the two men who were ready to lean back against the rope, their feet against the base of the wall they faced, while he climbed. He nodded. And he went up.

The two men gasped, and Lugh cursed without heed of the druid beside him. Each held fast, and Cormac's strength and superb physical condition steaded him well. Hand over hand, not hurriedly so as to avoid jerking Bas and Lugh, he went up, and up.

Lugh's arrow had had to go far higher than Cormac. He'd snugged the rope in close to the castle itself, and the narrow window he sought was little more than a dozen feet above the ground. The sun-ray projection held; the rope held; the men below held. Cormac climbed.

When he peered into the gloomy niche, he saw no man within the room. Muscles knotted and strained then, for he could not edge through that air-and-arrow embrasure while wearing his buckler behind. Dangling by one hand, he reached back and untethered it. He eased the targe into the slice in the stone wall, which was thick as the length of his arm.

Cormac glanced down. Then he put out his bare right foot and set it into the niche. In a swift movement then that scraped chainmail on stone, he lunged into the open window.

There he stood a moment, drawing shallow breath, for chest and shoulderblades touched the sides of the embrasure. He was wedged snugly into an opening that was as if designed to accommodate his body—sidewise.

A gliding step rightward, another . . . and he eased

himself silently as a stalking panther down into the room. He stood in one of the several chambers that lined the castle's pillar-supported second floor—or half-floor, for the vaulted ceiling of the main great hall soared to the roof.

Ancient hangings that surely were once more beauteous than the famed product of Eirrin's women hung now in tatters and were dust at the base of the walls. Yet two chairs and a low table, brassbound all, somehow remained. Cormac looked upon them, his teeth pressed tightly together; only through some sorcerous means surely could those furnishings have survived the millenia.

The *feeling* came upon him.

Hair prickled at his nape and cold fingers seemed to trail up his back. He'd been here afore of a certitude . . . but not in this lifetime. Neither had anyone else: the floor's thick layer of dust was long undisturbed.

Slowly so as to be more silent than a mouse seeking indoors for sustenance in winter, he picked up his buckler and drew his sword. There was no door; only a doorway, where long ago had hung a curtain or arras. Cormac paced to the portal. His bare feet were silent in the soft dust. No sound stirred the stillness. He peered out. There was no one in the corridor.

Cormac mac Art sat down in the dust and put on his buskins.

Out he went into the dingy hallway, and he turned right toward the castle's front. All was silent and gloomy; only the single window-niche in each room admitted light, and that but little, so that by the time it found its way out to the hall it was the merest glim. In that upper hallway of the anciently brooding castle, it may as well have been night. On a carpet of dust, in silence, Cormac walked through night at nigh-midday.

He was unable to understand the total lack of

sound, unless all the Britons were somewhere outside. In that event, they and his comrades—and Samaire, far more than comrade—might well be at the grim business of death-dealing even now. But he forced himself not to hurry, and paced forward in a semi-crouch. He let his soles glide over the dust, so as to make no sound of footfalls.

He moved only as swiftly as he thought he dared, with no more noise than a pacing cat.

Cormac passed the room wherein Wulfhere and Ceann had spent a night, while he had preferred to sleep out under the watchful moon. He passed the room in which Samaire was to have spent that same night. Almost he smiled; she had instead joined him outside, though he had stated clearly that he was ex-ile, and would not return to Eirrin. In the morning, he had announced that he would . . . .

He reached the end of the corridor, and was wary anew.

There was no man in view. There was no sound.

With caution, he moved past the stairway that led down to the narrow cul-de-sac of an entry hall. Here had knelt Norse archers; here was the window from whence they'd sped their whistling shafts at himself and Wulfhere and their approaching band of Danes. Now Cormac obtained the same view those Norge-born bowmen had. He peered without, and caution eased.

There was only the empty plain and, far off, the entry into the twisting passage through the rock that connected this valley with the beach.

A new feeling of nervousness akin to fear drifted over the Gael like a dark mist. The castle . . . deserted? And without . . . no matter how he turned his head to peer this way and that, and strained his ears, there was no sound of shout or clash of arms to seaward.

Cormac mac Art walked the length of that defense-hall, hardly pausing to peer out at each of the other three windows. At the head of the second flight of steps, he glanced back. He saw nothing, no one. He crept down the stairs to the landing, peered around.

Below was nothing, no one.

Re-ascending, he passed around the hall's back wall and onto the railed gallery that overlooked the vast main hall of the eerily silent castle.

Below, sprawled amid great dark splashes, were the bodies of strong men.

Cormac's and Wulfhere's Danes had died down there, three months agone, along with fifteen Norsemen. Cormac had been pursuing Samaire and Cutha Atheldane, a druid among Vikings, and had no part in the terrible battle. Only Wulfhere and Samaire's brother Ceann survived.

Despite some objection from the more civilized prince and princess of Leinster, Wulfhere and Cormac had deemed this great structure a fine tomb indeed. They had left the dead here, friend and foe alike, corpses all. It was these considerably decayed bodies Cormac expected to find this day.

He did not. Not even the bones of those two-and-twenty men remained.

Instead, the scent of new-spilled blood was on the air. It lay barely dry below in splashes and pools, amid the hideously staring, sprawled corpses of eighteen . . . Britons!

Chapter Five:
The Living Dead

Cormac was outside in the bright sunlight, summoning Bas the Druid and Lugh, the Meathish hunter whom the Gael had surnamed the Manhunter.

Then came the clamor, and the three men whirled. A clot of weapon-men burst into the far end of the Valley of the Castle. A huge red-bearded, ax-wielding Dane . . . a small warrior in leathern boots with a bronze-studded leathern helmet . . . three chain-mailed men with bows and feather-bristling quivers . . . others: all of Eirrin. And with them, a stumbling, mumbling Briton.

The man appeared mad and his gibbering was audible to Cormac long before his main party reached him. Great glazed eyes stared awfully from out a pallid Briton face twisted and set in horror.

"That man looks as if he has gazed upon the face of Death itself," Bas said.

"Mayhap he has," Cormac said very quietly. "He is the last of his entire crew."

The three waited; the fourteen came on. All were united before the gaping dark maw of the castle, where its big iron-bound door sagged forlornly from one rotting hinge.

"You've been within?" Wulfhere demanded, ere any other could direct coherent words.

"Aye."

"What . . . did you find?" Samaire asked.

Cormac jerked a gesture at the sagging Briton. "This one's companions. All of them save the three Wulfhere and I accounted for. All are dead; all of them. Hacked and stabbed and cut to pieces."

"Gods of my ancestors," Samaire said, little above a whisper. "This sniveler spoke true, then."

Wulfhere's big hand clamped the back of the Briton's neck. "Tell this man, Briton. Tell him—and the druid."

The Briton made as if to hurl himself to his knees before Bas; Wulfhere held him back and on his feet, by main strength. *Speak!*"

The man did not speak; he babbled, high-voiced, "Druid, Holy Druid, call upon—uhk!"

"I said *speak,* not beg," Wulfhere rùmbled, squeezing until the Briton's eyes bulged and his lean fox-face gained a bit of colour.

"I . . . I . . . we were . . . within," he said, and he shuddered when he cast a fearful glance in the direction of the castle's doorway. "Drinking, talking of what we'd do with our booty on our return to Silurnum. All was merriment—this demon-haunted keep is overflowing with the loot of a dozen raids!"

"We know that, man," Cormac said impatiently. He drew deep breath. His gaze flickered up to Wulfhere; back to the Briton. "Your name, man. What be your name?" He'd never seen a man so in need of calming.

"Os . . . Osbrit son of Drostan, of Wroxeter."

"And I be Cormac, Art's son of Connacht, Osbrit of Wroxeter. Be mindful of yourself as a surrounded captive, Osbrit Drostan's son, and attend me: no harm will come to ye. My word on it, before the druid. Now tell me how died those men in there, Osbrit. Who else be on this isle—and how is it you alone made escape?" Cormac raised his eyes. "Wulfhere—let go his neck. He's a man. He can stand."

"We . . . we were . . . they just *appeared,* among us, about us! Men of the north countries oversea, all of them. Most were Norse, though too there were Danes—"

"Danes and Norse *together?* Allies?"

"I swear it! Behl witness—I swear it! Danes and Norse, aye. They just . . . they were just *there.* Out of the very air they came, all with axes and swords naked in their hands. No word they spoke—not ever, not one among them uttered aught that I heard. Their faces were grim-set, awful . . . their business was *slaughter!* Naught else but to bring red death upon us. Four of our number were down bloody ere we even knew, realized! My cousin Anir . . . Bedwyr's brother Cei . . . oh, ye GODS!" The man paused to shudder and draw a deep uneven breath.

"Then we were snatching up spear and ax and sword and bucklers," he went on, "wallowing on the floor, stumbling to our feet and defending ourselves as best we could. But . . . what boots defense, when a man cannot injure his foe!"

"What?"

"Truth! They would not bleed, they could not be hurt. Struck, they bled not. Arms, slashed through, remained attached to body." A terrible shudder took Osbrit's body. "They would not die, not even when I passed my spear through the belly of one till the point brast through his backbone."

"What?"

Osbrit babbled. Tears shimmered in his eyes and spittle flecked his lips to drool upon his chin. "I SWEAR it! I myself faced a Dane, a man with a scar on his cheek like a fork for the snaring of hares, and an ax-haft dyed red and what I took for the emblem of the new faith on his black shield. He—"

Cormac stared with stricken, fixed eyes. "Wait, man. This Dane . . . his belt buckle . . . his buckler . . ."

"The bands of bronze on his black shield I at first thought was the cross of the Christians, and aye, his belt buckle . . . the face of a wing-eared man it was, moulded of br—"

"Crom and the Dagda!" Cormac gasped. "Wulfhere . . . it's Guthrun he describes!"

"He lies! Guthrun Jarl's son fell beside me these three months agone, in that same great hall of this keep! You yourself saw his body, with his head attached by only a string of tendon. This fellow *lies*—he saw Guthrun's remains within—"

Cormac interrupted. "There are no remains within, Wulfhere. All are gone. There are only the new-dead: eighteen Britons."

"Aye, Behl show mercy," Osbrit said with a sobbing catch in his voice. "All eighteen cut down by men who would neither wound nor bleed nor die! I slashed a face, I tell you, and that Norseman did not even bleed! At that I backed away in horror, for I knew there was evil upon us, dark magic. All around me good men screamed as they were hacked to death by . . . by man-*things* they could neither slay nor even wound! He came on, him whose face I slashed. He said nothing, he neither grinned nor frowned, but only just *stared,* stared into my soul, like . . . like a dead man! His ax caught in my shield. I fell back, stumbled—and then to catch my balance I was sitting in that huge curule-chair in there."

"The huge . . . what?" Samaire asked.

"The Roman influence," Cormac said. "He speaks of the throne. So you gave ground because ye must, in horror I've no doubt, and ye lost your balance and fell back into the lord's chair."

"Aye!" Osbrit nodded madly. "And—and . . . he drew back. He turned from me! I *saw* Dyfnwal thrust into him . . . *I saw the point of Dyfnwal's sword emerge at that man's back!*"

With a great shudder Osbrit sagged. Samaire gripped his arm and the man beside her held the Briton up merely by his presence; Osbrit leaned weakly against lean young Ros mac Dairb, nor did either seem to take note.

At last, dully, Osbrit regained life, and talked on.

"They . . . they killed them all. All my companions. All . . . all of them. No Norsemen fell or bled, no Dane, none of them, and they must have numbered a score. Then in the midst of the red carnage they'd wrought, they . . . they turned. *All* of them, as though one had given a signal, though none spoke. They turned to face me. They stared. None spoke. They looked upon me like hungry wolves just beyond the firelight, staring in, waiting, hoping . . . Gods! O mother . . . in awful silence they just stared at me thus, and none spoke ever, or so much as *frowned.* Like masks their faces were, with burning pale fires for eyes. I . . . sat. Behl's Name, Fire of Life, I could do naught else! I admit it—nay, I swear it: I was frozen with fear! There must have been a score—"

"Sixteen Norse," Cormac mac Art said in a quiet, dull voice, and he knew horror at his own thoughts, hearing his own matter-of-fact tone and chilled by it, "and . . . six Danes, I should say."

Wulfhere stared at him with wide eyes. *"Cormac!"*

Cormac met those blue eyes. "Aye." His gaze returned to what had been a man and was now a frightmad, gibbering creature for pity. "Osbrit . . . and then . . ."

"I remained where I was. And then . . . Fire of Life! I swear it by the sun and the moon—they *vanished!* Like smoke, like mist in the morning sun."

Cormac laid a hand on the man's shoulder; he did not drop it there, but laid hand on the other in commiseration, in a strange, understanding tenderness. "I believe you, Osbrit. Think. Describe others . . ."

Osbrit described two Norsemen, to be interrupted

by Wulfhere; with an oath, the Dane swore he'd cloven the head of one of those Vikings from crown to chin, three months agone.

Cormac nodded. He accepted what he must, and turned to Bas.

"It is a castle of dark sorcery, my lord Bas. The Britons were attacked by men already slain . . . when last we were here! And when we left, those same slain slayers lay on the floor within. Now there is no sign of them. Only the Briton dead. And the throne . . . somehow it be safe from their attack."

Bas was silent in thought. None broke that reverie.

"Such things," Bas said, "are said to be possible . . . to *have been* possible. We druids have no such power, nor do we covet it. It is black sorcery, the sorcery of death, the Old Magick. To raise the dead against the living . . . to cheat the dead of their rest and return for any purpose . . . Behl protect and Crom defend! It is too horrible. It is against all that is decent on the ridge of the world. Kull's or no, this is a place of evil!"

"It's not Kull's evil, I'm thinking. Will ye go in with me?"

"Cormac! No!"

Cormac ignored Samaire and her hand on his arm. He continued to look questioningly on the green-robed servant of Celtic and Gaelic gods, Bas of Tir Conaill who had been a noble of Eirrin.

Bas nodded. He looked about, seeming taller with purpose. He fingered his mistletoe pendant. "Who among ye bears oak? Be there the All-healer among us, *an t'uil:* Mistletoe?"

"The haft of my ax be oak," a man said, and so called another, hefting his shiny-bladed ax. Hopefully Ros mac Dairb bared a lunula from under his mailcoat; another drew forth, almost embarrassedly, a dried old sprig of mistletoe from his sword scabbard. His wife, he claimed, had insisted on his carrying it . . . .

Bas took the mistletoe, and an oak-hafted ax Cormac thought too light for war. Its owner had a Briton sword now, given him by Wulfhere in a moment of camaraderie the night previous.

Of course the druid wore a lunula, a moon-disk on a cord woven of gold wire about his neck. Larger it was than those of the three men present who also wore them, and surely more potent. Bas looked at Cormac, who wore the usual Celtic torc, and no other jewellery; the leather band about his right wrist was a brace for his sword-arm, not decoration.

"Yourself?"

Cormac gestured helplessly, in some embarrassment. He had little to do with gods, and never had, nor did he encumber himself with their trappings. Bas only put his hands on the other Gael, mistletoe to flesh, and murmured to himself—and to his gods. All heard the names, Behl of the shining sun and great Crom who was older than Eirrin, and the Dagda— the Good God—his son mac Og, and others as well.

Bas's voice rose and his words became discernible: ". . . who protected Cuchulain and the first mac Art, Cormac Mor, and the great Finn . . . protect this Cormac mac Art too, for no more loyal servant of your reverendness exists on all the ridge of the sprawling world."

Cormac looked around at the others. "Remain without. Bas and I go within, armed by our faith and his knowledge."

"I go with you, Cormac mac Art," Brian na Killevy said, a not-unhandsome young man whose face, Cormac felt, was so smooth because fair young Brian could raise no fur on it. The youth's hair was the colour of flax.

Another young man pressed forward. "It's not here I'll be remaining whilst my captain go into danger." Ros mac Dairb said, just as firmly.

Samaire said only, "No. I choose not to remain without." Her lower lip pushed forth, nor did it tremble; Cormac knew the sign.

Wulfhere's rumble summed up: "Lead on Druid. We go where you go; I go where Cormac goes. Damn you, son of an Eirish pig-farmer, I owe you this life!"

"No," Cormac said. "No. Wulfhere, ye *must* stay here with these men, who will not object to being termed . . . indifferent sailors." He looked at Brian and Ros, like eager-eyed pups when the master makes hunting preparations. "It's death inside, and sorcerous death at that. I would not bring the red blood on your bodies for it, south or north, east or west."

"Would be grief to me all my days, Cormac mac Art, if I went not with you after I've declared!" Brian of Killevy in Airgialla showed in his face that he'd not remain outside. "And ye know," he grinned, "I *love* to fight!"

"And I, son of Art," Dairb's son Ros said, a fair young man and lean, with a golden bush of hair like a halo. "And unless the sky fall on me, or the earth gave way beneath these feet, I will not move from your side."

"Ye be insane both," Cormac said. "And ye honour your mothers and your people. Very well. It's this we know: if we be set upon within, it's no living hands will bring steel upon us, but dead men. No. You two are ordered to go up onto the gallery which I shall show you, and there remain. On your oath."

Neither looking very happy, the two young men agreed. Cormac looked at Wulfhere. "An we shriek and scream and there be the clangour of arms, come not within. Wulfhere old cleaver of skulls, d'ye hear?"

If Ros and Brian were young dogs eager for the hunt, Wulfhere was an old hunting hound, envious, morose; saddened that he was to be left behind. Stiffly, sadly he said, "Aye." His right forefinger scratched within his beard.

"If such be the case, if ye hear us attacked and we come not forth . . . *take these men from this place, Wulfhere*. And slay a fine calf to the end that this dread Samaire-heim joins her mother Atlantis beneath the eternal sea. You're agreed?"

Unenthusiastically as before: "Aye."

Cormac nodded. "Bas . . . Brian . . . Ros . . ."

The three stood ready. Bas muttered, but naught that he said was understood by any present.

"Wulfhere?"

"The All-father's one eye be upon you, blood-brother."

Cormac nodded shortly. "Wulfhere . . . *seize Samaire, and hold her fast!*"

Though he'd paid her no mind while he issued his instructions, Samaire was unprepared for this treachery. For a moment she was still in shock. Then she started forward, her grass-green eyes widening.

The man who towered behind her, topping her height by more than the length of her two hands combined, enfolded her in arms that were like tree limbs. Instantly she was kicking and squirming.

"NO! Cormac! No *no*—Wulfhere, you ugly goat-smelling bull—let me GO!"

Wulfhere held fast. Without a word, Cormac and his trio turned to the castle. They passed between the pillars, and were lost to sight.

Behind them Samaire still combined pleading and demanding in no small voice as Cormac pointed to the stairs and issued swift instructions to Brian and Ros. They all ascended. The younger men went round and out onto the gallery; Cormac and Bas descended into the prodigious expanse of the castle's high-domed main hall.

Great pillars rose from the tiled floor, propping the gallery and the semi-floor that ran all about the walls, ten feet and more above the floor. The walls were engraved and indited with scenes not discernible until one went close, so that all appeared to be mere decor. The bodies of eighteen Britons still strewed the floor, in pools and splashes of the blood that was solely theirs, amid weapons and pieces of their corpses. Full forty good paces away, back of the sprawling hall's center, rested the carven throne. Despite the lofty pillars, the closely-etched walls, the decorated ceiling; despite even the dead, that regal throne dominated the hall and the castle; it surveyed all and seemed to *own* all.

Bas stopped suddenly as if he'd run into some barrier Cormac could not see. The druid looked all about, then lifted oak and mistletoe at the ends of green-robed arms.

"Hail O warming Sun in your bright rising, our shield of gold and our eternal heat-fire; give us good fortune! Hail O Behl lord of earth and sky; You we call now upon to perform a work only you can! A work of the Light to hurl down foul work that comes from the Dark!"

Bas began walking forward, among the corpses toward the throne.

"Soothe pains until they are painless . . . let the dead sink in rightful unpained slumber with woundy hurts smarting no more . . . let them rest and begin the Ring of Return, not as shades bearing evil but as Rightful Men in your Name!"

Cormac stood still, feeling a horripilation on him, as the man in the forest-green robe advanced into the immense room, walking amid corpses without looking down to guide his steps, without stilling his voice. But his steps were guided; his feet touched neither blood nor sheared away member nor corpse nor fallen weapon, and Cormac knew that the god was upon the druid.

"Agron, slaughter's noble mistress: attend us not!

"Shadowy Scathach who did tutor Cuchulain of Muirthemne, grant us invincibility as ye did him!

"Cu Roi mac Dairi, twice-noble master of sorcerers, note ye here Cormac mac Art—lend him your sword!

"Go along now those unneeded, come along now those we need, and perform for the sons of men the work of laying the dead, the word of the Light against the Dark! Hear us, warming Sun in your bright rising! Let not this mortal blood be spilled—we BEG! Let not evil strike down these fair mortal forms—WE PLEAD! Behl, Crom, Cu Roi, Great Dagda . . . behold your servant Cormac, behold your servant Bas, behold—*an t'uil!*"

Bas lifted high the all-healing mistletoe to the unseeing walls and the high-domed ceiling and, Cormac fervently hoped, to observant gods. All-healer was the wax-green plant that grew not from the ground but magickally on the sacred oaks in Eirrin, and in Gaul, and in Britain, and put forth its pure white berries: *an t'uil!*

"By mistletoe and oak, by Sun and moon, *by fire and water* we call for help, we pledge the good, the Light; we abjure the Dark of sorcerous evil; we proclaim that we be not ready to face Donn, Lord of the Dead, that so well we like this land we are not ready to view splendid I-breasil . . ."

Cormac's voice rose, and it seemed of its own accord, for he had no thought of speaking whilst holy words were intoned. The words merely . . . emerged.

"And I pledge body and brain," mac Art said, "spear and sword, voice and arms, to drive out from our fair green Eirrin those raven-robed, raven-tongued usurpers and proclaimers of the New Faith!"

Cormac frowned, shocked and astonished he'd spoken so.

Bas had stopped still at that sudden interruption of his speaking to his gods. But then, there amid the gory dead of Britain, he nodded, and bent, and took up a sword and a dagger. These he held high, one across the other so that they formed the execution symbol of the Romans and the priests of Rome.

"Behold the Cross, symbol of slow and agonized Death!" he cried, and dashed down the two blades with a great clang.

The druid was at pains to tread upon the broken cross as he resumed his slow trek to the throne. Now he muttered, and Cormac, understanding no word, knew that Bas spoke in the Old Tongue that only druids knew.

"In the name of the Sun and the moon," Cormac said, rather haltingly, wondering how to pray, wondering if indeed the gods of his fathers would listen to such a red-handed dealer of death as he. "This I say truly and swear by the gods the great clans of Eirrin swear by: All foemen I face. And this I ask: if foes must come, let them be of living flesh, that I may fight as a man fights."

At the far end of the sprawling room, ringed about by pillars with squared decor of bronze and gilt, the stately chair rested. From it, Cormac remembered, had one of his own men swept a fine bale of rich cloth, to cover one of their dead. Now green-robed Bas reached that kingly seat, and turned, and sat. Cormac stared, taken aback.

Kings Cormac had seen, and kings he had served, and on him by kings had treachery been done. But only one had he seen who looked so kingly, so made for such a chair, as this Bas mac Miall of the Northern ui-Neill of Tir Conaill; grandson of a king, brother of a king, brother in law to Eirrin's High-king—and by choice Druid of the Old Faith.

Then, as the seated Bas spoke on, droning now, Cormac took note of that rich and outsized chair.

It was of wood, bound with bronze, decorated in silver and onyx and gold itself, and all the decor in squared figures, for those of Atlantis and Valusia of old never broider'ed with reminders of their dread enemy: the sons of the Great Serpent, who owned the earth before man.

But the chair . . . the chair itself . . . that huge high-backed throne of wood . . .

Cormac mac Art strode out amid the gore and weapons and ghastly remains littering the floor, treading with care to avoid the awful clutter. He turned, and looked up. From the gallery at the front of the castle, Brian and Ros gazed down upon him.

"Go ye together. *Remain* together!" Cormac gestured. "Go along that corridor until ye come to a room piled with booty like the treasure trove of an Eastern prince. Gather what your arms can carry, and proceed back, and down, and out the door into the sun. An ye succeed unchallenged, return for more. WAIT! If aught amiss occurs . . . if it's foemen ye see . . . drop the booty, lads, and RUN! Draw ye no sword and stand to fight—FLEE, for heed me: it's fleeing mac Art will be!"

Without waiting for an answer, he whirled again and strode, a dark and lean man in rustling chain who stepped over a headless body and a cloven shield and then an armless hand as he paced to the stately chair where sat Bas.

"Bas . . . your pardon, Holy Druid . . . what say ye this chair be made of?"

Bas stared, blinking, obviously having been far and now coming back but slowly.

"Cormac mac Art," he said in a strange voice that came as if from that faraway place, "see ye that so long as ye live ye do never again interrupt a Druid in converse with Those he serves!"

It was Cormac's turn to blink. His armpits prickled and a chill touched his back. Almost, he who bent knee to no man, not even crowned head, considered kneeling . . . almost. He made no reply, for he could think of naught to say.

Now Bas, with no visible rancor whatever, looked down at the ancient throne, ran his hands over it. The druidic ring flashed. His head came up, long dark hair flurrying at his shoulder, and there was enlightenment in his clear eyes.

"Oak!"

"Aye, so I thought even from afar. Oak! From the tree holy and beloved to Behl and—"

But the druid's grey eyes had swerved to look past him, widening. Cormac broke off. He knew what he'd see ere he turned, for he *felt* it: Silent menace and the chill of the grave had entered the lofty hall of Atlantis. The air hung thick with a loathsome aura of blood-freezing horror and the cruelest sorcery devised by demonic mind.

He turned, and *they* were there.

There had been no sound; there was none now. *They were there.*

Men in plain helmets of iron bands and helms with horns like the Old God, Cernunnos the Horned One; men with eyes of blue and grey, and drooping pale moustaches; men carrying axes and swords and the round shields of far Norge. And . . . others . . .

Cormac's body went all overchill and damp, and the sweat was atrickle in armpits and palms. Ah, gods! He knew them, those Danes . . . Hrothgar of the bent broken nose and brilliant swordwork, and Hrut Forkbeard with his ornately hilted sword and silver-chased leather jerkin and vainly twisted mustachioes . . . and there Edric, aye and Hnaef . . .

"Gods! Oh my old comrades . . . *I saw ye all dead on this very floor!*"

Chapter Six:
The Throne of Kull

Dull eyes staring fixedly from faces like pasty masks, the men who were at once dead and not-dead began to move forward.

Bas rose to his feet. Deeply green sleeves slid back over surprisingly thick wrists as the druid extended his arms. Toward those stalking shades he held out mistletoe and oak. They stared, every one with naked sword or ax in hand, and no wounds upon them.

"Be at rest! By Sun and Moon, fire and water, oak and the green mistletoe that lives all the year . . . BEGONE! Mead awaits you in Valhal . . . your Valkyries cannot find you . . . bodies unborn await you in the land of the living! Your mighty god Odin of the Single Eye awaits you! Journey to him—*Leave us!* This is the realm of the living, where there is no place for slain men . . . and . . . ye be *dead!*"

They stared dully, fixedly, those horrid spectres that looked so unlike spectres, but living men. Two-and-twenty, they ceased their slow forward movement. Every eye, Cormac saw, was on the druid's hands. . . .

Then they began their ghastly silent moving again, edging around sidewise, avoiding Bas . . . coming at

Cormac. In winged helm and shining scale-mail, one
Norseman was well ahead of his fellows. Blue eyes,
dull as though mindless, stared at Cormac mac Art.

Cormac's buckler was on his arm and sword in
hand. The Gael attacked, for all the prickle of horripilation up his back and on his arms.

His sword swept out and around like a gale, hum-
ming through the air, and he watched it slash through
the Viking's bronze-cuffed sword-arm. Watched it
slash . . . through . . . without resistance . . . without
blood . . . and with no effect on the arm, which continued rising. It descended in a rush. The Gael's
shield leaped up and he shuddered as the descending
sword crashed onto its metal-ringed edge.

"By all the gods! My steel has no effect on him—
none! But *his* blade's as deadly as ever steel is! A man
has no chance against this horror—BAS!"

Cormac could only retreat or die; a swift jab
showed him that the Norseman's shield, too, was fit
to defend a living man. An unslayable kill-machine,
the Viking swept up his terrible ax.

For the first time in his life, Cormac mac Art
turned and ran from a foeman.

From the shocked druid's hand he tore the oaken
hafted ax of Ruadan mac Mogcorf. He was unsure
why; it was as if some instinct drove him. His sword
he left against the throne-chair as useless, nor did he
wield the ax as a man should. Holding it close to the
head he'd thought overlight for a fighting man, he
drove the end of the haft at the Norseman who had
followed—but had stopped three paces from the
throne.

The ax was poorly balanced for a thrusting weapon, held thus wrong end before, but with it Cormac
thrust. Nor was he averse to using the Saxon tactic of
feinting at the body and stabbing at the face.

The tip of the haft jolted home as if against living
flesh and bone. Cormac could have wept for happi-

ness at the shock to his arm.

A horrid groan filled that soaring chamber, and seconds later an equally horrid stench, the stomach-turning fetor of putrefaction and decay. And the Norseman seemed to melt, the flesh fading from his bones, hanging in tatters, vanishing into the air. His body quivered all over.

While his back crawled, Cormac watched what oaken stave had wrought, when steely brand was of no avail.

Bronze armlets dropped to ring on the floor, and one rolled noisily. Coat of scalemail *caved in*, cleaving to a form suddenly fleshless. For a brief moment Cormac stared into the eye-holes of a skull, a white-boned death's head bereft of so much as a scrap of flesh.

Then the lifeless skeleton crumpled to the floor with a rattle. It lay there, as should have done the bony structure of a man slain three months before.

"It's the O-O-O-OAKHH!" Cormac mac Art shouted, partly in triumph and partly in a release of fear and horror, tension close to hysteria. "The OAK, Druid! Behl's symbol of LIFE—the dead cannot withstand its touch! *This* be why that man Osbrit alone survived, for he sat that *oaken throne!* Here is why they sought to avoid you and come 'round at me, Bas—you held this ax!"

Then Cormac did that which was alien to a weaponman, and against the grain of his very nature.

With all his might, he swung the ax against a broad thick pillar of smooth, time-darkened stone. His hands shifted so that it was the side of the steel head that struck with a great ringing thump and a terrible jar to his arms. A loud crack split the air as the haft broke. With another swift stroke Cormac smashed the head from his ax so that it hurtled through the air until it struck another pillar—and rebounded, and rebounded, and drove bloodlessly *through* one of those horrid foes to ring and clatter on the floor.

The Dane was unharmed; the ax was an ax no longer; Cormac held a thick oaken stave as long as his arm, to the fingers.

With it he drove at another man of the Norse. A whirring ax-blade rushed past his head, while he slammed the haft of what had been Ruadan's ax into the shield-arm of the Viking. An awful death-cry rose; again came the stench of a mouldering putrid corpse—and a second skeleton clattered horribly to the floor.

Bas stared with half-glazed eyes as the tall weapon-man of Eirrin fell to one knee to avoid a sword-thrust, and cracked that attacker's knee with his strange cudgel. And there were three skeletons amid the corpses on the floor of Kull's Castle.

They closed in now, and Cormac did what he must to avoid death-dealing thrusts and slashes of un-dead men whose blades his targe could not turn all at once; he hurled himself aside.

Then he *ran,* racing around the seated druid to come upon a Dane at the edge of the cluster. Cormac knew that lightly bearded man; had fought beside him and trod the decks of ships named *Raven* and *Wolfsail* with him. But the Gael was steeled, sure now that he had the means of providing rest for these men brought back from the land of the dead on the murderous mission of some unknown mage. Cormac *was* the means.

Before the Dane could swing his weapon into line, a truncated ax-haft struck his shield and then his arm. As silently as he'd done three months before, Cormac's comrade of erst died again, and there were four skeletons.

Bas jerked erect as though waking from some dark dream.

"Cu Roi mac Dairi," he said in a shaky voice as his hand closed around the hilt of Cormac's sword, "son

of Behl, servant of Crom, be with me! And . . . King
. . . Kull . . . *pardon!*"

With that the druid crashed Cormac's sword down
onto one arm of the priceless ancient throne. The
blade bit deep; wood older than old splintered and
broke. The throne shuddered—as did Bas's surprisingly powerful arm.

A man in an iron-banded helm of dented grey
rushed past the oaken throne to swing his shining
glaive at Cormac mac Art—and Bas the Druid
smashed a ragged chunk of chair-arm into the
Viking's back. Released by fingers from which the
flesh began instantly to dangle in tatters like old
draperies, the Norse sword rushed past Cormac to
clang and clatter far across the room. A thrice-
banded helmet slipped down over the shining white
mound of bone that had been a human head. A
skeleton once more, the Norseman fell.

Cormac too had struck, and six skeletons lay on
the tiles.

A sword crashed off Cormac's shield and he saw
another rushing in from the side. Desperately he
struck at it with his oaken club just as he'd have done
with his own good sword—which was now so horribly useless. Ax-haft deflected glaive-blade; the point
tore a channel up the Gael's forearm. Later he would
feel pain and be discommoded by the rip in the skin
and flesh; now he did not so much as notice. Ax-haft
thunked into mailed hip, jerked away, leaped sidewise swift as a striking adder. Oak met skin; skin became tatters; tatters vanished to leave only bone.

The two skeletons fell almost together, with a rattle as
of many games of knuckle-bones at once.

The ghastly battle continued. It was two against
fourteen now, and one of the two unarmoured. Un-
helmeted too he was, and cumbered by rustling robes
of woolen girt with a rope composed of four intricate-
ly plaited strands.

"Bas, Bas! Back to the throne, man, ere ye be slain for naught! Hack the throne . . . and *hurl the pieces!*"

Bas skipped away from an overweight man of Norge. He turned—and faced an ax that had already commended its downward rush. Reflexively the holy druid jerked up his splintry chunk of ancient oak, and up leaped his other hand to brace it with a grip on either end.

The ax rushed down to cleave through that time-weakened slab of wood so that it was two, and had only slowed the descent of steel death. Bas went to one knee. His shocked arms quivered. From one nerve-tingling hand, even as the un-dead drew up his ax for the death-stroke, a piece of ragged wood fell. It struck the floor and bounded, just a little, onto the buskined foot of the ax-wielding Dane.

From above his head Bas heard a grunt. Then there was the stench of death's decay eerily accelerated, and then that was gone, as Guthrun Black-shield died once more. Again he returned to pallid smooth bones that clattered on the tiles.

Ten skeletons lay on the floor in their mail or leather; twelve men who were not men shuffled on. Twelve Un-dead men continued to do what they must: endeavour to slay the living. Helpless voiceless minions of the ghoulish sorcery that had raised them, they clove blindly to their one purpose: murder.

Bas of Tir Conaill gained the throne-chair and turned to look upon the awful sight.

The floor was strewn with corpses and man-shaped collections of bones. Bleeding from right forearm and left shoulder where the capping sleeve of his mailcoat was shredded, Cormac mac Art leaped and dodged, ducked and skidded, lunged and jabbed and swung. He danced, armour a-jingle; he raced away to attack again like a great spitting cat amid harrying dogs. Succor he knew lay only in nimbleness; a dash here, a jab there with his headless ax, and duck and dodge to continue the grim work from a new direction.

One advantage was held by the living man among the Un-dead; when his stave struck other than shield or enemy blade, an enemy fell.

The wood of the god-tree met sorcery-driven steel. Another of the resurrected dead was struck. Another skeleton crashed to the floor. A hand broke, and fingerbones rattled free to roll about. It was then Cormac fell backward across a Briton corpse. Ghoul-men who had been enemies, allied now in death, leaped in concert to carve the fallen man like a ham at feast-time.

Bas groaned in horror. But the other Gael was lean and more than passing quick.

Cormac rolled, contriving to hurl himself several feet along the floor with a wrenching twisting exertion that would have crippled the back of a man whose body was not so agile and muscle-sheathed. Armour screamed on tile. A rushing ax chopped down the corpse of the Briton over which Cormac had fallen, and where he'd sprawled but a second before. Already he was scrambling to his feet, aiding himself with his hands like the animals that were his remotest ancestors. To such was he reduced.

A brief glance showed the Gael five foes converging on him. These were uncanny foes, unnatural foes, impervious to aught but the headless ax in his hand. Again he must needs run, fleet as a hare before hounds, racing around and between pillars tall as oaks—which he wished they were.

In shuddery silence, dead men followed, to join him with them.

Bas saw that Cormac was bent on making his way around and back to him. He saw too how the Dane hurried to cut off his former piratic comrade—and the druid hurled the broken piece of oak in his hand. The dead man moved too fast to be struck where Bas aimed, between the shoulder blades. The splinter-bristling chunk of wood fell short.

Yet again the druid was lucky or Behl-blessed; it struck the back of his knotty calf. In seconds he became mere bone. Again the ghastly cycle: man who had turned into corpse and then into bone and then into man—returned to bone.

With cries of rage and challenge that rang and echoed in the room, Ros and Brian burst into the hall of horror. Having heard the clangour and Cormac's shouts, they'd hurried onto the gallery to stare down at that which erupted their bodies into gooseflesh. The two youths withstood the moveless watching as long as they could without intervening. Swallowing all fear, they came now loping like young hounds with more enthusiasm than knowledge or sense.

"STOP!" Bas bellowed, and it was no small voice the druid possessed. "Hold—only oak slays them— *only oak!*"

The two young men looked at him, at Cormac and his assailants—who though eerily *silent* looked quite natural—and at each other, and back to the druid.

Bas chopped a piece of splintery wood from the ruined airm of the throne of Kull. As though he'd commanded men all his life, as though he wore a crown and mail rather than robe and center-parted black hair that was rope-held about his forehead above his brows, Bas the Druid called out again.

"Come ye hither, both!"

Cormac was parrying a vicious sword-stroke from a man whose sword-wound he'd once treated, off Rechru isle after an encounter with a boat too full of Frisians. His hurried swing of his makeshift stave at the attacker was well caught on oval shield, even as Cormac blunted the ax-swing of a second foe on his own buckler.

"GET TO BAS!" he bellowed, without looking from his foemen.

Brian and Ros, as confused as they were quiveringly excited, were already doing so in obedience to the sword-wielding druid. Like a man whose wife is dying for lack of wood on the fire, the robed man chopped at the magnificent old throne with Cormac's sword.

Diving headlong between two attackers and beneath their rushing blades, Cormac was able to strike a leg in passing with his strange weapon.

Nine of the Un-dead remained.

A flying chunk of wood struck one and rebounded to thud into the leg of a second. Brian of Killevy cried out in high glee at the double result of his throw.

Seven Un-dead stalked Cormac mac Art.

He fell before the simultaneous crash of two axes on his shield, which divided in twain nearly to the boss. Yet a moment later there were six of the enemy remaining, and then five, for Ros and the druid each hurled an oaken missile true. Brian's second throw missed his target.

Slammed into a knee with a jolting force and then struck with a rushing sword, the splinter-tipped stave in Cormac's hand bit his wrist . . . and went clattering and rolling noisily across the floor.

Without smiles of triumph on their mask-like faces, four grim, silent spectres from the other side of the grave closed on him. Blades rushed down—

And Cormac hurled himself, not between, but *through* the legs of one Un-dead enemy!

The cold of death stabbed through mail and tunic like an icy knife, and then he was landing on his hands without so much as a grunt. He skidded, rolled, came up running. The Gael sprinted for the throne and the three allies there. Ere he joined them, Bas had stepped away. His eyes blazed with an unearthly fire and his gesturing hands were like the claws of a rearing bear. Strange words issued from his lips, guttural words from the dim past of the race of man.

Three horrors that had been men—and more lately

corpses—stalked toward him with uplifted weapons. From the throne-chair oaken chunks whizzed. Two of the Un-dead became first putrefying corpses once again, then bones—and as they dropped, so fell the last of their number—with his flesh still sheathing his skeleton.

"HOLD!" Cormac called, and his hand leapt out to stay Brian's arm. "That be the last—and he remains flesh, if not blood! The druid has wrought a spell upon him . . . upon *it.*"

The eyes of three weapon-men of Eirrin turned their gazes upon Bas. Still gesturing and still gutturally murmuring, he advanced upon the fallen Viking. The man, if such he could be called, lay still in his horn-sprouting helm and fine scalemail corselet and steel-bossed seagreen belt.

". . . hear me?" the druid said aloud. "By all those names and conjuries and by the eternal golden sun and silv'ry moon, lord of day and lord of night, I conjure you . . . I *command* you. Answer! Your name, your name!"

The dead man's chest did not move. The dead man's voice rasped up from his throat like wood dragged over whetstone, and words emerged as though he had to think hard to form each one, and three men shivered who had never quaked in combat.

"Thor—gast . . . Shield - hewer-r-r—"

"Ah!" The druid stood now over the living dead man he had bound by ancient words to the floor. Now he forced him to speak on, by dint of powers greater even than the speechlessness of death. "And are ye dead, Thorgast Shield-hewer?"

Rasping and dry: "Ay-ye . . ."

"Gods," Brian whispered, and beside him Ros gasped out, "Crom Cruach stead me!"

"Why came ye back, ye who were dead, to war thus on the living?"

". . . sent—called, forced—I wa-as . . . had to—

commme ba-a-ack . . . co-ol-l-ld . . ."

"Aye, colder than your northern home it is, for ye were not meant to be here thus. Release is at hand, Thorgast Shield-hewer, but first—*answer!* Why came ye back? What was your mission?"

"Kill—all who ca-ame . . . herre—kill—Ku—K. . . Cor-r-mac—mac—Aar-r-r-tt . . ."

Brian of Killevy saw it, as the dead spoke, but never did flaxen-haired Brian tell what he saw: Cormac mac Art shuddered and paled.

"Why him?" the druid demanded. *"Speak,* Thorgast Shield-hewer!"

"Let—me-e-ee—go-oh . . ."

"SPEAK, damned spirit that was a man, answer! *Why* must ye seek to slay Cormac mac Art?"

". . . ha-ad to-ooo—ven—geann-ccce—"

"Vengeance? Ye knew him before?"

"N-O-oh—passst—pa-a-ast—li-i-ife . . ."

"Ah." The druid crouched close to the dead man, motionless but for the tortured moving of his lips. "And, Thorgast Shield-hewer, dead and not dead, poor cold shade dragged back from the Otherwhere . . . *who called you* here?"

"C—C-uth—no-o-ohh," the corpse moaned, as though confused. "L-et me—go-oh . . ."

"Speak the name, Thorgast Shield-hewer that was. *Who?* Speak—and these will be your last words; speak, and return where you belong . . . *dead man!*"

Staring, his face pale, Cormac strained to hear.

Thorgast Shield-hewer spoke two words, a strange name if it was a name, and then he was still, and the flesh faded from his white face to leave behind only the eternally grinning death's head on the skeleton he had been before he was called back by him whose name he pronounced: "Thulsa Doom!"

Chapter Seven:
Pacts

Brian and Ros were heroes. Both slim, and neither ill-
favoured, the excited young men reminded Cormac
of tail-wagging dogs after their first hunt. *The hounds
of Cormac,* he thought, and wondered if he were not
crediting himself with overmuch. His head had been
swelled a bit by that name the crew had begun ap-
plying to themselves after the successful fighting off
of the Pictish attack asea: the *Cormacanachta;* descendants or followers of Cormac.

So Ros and Brian-I-love-to-fight were heroes, and
the two youthful weapon-men strutted and figur-
atively wagged their tails before the others, while responding to questions with answers longer than necessary. If those who had abided outside did not quite
fawn on the two who with Cormac and Bas had
"slain" no less than two-and-twenty ghastly un-men,
they did certainly show their envy and adulation.

Most of the others, just as naturally, expressed the
wish that they'd been allowed to go within, rather
than remaining without; but . . . captain's orders.

During that great deal of chatter, Cormac caught
the eye of a rather sombre Lugh, and he winked.
Lugh's looks improved; Ros and Brian were the he-

roes of the hour—or moment—but that wink advised the archer that Cormac mac Art still remembered how initial entry had been gained to the Castle of Kull of Atlantis.

Bas ruminated apart, while Cormac, the dead man's words having discovered to him his extraordinary danger from whom or whatever Thulsa Doom was, brooded on his future. How, he wondered, as Ros na Dun Dalgan and Brian na Killevy received the adulation and envy of their comrades, did a mere weapon-man protect himself, much less do combat against a sorcerer so powerful as to raise the dead and turn them into fighting men?

Wulfhere meanwhile was grim. The Dane was essaying not to show his unhappiness at being left out of the steel-wielding action—and probably suspecting Cormac of having cheated him of his beloved sport: the splitting of shields and helms and skulls. Cormac said nothing to the giant from Dane-mark. He had no doubt that impatient and impetuous Wulfhere would have been slain within. The Dane's pride and concept of manhood would have prevented his employing the dodging, fleeing, circling, snapping-wolf tactics that Cormac had used—to the saving of his own life.

And Samaire sulked.

Wulfhere had held her fast, nor had she ceased struggling and railing at him until Cormac reappeared; four ashy-faced men emerging from the reeking charnel-house of the thrice-ancient castle. Released then, Samaire had not run to Cormac as all would have thought natural, but had turned from him. Nor would she say aught to the Dane or accept his bumbling friendly overtures.

Now, either forgetting their leader with two younger heroes to raise on high or perhaps respecting Cormac's withdrawal into himself, all trooped inside to see what little there was to be viewed: corpse-slain corpses and oak-made skeletons. Eighteen of the

former there were, mingled among a score and two of
the latter. Blood and cruor, weapons and rattly
bones, dismembered and beheaded corpses and a
chopped-up throne; these were what remained to be
seen.

And so they were noted and exclaimed over—
along with the excited words of Ros and Brian, but
one of whom was so much as a score of years of age.

Others remained outside in the still-warm sunlight
of early fall.

With his soiled robe flapping in a little breeze, Bas
walked away to be alone with himself and his gods.
Cormac sat on a rounded stone, heedless of his
wounds. Someone or other had salved and bandaged
them; someone or other not Samaire. Again and
again he examined and worked at his doffed coat of
linked steel chain, though he was hardly aware of
what he did. Cormac spoke not now to gods; he was
alone with his thoughts.

Samaire, too, had remained outside. Around the
castle she had walked, into the shadowy gloom
betwixt it and the cliff. Her helmet of lacquered and
bronze-studded cowhide she had removed, so that
her wealth of orange-and-gold hair stirred about her
shoulders and bounced when she walked.

Cormac noted well her departure, while making
sure his noticing went unnoticed. He assumed she
had gone to relieve herself; it was no privacy she'd
had on the ship, and soon they'd be aboard again.
Morosely, he ruminated.

Thulsa Doom.

Thulsa Doom, Doom, Doom, Thool-sah . . . Doooommmm. The name and its ominous sound pulsed
within his head like a gloomy drum, thrumming there
and somberly booming. Thulsa Doooommmm. . . .

What was a Thulsa Doom?

Who was Thuls—

He knew.

He *saw.* It was what his former crewmen had called "the remembering" that was upon him once again; the pictures, the words and memories or "memories" within his brain.

A bronzed hand tore away the shielding veil from a tall, spectrally thin man in a dark, well-made robe. A woman screamed; white faces, including those of soldiers in uniforms and with weapons unfamiliar to Cormac mac Art, shrank bank. Revealed behind the veil was the face of the living man in the robe. But it was no living face; it was a bare white skull, *in whose eye sockets flamed livid fire!*

Cormac *heard* . . . a voice thrumming in his mind as if in an echoic cavern, and he knew that this was the voice of the faceless man . . .

"Aye, Thulsa Doom, fools! The greatest of all wizards and your eternal foe, Kull of Atlantis! You have won this tilt, but beware, there shall be others."

Cormac *saw* that death's head man burst the cords that bound him; saw him swing to stalk, dark robe whirling and flapping about his heels to the tall ornate door. The back of his head, too, was the skull of a man long dead. Cormac *saw* a sharp blade transpierce the tall figure . . . and emerge unblooded. Seated on a stone on a lonely island plain incalculable years later, Cormac *saw* the skull-faced mage turn, saw him laugh, heard him speak, sneering—

"Ages ago I died as men die! Nay, I shall pass to some other sphere when my time comes, not before. I bleed not, for my veins are empty . . . Stand back, fool, your master goes. But he shall come again to you, and you shall scream and shrivel and die in that coming!"

Cormac saw. . . .

The skull-faced wizard step to a door bordered all about with squared, runic decor, and pass through it, and . . . vanish.

He heard . . . a man's voice—what man? Could there be men with names such as Ka-nu, and Tu?

Aye, there had been, time out of mind.

"Next time we must be more wary," one said, within the mind of the seemingly stricken mac Art, *"for he is a fiend incarnate—an owner of magic black and unholy. He hates you, for he is a satellite of the Great Serpent."*

"Me? Hates me? I broke? I broke his power, I? But I am . . . I am. . . ."

"He has the gift of illusion and invisibility . . . you must beware of Thulsa Doom, for he vanished into another dimension, and as long as he is there he is invisible and harmless to us . . . but he will come again."

Dimension? What other dimension?

What is a "dimension"?

And Cormac saw . . .

. . . a death-duel with swords, all shrouded in a swirling eerie mist not of nature born. One man fought with a green-glowing blade, and his face was a pallid, awful skull . . . Thulsa Doom once again! The other man Cormac could not see . . . the other man was himself.

And they fought well and with the clangour of blades of steel within the mist, and the wizard's flashing green glaive was ensorceled, so I (he? I? He? He is I; I was he; I am he!) contrived to switch swords, warned by some shade or god from without the machina *and aye, he was stronger at once, for the enchanted green brand of the wizard drank the source of life and energy itself, and gave it to the wielder that he became ever more strong and virile.*

Cormac spoke aloud, dully, sitting and staring down at the earth. His voice was that of an old and weary man.

"And I grew strong and he weak, until he was drained. Then sank he down into naught but dust for the fickle winds to play with. For dust he was or should have been afore, a man long dead, a servant of . . . a servantish minion of . . . *ka nama kaa lajerama!*"

Well away along the plain of the Castle of Atlantis, another robed man with knowledge arcane stood, ruminating. At sound of those words he whirled about. A great look of surprise, of astonishment was writ on his well-boned face . . . well-boned, but fleshy that face, and not unpleasant to look upon, while his robe was of Nature's green, not night-dark like that of the mage whose age was measured in millenia. A servant of the gods of *men* was this man, not of rustling spiteful serpents who must ever hate the race possessed of voices and legs.

"Ka nama kaa lajerama," Bas repeated. *"La ka nam'an vorankh amarejal!"* Sweat stood out on the druid's brow as he stared at the hunched and slack-faced Cormac mac Art. "And he thinks he be but a descendant of that great ancient Kull, King Kull, that once and *always* King Kull! For it is all the same, Celt and Kelt, the *Keltoi* of the Greeks and the *Celtii/Keltii* of the Latins. All the same: Cormac and Kull, Cull and Kormak!"

The druid shook as with palsy. He murmured on, "And that I, *I*, Miall'sson Bas of Tir Conaill, am alive at this time, and him alive and abroad in goodly body once more. Aye . . . and menaced!"

Bas the Druid strode to the seated, bowed man. His hand fell gently on Cormac's shoulder.

Up jerked a dark head, and eyes like ice from within the crevasses of their slits stared wildly up at Bas. "Tu! It's he! We must—"

Cormac broke off. Bas waited a moment longer, feeling his own hand quiver on that powerful shoulder. He saw Cormac's eyes come into focus. Then the druid said what he had come to say, what he must say.

"Cormac mac Art! You are in more danger than any man on earth, for a timeless master of evil and illusion has marked you for his own. Vengeance he seeks, not on you whom he knows not in this life, but on him ye once were. Cormac mac Art! I who was there too, as councillor and enemy of the same enemy . . . I shall not leave your side, for sword and prowess alone will not prevail against the one who seeks grim vengeance from a time so far removed from this that men have not the numbers to count the years!"

Cormac did not move; it was as if the powerful weapon-man did not hear, so lost was he in visions and memories that were not memories, and voices of the past that was never past, never wholly gone, but one more portion of the flowing river of the eternal present.

With a hand on the shoulder of that seated, hunched man, Bas looked about. His chin rose and he put back his shoulders. The robe flapping like massy foliage in the wind, he strode to the far corner of the Castle of Atlantis. The druid looked into the gloom alongside it; he spoke into the gloom.

"Woman! One knows of tears shed, of fears that rise unbidden, of imagined gulf betwixt princess and exile! One knows of love, and who holds love for whom in a stout heart and firm, stubborn mind. Woman! Know that ye love not alone, know that ye are needed and that what ye do, weeping and nurturing fears and self-pity in the dark is an unworthy luxury—and an unaffordable one. Be ye woman indeed, Samaire of Leinster, or mere mewling whimpering girl? For there's another who too would weep, were he able, and the better be for it.

"Woman—he *needs us,* this man, for that is coming which shall shake the roots of his soul and aye of the world itself, the foundation stones upon which is builded the ridge of the world—shall shake and echo among the dimensions that are, and it's he will be at fulcrum, hated and menaced and tormented. Power ye have, Samaire of Leinster. For ye can add to that torture—and he to yours—or ye can be great."

Bas peered into the shadows betwixt natural walls

of granite and basalt and castle walls reared eighteen thousand years agone.

Bas said, "Decide!"

And Bas passed into the Castle of Atlantis.

The sun shed warmth and light on that castle, and on its valley and the man who sat as if struck by the hand of Death or powered over by the grim claws of age. He stared at the ground . . . and after a time there before his eyes were two small feet in unusual dark boots. Another voice came to his ears, and not, this time, from his mind or from Bas.

"It's like children we are, my love," that voice said, softly. A hand came onto his bowed head. "You hurt me, and so I sought to hurt you. Too there was confusion upon me. It's companion I must be, hulking hero, boon companion. For I be no squirming flirting fluttering woman likely to swoon, but Samaire of Leinster, *companion* to Cormac mac Art. It's destroyed I'd be an ye treated me as no *more* than comrade, but . . . when ye seek to protect me, it must be as companion, not something soft and vulnerable that belongs to you and that you want not marred."

The woman in the tall soft boots and loose coat of mail heaved up a great sigh. "Thrust me from yourself no more, my love, my dairlin boy, for it's no favour to me to force safety upon me whiles you face that which may slay you out of my sight. We must face together what is to be, as once we did here, as we did those Pictish raiders on Munster's coast and again on our ship just yester day but three, as we did in the wood of Brosna, as we did in treacherous Cashel. Lovers, aye . . . but *companions,* Cormac, by night *and* day!"

He looked up. "Princess born, you must not say 'my love' to me."

"Och! Fah, I say it by night, as do yourself . . . companions by day *and* night, aye, and my love by night *and* day! Now come up, my love, and let us go inside this ancient keep you have made your own."

My own, Cormac thought rising. *The Castle of Kull of Atlantis . . . my own . . . my castle. My. . . .*

"My woman!" he said hoarsely, seizing her arms above the elbows.

Samaire strove for control, and she looked at him and spoke as coolly as she was able. "Of course. My man."

They looked at each other a long while in the sunlight. Then, each with an arm about the other, they went for Bas, in the Castle of Atlantis.

Chapter Eight:
Footprints

"It was in this room that the man held her, Bas, that druid out of place among Vikings. Cutha Atheldane. Some plan he had for Samaire's marriage to one of the Norse. As I think on it now, I remember me that we've talked not of that, Samaire and I; I'd forgot. I came upon them, and saw him staring into my eyes with a gaze sharp as a raven's. Ere I knew what was afoot, it was *Wulfhere* I was looking upon!"

"Seemed to be looking upon," Bas corrected, nodding without apparent surprise.

"Just so," Cormac said. "I like to have died then, until Samaire made a great shout. Then it was like waking from a dream-fraught sleep. Not Wulfhere I saw then but the man Cutha Atheldane in his night-dark robe—almost upon me with a dagger naked in his hand. In avoiding his attack with my mind still befogged, I fell—here, across that chair. I only just saw him as he oped a door, here in this wall, and with Samaire fled within."

Cormac had found the mechanism he had marked; after a few minutes of striving, he sprang open the panel in the wall. Beyond was the corridor that became the tunnel he remembered too well. Bas peered

93

within. The druid's nose wrinkled as it was assailed
by the musty, mephitic odour of ages agone.

"It was with that chair I propped open the door,"
Cormac told him, "that it might not seal us within. I
pursued. But he had a torch, taken from that sconce
there, while I was in darkness. The tunnel twists.
Here."

With the strike-a-light of iron and flint that no sensible man went without, Cormac mac Art raised a
flame on a slow-burning torch. He looked at Bas and
Samaire; the three of them entered into the wall.

"Ah, see how the corridor runs straight and seems
to end at a wall—I ran up against that, and with
force! After that, once I'd found the turn, I was
forced to less speed."

The three came to the apparently blank wall, but
the flickering torchlight in Cormac's hand showed
them how the tunnel continued, merely bending
sharply leftward. A short distance past that, they
turned again to the right.

"I soon learned that these constant turn-asides run
ever in twos, so that this tunnel proceeds ever in the
same direction."

"The musty odour of this place has not improved
since last we trod here," Samaire said.

"Age, mere age," Bas said as though to himself.
"And the tunnel must be open at the far end, since
there's air to breathe and to burn."

The torch burned; Cormac nodded.

"Ah—we go down," Bas said.

"And we turn. An ancient escape-route,
methought, made so full of turns to slow and baffle
pursuit—as it did me! And man-made all, as ye see by
the smoothness of the walls. Else I'd have thought
this tunnel was carved out here by a man both blind
and blind-drunk—and led the while by a lazy serpent." Remembering, he added, "Perhaps I was partly aright. . . ."

Their feet scuffed through dust that lifted up and hovered about. Their nostrils were constantly assaulted by fetor. Once Cormac had blown through his nostrils like a tracking hound, Samaire and Bas did the same. The dust was instep deep, for in centuries no feet had trod here but Samaire's, and Cormac's, and Cutha Atheldane's. The men's buskins and Samaire's boots hissed susurrantly through dust older than they could conceive in their minds. Each essayed to breathe shallowly, to inspire less vitiated, fetid air.

"Ah! Here, Druid, I stopped. For it was here I beheld a woman of passing beauty of face and form. Like a queen she was, with plaited hair like corn and soft folds of silk robing her. I remember sandals . . . of white bronze they were, and so too was she: white as though she'd known no sun. She spoke; she strove to tempt me. She warned that for me to pursue was to find death before the next dawn. I demanded her name. Only one who wished me well, she said, and I bade her swear on my sword."

Bas nodded.

"Was she fairer than I," Samaire asked, "this temptress you say was of such passing beauty?"

"Aye, for of what avail a sorcerous temptress, an she were not more beautiful than normal folk . . . companion? But she called me handsome, and would not swear on my sword. Then knew I she was not what she appeared, for none can call me handsome in honesty! And whether she was a shade of the sidhe or a demon of those cold Northlands whence came Cutha Atheldane, or indeed he himself in a new disguise, I knew she was no woman of woman born!"

"She would not swear on your sword," Bas said, nodding again. "For though the walking dead can, no demon can abide iron!"

"Aye. And I lunged, and spitted her on my blade."

"Whereupon she vanished?"

Cormac looked at Bas, and his lips made as if to smile; it was good, these reminders that the man was wise, and not one to come apart like old cloth, as that Briton Osbrit had done.

"Whereupon," Cormac confirmed, "she vanished." Then he turned about. "And I walked on, in the dark, though were we without this torch, ye'd see that the walls themselves emit some strange light of their own. Around this bending. . . ."

They turned to pace leftward, then were forced by the smooth walls to turn right again.

"Around that bending, even here," Cormac said, halting again, "I stopped once more. My short hairs stood right up! There facing me were three men, war girt and with their swords naked. One a Norse, and one a Pict, and the third a Norse as well, though he served in Dalriada of Alba when last I'd seen him . . . and slain him."

Bas stepped past Cormac, turned so that he could look into his face. "This ye've told me not—that ye'd fought the walking dead before this day."

"There was a difference, Bas. Mayhap the spell was of less power, or mayhap it was more. One called Sigrel and I fought briefly, just here, and I broke his wrist and skewered his belly. And he laughed. Then did I remember the woman I'd just stabbed in the same manner, and I shouted to them to get hence, that I had business beyond, with their master—and I charged them. Whereupon, like smoke in a goodly wind, they vanished."

Bas thought upon that. "A spell of less power, I'd venture to say. If a spell at all—thus Cutha Atheldane had the power of the *eyes,* Cormac. The illusion-power over men's minds, as did he who sent darkness on ye in Eirrin that day of your testing. Only your eyes beheld that darkness that was not. Nor were there dead men here, nor was the woman a demon. All sprang from the mind of Cutha Atheldane as did

the darkness that later came from that foul
Leinsterish druid—and from your own mind, Cormac mac Art."

"So it can be done, the seizing of a man's mind and
making him to see what is not there, without
sorcery?"

Bas nodded. "It can, though whether it is of
sorcery or no—who can say?"

"You have this power, this knowledge?" Samaire
asked.

"It is available to me."

"I'll be asking ye about that again, Druid," Cormac mac Art assured him. "And methinks yours is
the explanation, for those men in the great hall today
were *there,* and so are their bones still. But the woman and the men who braced me here, all three slain
before by me . . . those were not here, sure, for they
left no prints at all in the dust, no sign."

Automatically Samaire looked down though Bas
did not.

"Cormac! Bas!"

They whirled about; they followed her down-di-
rected gaze. The trio stared at the footprints in the
dust, only a little of which had dribbled down into the
depressions. Cormac stepped forward, moving the
torch. The prints of shod feet continued. They faded
away into the darkness ahead of them whence that
walker had come—for these prints led *to* the castle,
not from it. In the darkness before, and with the
torch held well up, none had noticed.

"Yours," Bas said, "from that other time."

"There be but one set," Samaire said.

Cormac squatted. "Nor are they yours . . . nor
mine! Here, look here. These are ours, nearly gone
now in the three months since we were here."

The three looked at the impressions in the dust
and, in the light of the flickering torch, at each other.
None needed to speak. The evidence was there.

Someone, a man wearing buskins or sandals, had paced this subterrene corridor since Cormac and Samaire had, nor had it been one of the slain Britons. For there was but one set of prints, and they came from . . . wherever this tunnel led. To the sea, Cormac had previously assumed; he'd not gone on to be sure, for he'd been in haste to return to the great hall and the battle he had known was taking place there. It was in that fierce and bloody fight had been slain the Danes and Norse who had returned to slay again.

"Cutha Atheldane we left dead," Samaire whispered.

"Aye, and the serpent," Cormac said. "There was no other. But . . . from the sea, one must think, someone else has walked this ancient corridor—*to* the castle, but never *from* it."

Bas straightened up. "A mystery we can think on later," he said. "He be not before us, and he be not in the castle either."

"Nevertheless," Samaire said, and she unsheathed her sword.

The three went on, in silence.

The odour of the decay of death came to their nostrils before they reached the physical evidence. With wrinkled noses, they came to where lay the remains of the mighty serpent that had attacked Cormac.

He told Bas of how he had nearly died from his error then; since he had been twice set upon by those that were not truly there, he had assumed the serpent —three times his length and more thick than his arm —to have been the same.

"It was real enough," he said. "And it took a lot of killing."

Despite the odour of putrefaction, Bas was pacing along the curving length of the dead reptile. Turning away, he sucked in a deep breath and released it, then sucked in another, which he held. The druid squatted beside the dead monster.

"What is it, lord Druid?"

"It is a dead serpent of impossible size, Cormac. A sea monster, one must suppose, for all know such frightful monsters inhabit the keep of Manannan mac Lyr. A serpent . . . *dead, from the smell and the extent of its decay, less than a month.*"

Nor could all Cormac's and Samaire's gasping and denials belie the evidence.

Fact: near unto death in squeezing coils and with his shield ruined and his sword-arm pinned to his side, the son of Art had drawn his dagger, left-handed, and stabbed his reptilian attacker many times in the space of a few seconds. Fact: he had slain the serpent, and gone on in pursuit of Samaire and the anomaly of a druid of the Norse. Fact: when they two had come back this way not long after, the great creature had lain dead as now, though without any decay at all. There had been a lake of blood, and Cormac had retrieved his sax-knife from the monster's mouth.

Fact, then: this enormous snake had been slain three months agone.

Evidence: that it had begun to decay but a few more than a score of days before now; it had lain here two full months before began that ugly and stenchy process that begins in all creatures immediately after death, whether there be flies to lay their maggot-spawning eggs in the swelling corpse or no.

There was no explanation. No . . . *natural* explanation.

They went on, and soon Cormac was saying, "Ah. It was just beyond this bend that I came upon them at last—Cutha Atheldane and Samaire."

"I like not the way ye do put his name first," Samaire said with a smile.

Bas did not smile. "And here ye killed him."

"No no—here *Samaire* killed him! It was she who

was the captive maid, ye see, and I the pursuing warrior. I suppose he heard my approach, and turned from her to stand ready to face me—doubtless to use his eyes and brain, and my eyes and brain, to confound me with more illusions. But the poor son of a donkey had turned his back on a *warrior*, not a helpless girl he'd kidnaped! He dropped to his knees and then stretched his length just as I caught sight of him . . . it was his own dagger he wore in him, to the hilt."

About to follow the turn of the passage, Cormac glanced back to show one of his almost-smiles. He directed at Samaire a look that saw past the prettiness of face and well-wrought womanly form. Then he went on and stopped with an oath.

The others crowded in to look upon what his astonished eyes beheld: nothing.

Of *course* they were certain, Samaire and Cormac told Bas with some heat; here had lain Cutha Atheldane. Aye, and he was *dead*. Here, this was his blood, Cormac said, holding up the dark-threaded dust.

But Cutha Atheldane lay there no longer.

The three stood close. None of them even approached comfort in the mind.

"The footprints. . . ."

"Aye. . . ."

"A dead man . . . walked out of here. . . ."

"And . . . raised . . . others to await our return!"

"Bas!" Cormac's eyes were grimly bright. "That dead Norseman ye made to speak—can you remember that ye asked him *twice* for his name? First he commenced to reply 'Cuth,' and then said 'no,' for it was *the wrong name*. It was after ye asked him *again* that he pronounced that other name."

Bas nodded. "It's right ye must have it, Cormac. It's Cutha Atheldane Samaire slew, and Cutha Atheldane is dead. His *body* walks the earth, though, a husk now, guided by the brain of another. An undying brain, and how it came to be here, or where it lay all these centuries, who can say? But that brain is amove again, within a human body, and it seeks an ancient revenge, Cormac, on you."

"O ye gods," Samaire murmured, "why talk ye so? Surely such things cannot *be*—a man from the *past*, who can resurrect the body of a man slain in the present—his future, and—"

"A man," Cormac said, with an arm across her back and a hand on her waist, "with naught for a face but bones—a death's head!"

Bas spoke, and in that place of eeriness and death-conquering sorcery his voice was passing quiet.

"The man ye slew here, Princess Samaire, is dead, make no mistake. Like those we defeated today, and yet unlike them, he is . . . *un*-dead. For though he lay here in death, now he walks and plots again—Cutha Atheldane, driven by the vengeful mind of an ancient wizard . . . Thulsa Doom!"

Chapter Nine:
Memories

The men of Cormac mac Art went through the halls and rooms of the castle, collecting the booty stored there by Norse rievers or reavers: raiders from the sea. They gathered it in a glittering pile along the defense-hall across the fore of the castle. From there it would be carried down and through the winding pass to the shore, and thence onto the ships.

Aye, ships, for now they possessed two, though their number totaled but fourteen: Cormac, and Bas the Druid, and Samaire and Wulfhere Skullsplitter of the Danes, and their Briton captive Osbrit, and nine men of Eirrin.

Few of the company had ever seen so much wealth or such splendour. Often they paused in their work to exclaim or merely stare, dazzled by the brilliancy of jewels and the handsome richness of fine fabrics.

There were bales and folded piles of standard fabrics—and of fine linens and silks and wools that were dyed in divers hues and often purfled or cunningly broidered with panels and strips of other colours. There was even a strip of cloth-of-silver, twice the length of Cormac—the second tallest man among them, after Wulfhere—and just under half as wide.

Men blinked at its lustre.

Earrings there were, and brooches and torcs, and other ornaments. Two of the torcs were so large and ornate as to constitute carcanets rather than the normal neck-rings worn by nearly every Celt of every land, whether Eirrin or Gaul or Britain. No less than a dozen good bracelets from the hand of the same artisan they discovered, in folds of the imperial red cloth of the Romans. Trade articles, Wulfhere opined. Of wrought bronze the wristlets were, and inlaid with gold, each decorated too with insets of agate and jasper in dark green and opaque yellow.

Cormac and Samaire conferred briefly; soon nine men, aye and the armoured woman among them, happily wore each a new bracelet.

Pearls there were too, though few really precious gems. A number of belts, scabbards, and two bracelets were studded with the red volcanic stones so popular among the Romans, porphyry.

A single gold plate, so finely wrought that it must have been stolen by the Romans from the Greeks, they found too: surely it had been stolen in turn by the Vikings off the ship of some wealthy Roman en route to—or, more likely, from—Britain. Its value was obviously considerable. Samaire soon made it vanish amid folds and folds of excellent white linen—which was surely of Eirrin.

Wulfhere approached the expedition's leader, who stood thoughtfully in the great hall of butchery. The giant gestured.

"The gold and jewels in that throne, Wolf, would ransom a king—and perhaps buy the retainers of one . . . such as Samaire's murderous older brother."

"I'll not be touching it, or have it touched," Cormac said, gazing upon the great chair. It remained stately, despite the sword-hacking inflicted upon it by Bas. It was as if the chair itself owned and presided over the broad hall.

Wulfhere thought upon that, and nodded. "Another time I'd call ye mad, Cormac. Now, knowing what I know of this place . . . I'd not touch it either."

"Then we'll be asking no other man to theft from the king that caused this throne to be placed—to brood here for thousands of years."

"Some time," Wulfhere said, "this year or next or twenty or fifty years hence, others will come here. It's they will pry forth that silver chasing, the gold inlays, those emeralds and rubies and those strange stones that are like clear glass with their many faces."

"Diamonds," Cormac said, "stones that cannot be cut. Aye. But not us." Then he said, "But there's naught to stop ye from returning, splitter of skulls, to collect what be here."

"There is," Wulfhere assured him. "It's happy I'll be to leave this isle behind—and alone!"

Cormac's voice was almost a whisper: "Aye. . . ."

"It's Samaire and Ceann her princely brother have such need for . . . the financing of their enterprise, Cormac. Is it fair to them, to leave all this?"

Cormac looked into the other man's eyes. Around them, as around his own, years in wind and sun and salt spray had worn and incised fine lines like the nascent erosion of a rain-swept plain. Above the flaming beard, Wulfhere's face was like old ship's wood.

"An Prince Ceann wants that throne—I'll tell him of it—he may return here for it himself!"

Wulfhere's grunting noise was a comment. He smiled, not with humour. "Ye have little love for our onetime companion . . . though much, methinks, for his sister."

"There's no quarrel I have with Samaire's brother, Wulfhere, and naught I harbour against him. He is the king's son of Leinster, and the time I have spent in his company, good times and bad, convince me it's a good ruler he'd be making."

"Still. . . ."

"It matters not," Cormac said, with an impatient jerk of his head.

Ceann he knew only tolerated Samaire's relationship with him who'd once been a weapon-man in her father's employ—and more latterly a pirate. Too. Ceann seemed at times to forget his own anomalous position—and who had rescued him and his sister from their Norse captors. Ceann Red-hair acted the role of the king he was not. To Wulfhere, though, Cormac mac Art saw no reason to tell any of this. He had braced Ceann Ceannselaigh afore, and doubtless would again. They'd also fought side by side, and endured and won through much, and accepted each the other's counsel.

And . . . though it might mean the state *marriage de convenance* of a kingly Ceann's sister and Cormac's last sight of her, he knew that the time would come when he'd be working to topple Feredach an Dubh and place Ceann on Leinster's throne.

Cormac glanced over to find that Wulfhere had departed from his side. They had long been companions; the Dane recognized at once when thought came heavily upon mac Art. Thinking was not Wulfhere's province, and he well respected it in the Gael. Neither of them had a better friend than the other—until, perhaps, Samaire. Cormac noted that the fiery-haired giant had appropriated the largest of the axes dropped on this floor of bloody tiles, and the mailcoat that had belonged to the burliest of the Norsemen.

Alone with the dead, the Gael returned again within himself. Wulfhere had called up Ceann into his mind, but it was of the prince's sister Cormac thought.

Samaire.

He'd known her long, the princess with the Eirrin-green eyes. Long before his own years and years as blood-splashed reaver, an exile. . . .

Both bright and sturdy had been Art's boy Cormac; the old druid Sualtim saw to the training of the lad's mind while his father taught him the wielding of arms. Auspicious the name of Cormac son of Art of Connacht, for it had belonged centuries before to one of Eirrin's very greatest kings. Unfortunately the boy's stoutness and skill at arms, combined with the very name, attracted the notice of a man whose crown rested shakily on his aging head; High-king Lugaid was a fearful man on a throne that had been sat afore him by giants among men. Young Cormac knew naught of plots and scheming. His father paid no heed, he who was a descendant of great men though he wore no crown. But treachery was done by a man with fear upon him, and came the time when Art of Connacht was slain, and that mysteriously by an unknown hand.

Young Cormac mac Art was not slow, either to learn or to adapt. His judgment was astonishingly logical, and good, for so Sualtim had trained his good mind. There could be no blood-feud with the *Ardrigh,* the High-king, not for a boy of Connacht and him both fatherless and motherless.

Not yet a man, Cormac did what he must: he fled Connacht, ere his father's fate could overtake him.

The Connachtish youth was not recognized as the "Partha mac Othna of Ulahd" who—lying about his years—took warrior service in Leinster. He proved a good soldier and a good man, for all his being not yet a man. He remained apart from his fellow weaponmen in Leinsterish blue, lest they learn age or origin. Partha mac Othna kept his counsel, and was promoted even to the Command of a Hundred. Eventually he had still another secret, a dangerous one: a friend who became more than a friend, a girl but a year younger than himself. Fair and freckled she was, with eyes of a startling green and hair like a rich October sunset.

Forfeit would have been the head of Partha/Cormac, had His Highness known of the young weapon-man's friend and paramour—the king of Leinster's own royal and well-betrothed daughter Samaire.

Came the day when young Partha mac Othna well represented Leinster in the too-frequent warring between Leinster and Tara over the latter's collection of the ancient and much-hated Boru Tribute. Spawn of a long-ago quarrel it was, and like a wedge driven into the heart of Eirrin or an insurmountable fence across the land. But it lingered on; no High-king forewent its collection or declared it banned. Leinsterish kings but tried. . . .

In that year, though the "tribute" was gained, the hero of the skirmishes was Partha mac Othna.

He was so accomplished and valiant a weapon-man that some compared him with the legendary Cuchulain of old. And soon, on Tara Hill of Meath, High-king Lugaid learned the real name of the so-called son of Othna. It was High-kingly gold brought to an end that era of Cormac's life. He was goaded, carefully and deliberately, into drawing steel at the Great Fair. Thus he slew; thus he broke the King's Peace; thus he condemned himself. For he who broke the King's peace at Fair-time stepped instantly outside the law, and must die—or flee.

Samaire had wept that night, and assured him that she loved him. And then Cormac mac Art, driven already from home and home-land, was driven from Eirrin. He fled, outlaw.

Then came the long years in which he was a farmhand, little more, in Dal Riada, on the southern coast of Alba. Next he was a warrior in the service of that king—until once again royal treachery was done on him. Pictish captivity followed, a captivity during which he'd have died had it not been for a Pictish girl, widowed but recently in her youth. After that came escape and the years as coastal raider, and then capture and imprisonment anew . . . and escape with a prison-made friend, a mighty and outsized man from the cold north.

It was then Cormac and that new friend and comrade, Wulfhere the Dane, became a perfect pairing. With a crew of Danes, they raided every coast save that of Dane-mark and Eirrin—and far Norge.

Was a vicious wind swept them here, an unfathomable whim of capricious gods. Then, by similar caprice, the gods saw that the life-line of Samaire of Leinster again intersected that of Cormac of Connacht, after over a half-score of years.

That first night she had joined him as he lay beneath the sky, in whose chill starlight he'd slept so often. That night he slept but little, and he and Samaire had not been apart since. And now *she* had told *him* they'd part no more. . . .

She *told* me, aye, he mused, *and I said naught to the contrary!*

Standing in the great hall of Kull's Castle and gazing in silence upon corpses and skeletons and a floor cluttered too with dropped weapons and shields and helms, the memory-bound Cormac heaved a great sigh—and heard the approach of footsteps from behind. Instantly he turned, to see bright-eyed young Brian.

Once I was bright of eye and clear of mind and bushy of tail, Cormac mused, cheerlessly, but he showed nothing.

First making apology for the interruption of thoughts, Brian said, "All the booty be gathered at the tops of the stairs, Captain."

Cormac nodded. "It is late of afternoon for the loading of ships—and after that too late to launch them. It must be tomorrow we leave, Brian."

Brian looked about them with distaste, though Cormac saw no fear on the youth.

"It's another night we'll be spending on this isle, then."

"Aye," Cormac said. "Though some prefer to be away from this place and remain with the ships, I'll wager there are others who'd be averse to leaving the amassed treasure!"

Brian grinned. "True. And . . . Osbrit?"

"Brian," Cormac said, seeking to be gentle, "it's . . . not my second ye be."

Brian slapped his head. "Och, it's the Dane who sent me, my lord."

"Oh. Wulfhere." Cormac nodded. Without appointment, Wulfhere had become his second in command. "But I be no man's lord, Brian na Killevy. Hm; Osbrit. A badly frightened man. Not likely to attempt aught against one man, I'm thinking, much less a dozen. Nor likely, either, to want to be apart from the company of others . . . nor will he be attempting to sail off alone! Only Wulfhere could ever accomplish such as that. A man not to be worried over then, is Osbrit of Britain. Nor I noted has Wulfhere aught against him that be personal, from his captivity of the Britons."

"I think not, Captain—other than that Osbrit be neither Dane nor yourself! He be unsure of us, methinks, and . . . we be of him."

"Osbrit."

"The Dane, Captain."

"*Wulfhere?*"

"Aye," Brian said. "It be obvious he trusts none and is friend of none save yourself, Captain. We others are, after all, of Eirrin save Osbrit, who is a prisoner. Wulfhere is . . . neither."

Cormac faced about to fix Brian's clear large eyes with his own dark gaze. "Brian: see you that all understand this, though quietly apprised. Wulfhere

Hausakluifr is my blood-brother. It's five men he's worth, in any passage of arms."

When Brian looked not just doubting but shocked, Cormac twitched his mouth in what might have been taken for the hint of a smile. He said, "Very well then, Wulfhere be the worth of any five men—save myself. Ah, I see that goes down better—but see ye that ye make me no god, Brian I-Love-To-Fight of fair Meath! And see ye that all know this: it was for years *I* was the only man of Eirrin among a crew of *Danes* . . . *his* Danes . . . and we were comrades-at-arms, Brian; it's brothers we all were."

Brian blinked more than once. "Champion of Eirrin, I meant not to imply that we respect him not, or that there be any sigh of trouble among us. Only a . . . certain . . . lack of comfort."

Cormac nodded shortly. "My name for that is foolishness; see that all know it. Now there is a place I wish to go, alone."

The young man took his dismissal with aplomb, as Cormac's due. He returned to carry the plans to Wulfhere—and the leader's words, quietly, among the others. Cormac, knowing where he went though not what he might find, took with him the long, long coil of rope he'd used to gain entry to the castle.

Drawn somehow though he knew not by what, he ascended to the second floor again. He paced thoughtfully along the corridor until he reached a well-remembered room. Carrying a lighted torch in his hand and with sword loosened in sheath, he entered the fetid passageway that became subterranean tunnel. The old secret door he braced open after him.

Chapter Ten:
The Roof of the World

Cormac mac Art was not certain why he paced again along this gloomy stone-braced corridor that had been so haunted by sorcery . . . and was now haunted by footprints of mystery. Perhaps he was deliberately —foolishly—tempting his new enemy, him he had not laid eyes upon.

Foolhardy this trek again beneath the earth, and especially so with Bas, and the Gael knew it. Yet it was . . . irresistible. He was as if compelled, drawn by unseen hands or command, as those strange ship-guiding stones were drawn ever to the north. Nor was it any new mood of Cormac's, this need to be alone with his busy mind.

Busy his mind was—and confused.

It hummed and thrummed now with that sonorous name of menace: *Thulsa Doom, Doom.* . . .

Dust whispered beneath his feet and he fought the ugliness, the foreboding drumbeat inside his head. With will and stern determination, he wrestled his mind from its ugly thoughts elsewhere, to beauty. . . .

Samaire.

Face and form to stir a man's blood and rouse his body, to make his fingers fair tingle for the feel of her

111

under them; these were Samaire of Leinster.

A woman with the highness of pride in bearing and in those wide eyes the colour of grass in high summer, was Samaire daughter of Ulad Ceannselaigh. Slim and well-curved her body, full and well-curved her lips, which, as their ancestors in poet-honouring Eirrin would have told it, were red as the berries of the rowan-tree.

Firm those lips became against him, and warm as if fiery so that there had been times when her mouth had seemed to burn while he listened to her quickening breath and felt her arms about him, felt her straining against him until his own arms were pulling her feverishly close.

Yet there was more to Samaire, far more. Swift and skilled and unblanching in danger and combat she was; a warrior's companion for she was herself a warrior.

Cormac let his mind slip to her as he paced along the tunnel beneath the earth, breathing its fetid, vitiated air.

She'd been wed, naturally enough, betwixt the time of his leaving Eirrin (*when we were both but children*, he now thought) and their coming together again on this rocky speck on the ocean. She was wed by her father to a prince of Osraige, a small strip of land that was to all but its proud king a part of Leinster. Samaire was not long a wife. Whilst aiding the Munstermen in resisting a Pictish incursion into their lands, the prince of Osraige took an arrow in the chest. It gave him his death, even as his men carried him homeward. Childless Samaire was, and no friend of her late husband's mother. She returned to the home of her ancestors.

Already death had visited that home, coming suddenly and without blood upon her father. His first-born ascended to the high seat of proud but tribute-laden Leinster. That son sat the throne well. He became it, as it did him. Though he retained close to hand most of those who had counseled his father, he created his brother Feredach high minister.

Another brother there was still: Ceann mong Ruadh, whose wife had died in her bearing him a child. Widow and widower, Samaire and Ceann became the good friends and companions that they had not been, as children, for friendship were a difficult matter for siblings.

The king was dead within a year, nor was there much doubt that it was his brother Feredach had him slain.

And Feredach was king. He was soon called *an Dubh,* the Dark. A mean, unpopular, grasping and ever suspicious man was he, with the schemer's usual suspicion that others were ascheming against him. Much time Ceann and Samaire spent together, for it was much they had in common. Feredach suspected them; Feredach feared them; Feredach did treachery on his younger brother and sister as he had on his elder.

In a scurrilous bargain made worse because it was with *Norsemen,* Feredach saw that there was no possible claim on Leinster's throne save his own. The men of Norge kidnaped and carried off Ceann and Samaire as one day they rode near the sea.

Then had chance or the gods taken a hand—if Chance were not indeed a god. To this haunted isle whirlpool and storm brought Cormac and Wulfhere; here too the Norsemen brought Ceann and Samaire. Soon Feredach's Viking hirelings were well paid in scarlet coin. Once he was freed of bonds and had snatched up sharp steel, the minstrel-prince Ceann took good toll among his own captors; all were slain.

Across the sea Cormac escorted Ceann and Samaire, and across a third of Eirrin; through Picts and a lustful Munsterish soldier and an honour-less Munsterish king—and his honourable son. Through

highwaymen in the Wood of Brosna and into Meath
Cormac escorted them, and to Tara Hill and the pal-
ace of the High-king. Nor was the relationship of
Cormac and Samaire less than one of friendship and
companionry—nor still was it limited so, for they
were man and woman. Each had been, long ago, the
other's first lover.

Now a protected ward of the Ard-righ, Ceann remained in Eirrin but durst not go into his own
Leinster. He was saying and doing the things that
princes without crowns say and do when they'd have
the throne of their fathers, but will not resort to
murder. Such activities had much need of financing.
And so Cormac had come back here, to a lonely, un-
charted isle of rock and its castle peopled by ghosts
and the crimsoned corpses of slain men. For here was
the price of many cattle, and Ceann and Samaire
needed such in their endeavours.

With Cormac had come Samaire, for she'd not stay
behind. And they'd met the grimmest and most horrible of powerful enemies, who sought dark vengeance on Cormac mac Art, though for nothing done
by Cormac mac Art. And if the subterrene corridor
were his haunt and den—Cormac walked now its
dusty floor, alone.

In that smooth-walled hallway of earth and stone,
the thoughtful Cormac of Connacht came again upon
the remains of the awesome serpent he'd slain. Called
back by sight and smell from his thoughts to the
present, he paused, staring.

Then he went on, for this was not his goal.

He came to that place where had lain Cutha Atheldane, and he paused. *Thulsa Doom, Doom. . . .*

Cormac gave his head a jerk to clear it of the drum-
thrum and went on. On both the previous occasions
of his being here—the second but a few hours past—
there had been reason not to go on, but swiftly to
return. Now there was no such reason. He would see

what lay ahead, toward what Cutha Atheldane had
fled. He walked on, through untrod dust, dust that
had lain here without stirring for . . . what man could
know how long? Dust rose in little clouds at each
step, so that he was able to see his feet only when one
lifted in a step.

Thulsa Doom, Doom. . . .

The torchlight flickered off smooth, close-set walls
and floor smooth and soft with its layer of dust. The
tunnel ran straight now, without the constant left-
then-right baffles.

Though he was not able to see ahead more than a
few body-lengths, Cormac knew by the sensation in
legs and broad back that he had begun to ascend. He
was surprised. He had assumed the tunnel ran on
down, to the sea. Instead, it leveled at about the place
where Cutha Atheldane had died . . . and risen again
. . . and then it began to elevate once more, though at
a most gentle incline.

Cormac walked on, ascending.

Was the tunnel turning, bending? He could not be
sure; he was unable to see far enough ahead to make
such a determination. It seemed so; he *felt* that he was
both ascending and rounding a long gentle bend.

He walked on. Dust puffed up about his legs. The
name walked with him, grimly stalking the hallways
of his mind. *Thulsa Doom, Doom. . . .*

Now he saw clearly a curve up ahead, for it was
somehow illumined. The tremulous light from the
glim he carried rayed out not so far, but by some other light he could see that curving wall, could see the
tunnel disappear to the left. A feeling of the eerie eddied about him with the dust. It strove to settle between his shoulder blades and chill his back, a nervousness and foreboding that had no name and could
not be explained.

Cormac shrugged and twitched his shoulders as if
to free them of something palpable.

He had reached across his lean, mailcoated belly to set hand to his sword pommel, shaped for enwrapping fingers. His fingers enwrapped it. He felt well-shaped, heat-hardened wood and the cool touch of insets of bronze and silver, tooled and chiseled. He drew the long sword slowly; there was only the faintest of sounds as steel blade slid from leather-covered, bronze encircled scabbard. Dust hissing and eddying about his feet and lower legs, he paced watchfully forward.

Cormac began rounding the long curve in the tunnel, and two facts made themselves known to his senses. The light came not from the walls, but from ahead. It grew brighter. And the air was better, far less stagnant, imbued with less of that unpleasant mephitic odour.

Tunnel's end at last, he thought, and stopped.

First he checked his strike-a-light. Then, snuffing the torch in thick dust, he placed it against the wall of the corridor. He gripped his shield; while he had carried the torch, he had but "worn" the targe, with his arm through its straps. Above, over his shoulders, was the coil of rope.

Sword and shield at ready, he advanced along the curving hall of earth and stone. The light grew and the air became sweeter still. He felt the stir of a faint breeze.

Then he saw daylight. A patch of fleece-decorated cerulean sky formed the very top of a slender oval opening; below the sky reared shadowed rock of grey and black. Unmenaced but silent and ready, he went forward. The patch of sky grew. He saw that the aperture through which he must pass was little more than the width of his shoulders. Clean air wafted in, bearing with it the familiar saline tang of the sea.

Cormac mac Art emerged from the subterrene escape-route from the Castle of Atlantis, and he drew in great lungsful of clear clean air, which he released in long suspirations. He looked about.

Above him: the sky of autumn, in late afternoon. To his left, a stony wall, slightly convex, so that a man standing above might well look down into the shadowy slice in the rock without seeing the niche that was the tunnel's mouth. Directly ahead: the same dark stone. Behind him: the niche; a doorway opening into the tunnel. And to his right: another niche, also slender and framed all in sky. The tunnel emerged through a cleft into another, then, a sort of roofless vestibule.

After a few moments, Cormac left it. The coiled rope on his shoulder brushed the stone on his left.

First he saw the sea, far below. At nearly the same time, he both saw and felt the existence of another natural phenomenon, a sinister one. Cormac stopped, very suddenly indeed. Simultaneously he did his best to lean backward.

He was on the brink of death.

Once, a long granitic slope had perhaps swept down to the dark sea. Surely only if that were true would the tunnel have been brought to its terminus here. But inconceivable time had passed, and wrought its changes. Now an escape tunnel ending at this place was no less than insanity. Over the thousands of years, wind and sea had done their work. The slope had been chewed up and swallowed, the ocean moving in as a predator on its quarry.

Yet Cormac knew how great rearing formations of solid granite could *break;* he remembered the "earth"-quake he himself had experienced so recently at sea, not far from here. Perhaps there had been no slow relentless chewing away at all. Perhaps the slope's death had not been the result of weathering, but had taken place all in a day—or within seconds.

Whatever the cause, the Gael was now on the brink of a cliff.

He stood on a short narrow shelf atop a sheer

beetling precipice that could have been laid with a plumb-line. The basaltic butte dropped from his feet straight to a jumble of jagged rocks against which the restless sea lapped. It was a nigh-straight wall, as though he stood atop an unusually high watch tower of one of those Roman forts in Britain, or a Cromlech raised to the glory of Crom by an army of devoted giants.

He stood as if on a natural balcony above the abyss.

How far below were those ominous crags and up-rearing rocks and lapping waters he could not know; there was no measurement available, no frame of reference. The vertical distance was many times his own height: many.

Nor yet was he at the very summit of this wall of rock that frowned down upon the hungry sea as though erected as a bulwark against it. Granite and anciently piled ejecta rose behind him a spear-length more.

Cormac stood gazing out over the ocean. It was dark from this height, not blue but a vast lonely plain of opaque, dark green glass. Well out—probably a day's journey away, were one able to walk that porphyritic plain—the water shone where the sun's slanting rays turned it into an opalescent mirror. On and on, out and out the ocean ran uninterrupted, until it met a sky going deep blue; the sun was behind Cormac.

Here was the nearest to any concept of eternity, Cormac mac Art mused, that living man could approach in his limited mind: Timeless sea becoming sky across untold distance, seen from many spear-lengths above.

That thought brought taunting horror and menace swooping back into his brain like hungering vultures. Their wings thrummed . . . *Any living man.* But Cutha Atheldane; was he a living man? This Thulsa Doom who had lived and practiced his evil sorceries so long ago, so incredibly long ago—was he a living man?

By some unholy and totally arcane means Thulsa Doom seemed to have survived the enormous span of years separating Cormac's time from that of Kull. The wizard must have a more knowledgeable concept of inconceivable eternity than any man on the ridge of the world, whether living or dead . . . or Undead.

Cormac jerked his head as if he'd been struck on the helm and sought to clear his brain of the awful sound-from-within known to many warriors.

Turning, he squinted to look upward. Then he lowered his head to peer within the sheltered crevice into which the tunnel debouched. Aye . . . that was a handhold sure, and that little eruption of basaltic rock would bear his foot, and that depression would accept two fingers. . . .

He stood high up, but it were possible to stand higher still. The call to ascend to the summit was irresistible. Entering the little alcove of rock once more, so that a fall would not mean automatic death, he ascended.

A few minutes later Cormac mac Art stood atop what a swift sweep of his slitted eyes assured him was the highest point on the isle Wulfhere had named Samaire-heim.

Samaire-heim possessed neither the beauty nor warmth of its namesake. From Cormac sloped away a lifeless plain of granite and igneous rock. The sprawling desolate plateau showed the wearing of relentless time only by the dark shadows of pockmarks and small eruptions of harder stone that had resisted the weathering.

A desert of rock it was, and it mocked him with a taunting dead silence.

Glints in the rays of the lowering sun fixed the castle's location for him. He knew those glittery reflections marked the bronze projections set high up on the walls of the keep. From his feet this broad mesa sloped down to that point and flanked the valley that sliced through it. Studying, he tried to calculate. The distance between himself and the castle, he judged, might be just under that measurement the Romans had named after their own marching legionaires: a *mile*.

The roof of the world, Lugh Man-hunter had said. Lonely and desolate that roof, a bleak plain unmarked by the green of life.

Aye, Lugh, Cormac mused, *and if so, this spot marks the edge of the world! And it's nigh flat the top of the world is, and the world no more than two of those Roman miles long and perhaps one and a half across. And surrounded by water! Aye, and with but one valley, like a slice out of the middle of a loaf of bread.*

Almost he smiled. It was an interesting concept, but one for poets and philosophers. He heard the call of a wild goose and saw it flapping over the "roof of the world." Behind him, a soaring waterfowl screeked as if in reply.

Another sound from behind and below attracted his attention. He forgot the birds. Cormac spun, sword scraping out, and looked down. But he saw nothing, and had to step to the very edge of the cleft in order to peer down into the little rocky alcove.

Below, obviously having just emerged from the tunnel, a huge red-bearded man was looking up at him.

"Wulfhere! What—why be ye here, man?"

"Seeking a hand up," Wulfhere said, stretching up a brawny arm.

Chapter Eleven:
When Friend becomes Foe

First passing up ax and shield, a helmeted and mailcoated Wulfhere took the hand of his old comrade. With a few grunts on both sides, two and a half hundred pounds of Danish giant joined Cormac on the island's very summit.

"Now why came you here, Wulf, other than to strain my arms?"

Wulfhere bent to pick up his buckler and slide it onto his arm, then he fetched up the great ax. Its thick helve matched the length of his arm; its head was nearly twice the size of his hand.

"Not the ax ye took from our Briton friend on the strand," Cormac observed, "nor yet the one ye plucked up from the floor in the castle. It's fickle ye grow in your declining years, O drinker of overmuch Briton ale!"

Cormac's scarred, dark face had just commenced to form one of his almost-smiles. It died there as he called on battle-born reflexes to hurl himself away from the edge of the giddy precipice—and away from the rushing ax of his friend.

Cormac hit the ground and rolled. Without terminating the rolling movement, he came to his feet as smoothly as flowing water. And somehow, nearly exceeding the possible, his sword was in his hand. He much regretted having slipped his shield off his arm to aid Wulfhere's climb.

"Wulfhere! Has all sense of humour fled ye *too,* man?"

The Dane's only reply was in the form of motion. Already charging after the other man, he was bringing his ax back across in a new sweep to cleave Cormac in twain.

Too late for Cormac to adopt a favourite tactic and lunge forward within the sweep of the whizzing ax. Too late to parry or duck; he drove down with his right leg to hurl himself in the same direction as the ax's swing. He heard death *whish* through the air as it rushed past his head. Cormac kept moving. Swinging back, squatting and rising all in a single fluid movement while his gaze remained on the big man, he snatched up his shield.

"I put down this shield to aid up my *best friend,* man! Wulfhere! STOP! What are ye DOING, man?"

Cormac's voice slapped hollowly out across bare rock mesa and the darkling flatness of the sea. It seemed to echo from the thick broad form of Wulfhere Hausakluifr too; certainly voice and words had no other effect. Even while he brought his ax from its rightward-terminating backswing, the Dane was rushing forward to crush and overwhelm his chosen foe with silent ferocity.

Cormac backed, watching, thinking rapidly.

Cormac mac Art had never fought this man. He had battled beside Wulfhere, though, for several years. Each had saved the life of the other far more than once, directly and indirectly in the swift-moving matter of immeasurable seconds, split instants.

Lean and wiry, Cormac fought with swiftness— and brain. He observed even those who were his allies. He knew Wulfhere's fighting methods. He *knew* the mighty ax-swing that must be arrested by the arm that guided it, knew the almost inevitable looping backswing, lower, curving upward, during which the outsized man covered himself with heavy buckler. Occasionally he exerted some little offensive efforts with that buckler; seldom were they more than reflex-ive, defensive movements of his left arm until his right could launch its attack anew. He had seen, too, the way Wulfhere closed with opponents; seen him bowl them over with the momentum of his bullish charges. Backed by gigantic height, great bulk, and tremendous strength, those closing charges were ir-resistible.

Wulfhere fought as he was constructed. Wulfhere Skull-splitter of Dane-mark was not a thinker; he was animal, he was brute strength, he was nigh onto in-defatigable and thus undefeatable.

But not, Cormac hoped, irresistible and un-defeatable by a man who knew how he fought!

Though unusually tall, Cormac was a lean man whose musculature did not bulge, but flowed sinuously to knot here and there in stress. Like steel wire his muscles were, and yet, at the same time, *fluid*. Cormac's strength was great, shocking, because he knew how to use it.

The Gael's way was to hew and stab, aye, but not to seek to overwhelm. He pounced and struck, and was away and back again in seconds, like the gaunt wolf that was his namesake. There was no way his size could overwhelm a foeman, save in his reach; he fought viciously, and that overwhelmed. Nor could Cormac be bothered with what some called "civilized fighting." Battling for one's life could not, to him, be bounded about with rules. Thus with wooden sword and light buckler he had shocked his opponents in contests in Eirrin, and thus defeated them to become champion, but a month gone by.

He was a man who battled with sword or dagger or ax·. . . and *shield, and* knee and foot and rush. Strike and sweep and thrust, smash and delicately stab and withdraw; all were within his unwritten book of combat. He was the consummate fighter, in whom a barbarian leapt to the fore when he faced a death-bringing antagonist. On more than one occasion Wulfhere had avowed that his Gaelic friend had no specific *style* at which to point.

And Cormac was intelligent.

If he had a rule, it was a simple one: learn swiftly from successes and from errors, so as never to make the same mistake twice. He had become, in this the year the Christians were calling four-hundred eighty-eight or ninety, or ninety-one or -two, the most terrible of warriors: an intellect-backed barbarian of great strength, shocking swiftness, and few scruples; in combat, he had none.

These attributes Cormac mac Art was now forced to pit against the brutish strength and attack of his friend and longtime fellow reaver. With awful silent ferocity, Wulfhere charged him.

High above the lapping dark sea, the wolf fought the bear.

Cormac waited until the last possible moment as that great bulk rushed upon him, like a thick grappling bear.

Then the Gael dodged to his left with a speed Wulfhere could not match—and as Cormac made that gliding sideward motion, his sword leaped out like a striking snake. The point just touched, with a tiny *ting* sound, Wulfhere's coat of scalemail.

"Stop this, Wulfhere! Three killing strokes I've avoided—and could have slain ye, then. *Stop it, man!*"

Still the Dane said nothing. He lashed out with the edge of his shield at Cormac's sword. A blur of silvery steel, that brand flicked away to spoil, with its flickering serpentine readiness and speed, the short ax-cut Wulfhere made. That tactic, too, Cormac knew.

"You are open at this instant, Wulfhere!"

But the Dane made no reply.

Instead that grim silent killing machine lashed back with the ax in a cut so much more vicious that Cormac dared not meet it with his buckler. With a skillful twist of his arm he used the targe to bash away the heavy steel blade. Impact and crashing clang were enormous. At the same time he sought to give Wulfhere a bash in the side with his sword, a stroke that would hurt and leave a bruise without cutting the scales of steel mail. For still Cormac mac Art could not bring himself to launch a killing attack on his friend.

That gentler stroke the giant with the bushy red beard avoided with a writhing movement. Around came his shield, and Cormac's only just caught the blow. The two bucklers slammed together with a terrific crash and clanging thud, and Cormac was hurled backward.

Still the Dane came.

His friend flailed, backing precipitately inland along the sloping mesa of stone—until his foot came down on a fist-sized upcrop of rock.

Cormac felt himself falling back and knew that he was going to stretch his length. It was not instinct but self-control and the result of long experience that prevented him from windmilling his arms.

Before his buttocks struck unyielding ophitic rock, Cormac's sword-arm was before him, and not only to protect elbow and grip. His wrist was amove, his swordblade weaving a silvery net of defense and steel menace before him. And then above him, for with a grunt and jingle of steel links and a jarring impact that clashed his teeth, he struck the rocky mesa. His eyes saw lightning-shot darkness as he sprawled full length on his back.

His head continued to buzz; his eyes he cleared.

Wulfhere came on, still in morbid silence that was more blood-chilling than the man's usual battle-cries, curses, and fabulous threats. The battle-light was in his eyes, and Cormac knew horror. He knew, finally, that this was no joke, no game.

Wulfhere Hausakluifr meant to kill his best friend.

Already the Dane's shield was in position as protective barrier against the fallen man's sword. Wulfhere's other arm was rising. The lowering sun flashed off the broad steel blade. In seconds it would descend to hurtle down in a totally irresistible chop that would drive the terrible blade through the body of his longtime piratic comrade until it rang off the rock beneath him.

Perhaps Cormac could roll and escape, then in a swift movement chop into the back of the man's legs. But . . . cripple Wulfhere forever? No, better to slay him—if he could. Once that swift thought and decision had formed in his mind, it was too late to roll, and no sensible man would attempt to brace a shield against such a blow.

Cormac drove both feet straight up under the short skirt of the other man's tunic and coat of scale mail.

Wulfhere's eyes went spherical and bulged as he was jolted to a halt. His ax descended, but weakly and erratically. The Gael was able to turn that blow with his shield, though it split.

Wulfhere was busy trying very hard to breathe, and to see past the tears that filled his eyes, as though his crotch and his lachrymal glands were directly connected.

Cormac's body catapulted upward; his sword crashed against the Dane's helmet with a frightful ringing clang. The blade he was willing to sacrifice, if he could knock the man unconscious so as to hear what he had to say while bound and with dagger at his throat.

The blade did not break; Wulfhere remained conscious. Momentum, the weakness the other man's kick had sent into his legs, and the blow to his helmeted head drove him to his knees. Cormac pounced away behind him. Wedge-shaped sword point touched scales of steel where they lay between muscle-layered shoulder blades.

"Release the ax, Wulfhere. It's no wish I have to *lean* on this sword—and remember that I could have chopped or stabbed ye already."

Wulfhere swept back his right hand. Cormac had the barest instant in which to decide: drive with his blade into the big man's back, or get his legs out of reach of the ax Wulfhere sent blindly around and back to shorten him.

Cormac did both. Pressure on his point did not send it through the Dane's scalemail, but provided Cormac the leverage and pivot-point he needed to spring into the air. The ax missed his legs; his weight on his own sword drove Wulfhere forward and down.

The Gael alighted. He stepped back, unwinded and unscathed, and ran his tongue over his lips. He waited.

Wulfhere rolled over and glowered up at him.

"I had rather talk about whatever it be that's driving ye to attack me thus, my friend," Cormac said. "Twice I have had the opportunity to slay; twice I have not, for my last wish is to kill Wulfhere Skullsplitter! Now what means this maniacal attack on me your friend, man—and this silence that becomes ye not?"

Without a word, Wulfhere rose. He hefted ax and buckler. Looked at the other man. And bent his knees in warrior's combative crouch. Nor was there friendship in his eyes.

Still without a word, the towering Dane put up his shield before him, holding it like a battering ram, and came rushing. The mighty ax swung on high even as he charged—maintaining his eerie silence.

"DAMN ye, man!" Cormac bellowed in his horror and frustration.

He stood his ground. To the left he let his dark eyes flicker, a telltale act to a man of Wulfhere's experience and expertise. At the last possible instant in the face of the other's rushing charge, Cormac hurled himself to his right.

Wulfhere's stroke had already commenced, and the adjustment of his aim to his own right was begun, for the Dane knew when he saw an opponent's eyes picking out the direction of his evasive dodge!

But that sideward glance had been a sophisticated feint on Cormac's part. Nor was Wulfhere swift enough now to halt his charge and ax-swing . . . nor, disconcerted by his chosen enemy's leaping in the direction opposite the expected, to avoid tripping over the leg Cormac left stretched behind.

Wulfhere must have felt triumphant to see that his foeman had inadvertently got his back to the cliff and could no longer give ground with such facility. Cormac had given no thought to the cliff but indeed had backed to within arm's length of it without knowing, so overwhelmed was his mind by this inexplicable attack.

Without so much as a cry of any sort, Wulfhere Skullsplitter flew out into cavernous space and rushed down through the depthy void that separated cliff from sea.

"NO!" Cormac roared, and jerked himself up into a squat, twisting half about to stare . . . down.

Now he had his frame of reference for measuring distance from cliff's edge to tide-washed rocks. Now he had a point of comparison that enabled a man with a seaman's eye to judge distance.

The twisted, mailed body that lay on the ragged rocks below could be concealed by his uplifted index finger. Now Cormac could assume that the distance separating him from the broken, stone-pierced corpse of his former comrade and friend was more than twenty times the length of his own body.

Wulfhere did not so much as twitch.

"Ah, Wulfhere," Cormac muttered, and his voice caught in his throat. "Damn ye, man . . . *why?*"

Chapter Twelve:
When Companion becomes Lover

Cormac mac Art slumped, lying on his side and breathing through his open mouth.

He stared down and down at the moveless, broken body of him who had been his best friend. But the Gael's dark, stricken eyes hardly saw that smashed, twisted form that lay over a hundred feet below.

What he saw was behind his eyes. Wulfhere was dead. Cormac remembered all the years with Wulfhere. . . .

There had been the time on dreary little Iona, off Alba's rocky westward coast. He had been climbing, foolishly and rashly as it fell out. And fell was the word. Tumbling and rolling and flailing, Cormac fell —and Wulfhere Skullsplitter moved his bulk with astonishing swiftness. He broke the Gael's fall with his own huge body, not without a sore bruising to both men.

"It's wolf ye are, not goat," the Dane had said with equanimity, once they were again on their feet. "And do shout out next time ye be of a mind to try such a *leap*, Gaelic madman . . . this time I barely moved fast enow!"

Madman, Cormac thought now, and he heaved a

sigh. Surely he had just been attacked by a madman. *Why?*

Cormac recalled those several occasions on which he had, according to the battle-loving Dane, "cheated" him of his beloved ax-hewing.

"Selfish son of an Irish pig-farmer!" Aye, Cormac could hear the huge man's grumble even now, chiding him for such as having "slain more than his share," or silently, savagely striking down foemen ere Wulfhere had reached the scene of sword-reddening combat.

"This world holds no place for a *lone* wolf, Wolf," Wulfhere had told him once, off the Isles of Orkney. Aye, and it was a team they'd become.

Cormac remembered a daring raid on Saxon shores. He shook his black-maned head, remembering. . . .

Wulfhere, slipping in a glittering sheet of blood to fall with heels high, had been fair game for a grinning Saxon wielding an ax that rivaled the weight of Wulfhere's own. In his desperate rush to be there in time, Cormac had been forced to set foot on the fallen Dane's broad chest in order to drive his blade straight up through the Saxon's intestines. The man died with his triumphant grin replaced by a look of great surprise. His own momentum bore him down on the Gael's blade so that its point appeared red-dripping at his back. In toppling, the Saxon downed his slayer. Onto Wulfhere both fell. Beneath the two bodies, one quick and one stare-eyed dead, Wulfhere Hausakluifr had groaned.

"Get ye off me, black-eyed Gaelic hog! Think ye that ye be without weight?"

Cormac shoved away the corpse and scrambled off his friend. "It's your worthless life I'm after saving," he grumbled, dragging himself to his feet to find none remaining afoot but Danes; he and Wulfhere and their company had triumphed once more.

"HA!" Wulfhere bellowed, grunting his way to his feet. "I merely lay taking my rest, in wait for him! Wouldn't he have been surprised when I caught his ax in both hands and gelded him with it! And ye had to spoil it, *and* walk all over me withal! Think ye I be a carpet, Cormac, damn ye?"

"Nay, Wulfhere, only the greatest liar abroad on the Narrow Seas!"

The two battle-reddened men had looked at each other, and about them their crew, men of Wulfhere's Dane-mark, awaited their countryman's reaction to that insufferable word.

The tension lasted not long.

Dark, cleanshaven Gael and huge red-bearded Dane were soon both laughing, with the bigger man clapping a ham-like hand to each of the other's shoulders with force enow to stagger him.

"Liar am I, eh?" Wulfhere Hausakluifr roared. "Blood brother!"

"Blood brother!" Cormac called, and all about them gore-shining blades rose in a delighted Danish hail.

Blood brothers, the dark Eirrin-born Gael and the red-bearded ruddy-cheeked northerner.

Remembering, Cormac bit into his lower lip and sighed again, heavily. He recalled the depth of their relationship, their way of working together . . . For gold, the two reavers had undertaken to contract their crew to a mission for an unlikely employer: Gerinth, one of the Britonish kings. With care and shrewdness the Gael had worked out his plan. It was beyond Wulfhere's understanding.

"I am done seeking to reason out your actions," Wulfhere had growled. And he had acquiesced to Cormac's plan, which led to battle after gore-smeared battle. A fine scheme it had been—and that fine scheme might well have come to naught without the giant Dane and his flailing ax.

Aye, Cormac thought now. Wulfhere had said the same afore that time, and after. And always he had followed Cormac's stratagems natheless. But . . . what mad reason was there now for this action of Wulfhere . . . his last action?

Cormac stared down twenty times the length of his body at the corpse of the best fighting man, the best companion he had ever known. Misery and despair fell on mac Art. They added their burden to that of foreboding, the menace of resistless vengeance from an unknown sorcerer for reasons no better understood.

Why, Blood-brother?

Cormac turned away, blinking.

Lying there at cliff's edge, he touched his coil of rope. He considered the ridiculous: to make it fast and clamber down, back-walking the sheer seawall. To what purpose? To twist the blade of self-torturing remorse in himself by looking upon a dead friend?—he felt it sharply enow already. To see the bright too-familiar scarlet of Wulfhere's life all over those rocks? To look into staring eyes and force himself to tears? To see the face of a dead blood-brother whose blood had all run out? To ask of an unhearing corpse his torturing question . . . *why?*

He shook his head. No. Let Bas demand answers of raised corpses. Cormac would not—nor would Wulfhere be rising.

Yet . . . to let him lie asprawl there so, a huge robust hearty giant of a man now hanging like a bit of sail-cloth caught over stones to dry. . . .

Cormac mac Art ground his teeth. *Last night,* he thought, *I saved him from the sea. Today he tried to slay me. Now it's back at the sea's edge he is, and dusk comes soon, and then the tide. From the sea I saved him; on the sea he chose to live; let the sea have him in death.*

"Return to the sea, Wulfhere," he said aloud,

though without looking down again at the Dane.
Cormac would look on him no more.

"Cormac?"

Blood of the gods! So distrait was Cormac that he
started violently, an unworthy reaction in a man
who'd let a Briton serpent wriggle across his prone
body not once but twice, on that dusky day when
he'd lain in wait for a Saxon raiding party.

He felt himself quiver, and knew what a pitiful
state he'd let himself get to, over a friend who had
betrayed and attacked him and whose death was
none of Cormac's doing, but the same as suicide—
with justice for his last acts.

The voice came again. "Cormac?"

He turned over to peer down into the little alcove
of rock that was tunnel's end. It was darker now, with
the sun lower and the sky starting to frown at its
leavetaking. He could just see her face, a pale oval as
she gazed up at him.

"*Cormac!*" Samaire repeated, not merely question-
ing now but in fearful anxiety. "What's amiss—did I
startle you?"

He forced himself to make reply. "A—aye. You
. . . startled me."

"It's sorry I am. I heard you speak . . ."

He frowned. "No, I said nothing."

"It sounded like, uh, 'Turn to the sea, Wulfhere.' "

"Oh." Cormac strove to clear his brain, to adjust
to this intrusion on his anguish and to speak nor-
mally. "Oh. Spoke I aloud?"

"Aye," she said. She was still frowning. Her
knowledge that something *was* amiss prevented her
remarking on their odd position for such converse:
she standing below and craning her neck, he asprawl
and looking down at her. "But my love . . . *Wulfhere?*
I just left him, as I came to seek you."

Cormac's stomach lurched. He made two attempts
before he was able to form words. "You just . . . what

. . . what did Wulfhere, when ye saw him last?" Gods; it was as if worms crawled about on his body and within his guts.

"Why, it's back in the castle the overgrown boy is, and half drunk already." With amusement in her voice: "He was bawling out challenge to all and any from the Other Side of death who'd care to come forth and face his ax, dead foes or live sorcerer!"

Samaire chuckled, for she could not see Cormac's expression.

"Wulf. . . but—but Sa . . . Samaire. . . ."

"Cormac!"

He fought to control himself; *be strong, why alarm her so?* "He was thus, and ye came directly along the passage, along the tunnel, so that he can . . . he cannot be aught else but behind you?"

"Aye. O'course. Cormac, methinks—"

"Bear . . . with me," he said, more confused and truly fearful than ever before in his life. Resistless sorcery stalked him, loomed grim and threatening, and he could not know B from L or what was white and what black.

"I'm all right . . . dairlin girl," he said huskily, striving with all his might to give the semblance of truth to the lie. A thousand ants seemed at the running of footraces over his body, while his arms and back had gone chill under tunic and mailcoat. Seeking sanity, he fled the dread impossible and spoke the mundane. "Why have you followed me?"

Samaire answered with seductive softness, "Why, to be alone with you, love."

He stared down at her. "You came not to attack me?"

Again she cried out his name, this time more in confused accusation than apprehension. *"Cormac!"*

Before he could wrestle forth words from his clouded mind and tense lips, Samaire chuckled. It was a rippling throaty sound that he liked much and had so told her.

"Oh!" she said. "Aye then . . . I came to attack you, king of my heart. I followed you because I want you."

He knew that he was not responding properly, in words or body, to that frank statement. But he could not, not yet. "Samaire," he said with a grave seriousness that sent her smile afleeting. He heard his own voice shake. Cormac took control of himself as though he were a nervous but strong-willed rider on a worse than nervous horse. He had to. Else he'd be gibbering, and Cormac mac Art knew it.

"Behind ye," he said, intoning words in the manner of a druid at his most solemn rites, "is the only way out of that pit, save the tunnel. Have care—one step through and it's death. But . . . do you look forth, and down . . . and tell me what you see."

He clenched his teeth, angered that he'd let those last several words tumble forth in such a rush.

Samaire raised her hand to her cheek. An extended finger rubbed nervously in her hair, at the ear, where she had the wispiest of golden sideburns. She was frowning and a tremor rode her voice.

"What *is* it, my love? It's far from natural you are!"

He heard the pleading note and was moved—but he firmed his jaw. "*Please,* Samaire. Do you look as I asked."

After a moment, she did so without a word, and he knew he'd put hurt upon her. From above he gazed at her back, with the thick mass of curling vermillion tresses bright against the dark leather. Her hair appeared recently to have been much-combed.

Samaire emitted a startled "oh" on discovering the sheer drop at her feet, and clutched at the edge of that doorway that oped upon plummeting death.

"The sea," the woman said. "The endless ocean I see, and awful rocks like teeth directly below. Ugh! *Far* below."

O ye gods my ancestors swore by and found solace

. . . "Look . . . look ye to the left along those rocks!"
he commanded with a sudden desperate urgency. He
could not look.

She did, and he watched her head turn both to the
left and then rightward. *"Cormac . . . the sea.* Water.
And more rocks. Stones and great rearing boulders.
A spot of sand here and there. And it's not happy I
am looking down on such; it puts a dizziness on me.
Cormac? What—love, what am I to see?"

But Cormac lay shuddering, holding his breath,
clenching fingers into palms until the nails deeply
dented even that calloused skin. He nerved himself.
With a sudden lurch, he twisted onto his side. And he
looked down.

He remembered the words of Osbrit the Briton. *O
ye gods,* he'd babbled in his horror, and *Behl show
mercy,* and the most poignant, man reduced to boy
by horror and the unknown: *Gods! O mother. . . .*

"Behl help!" Cormac exclaimed, and his voice
broke as it teetered on hysteria's brink.

Wulfhere's body was no longer there.

Cormac fell back. He stared at the lowering sky.
Wulfhere was dead, he told himself. Wulfhere was
dead. He knew it. The man had *not* dragged his broken body off those rocks and crawled or walked *any-
where.* Cormac had seen him fall; Cormac had long
stared down. Nor had there been the merest whit of
movement.

A feeling of the eerie crept over him like palpable
fog.

The Gael moved now, though not voluntarily; he
was so tense that he shivered. His heart slammed at
his chest like a great fist within him and the pulse was
thunder in his temples. He was cold and hot both at
once. Dusk-shot and darkly streaked, the sky seemed
to glower above a world peopled with slavering fangs
and dead-who-walked and unknowable evil and a
lurking black abyss of unconsciousness and madness.

Cormac wrestled with his own mind. Desperately

he sought logic, some sane explanation.

Wulfhere had landed on the jaggedly rearing rocks below, and was dead. He had *seen* that. Yet Samaire said the Dane was in the castle a mile distant, drunk and foolishly challenging a power that hacked at Cormac's horror-distorted mind as with a blade steeped in some numbing, insanity producing toxin. Wulfhere lay dead . . . Wulfhere was in the castle . . . Wulfhere's corpse had vanished. At one and the same time Wulfhere had been here, and fallen to his death, and lain there—and had not been here at all; he had fallen/stood roaring out defiance; he had died, burst and shredded on rearing rocks like gigantic fangs/he was merely, predictably and characteristically, drunk. . . .

No!

No. Fight! Fight to regain control of a mind staggering like a man with an adder's venom turning his blood to consuming fire. Cormac shuddered—and was hot. He became aware that pain was on his fingers. So tightly did he clutch the edge of the precipice that his knuckles had gone white as the sea's foam on the rocks so far below. The Gael was hanging onto the solid tangible rock for fear of flying off into a red-shot void of black horror and insanity.

He heard her voice. He began breathing deeply, pushing out his stomach as he filled his lungs to bursting before expelling that air to the last flutter and dragging in more. She was begging, she was tearful in her fear for him.

"Samaire!" He spoke to the sky. "Step back. Into the tunnel and out of the way with ye, lustful woman!" he said, trying to cover his staggered mind with lightness. "It's down I'm coming."

"Ohh . . . I'd hoped to come *up*, love. Oh my love —let me hold you . . . the tunnel is so dusty, Cormac. . . ."

"Oh. Aye. Of . . . course."

Pretending all was aright, she was, that strong

magnificent woman he called dairlin girl. Almost, he smiled.

"Is that the very top, Cormac? Cormac?"

She's fearful as I and needs the sound of my voice constantly—and she has even less knowledge of the why! *Which of us be the worse off; I who know and yet know nothing, or she who—*

"Aye," he answered, "Lugh's 'Roof of the World.' "

"Won't you be giving me a hand up, then, love," she said, too rapidly, and he knew she was covering, too. "I want to see."

"All . . . all right," Cormac said, and steeled himself anew.

Rolling over once more, he gazed down at her wan face. Was that a sparkle of tears? The Gael lowered a hand, and she stretched up hers. But he had to rise and squat, to draw her up with her feet "walking" up the rock. With ease then he handed her up, and fell back as he drew her over the edge and onto the mesa. She fell upon him as he lay there at the edge of that sprawling flatland of stone.

"Oh love," she murmured, so close he could feel her lips move against his face, "it's *cold* you are!"

He was; there was nothing he could think of to say; he said nothing.

He felt a transfer of warmth, hers to him as the loving woman lay over him, holding him, though he wore mail and she her byrnie of boiled leather.

Tremulously, seeking the comforting texture of reality, his hands slipped up into the richness of her hair while she pressed her warm mouth down on his. Her lips seemed hot, which told him that his own were cold. Soft was her hair against his hands, soft as he'd known it in her cousin's manse on Tara Hill. Strange, after their days asea and her long wearing of a leather helm under a sun that boiled forth sweat, and them with no extra water for such as the washing of hair. But he had other things to think of now.

Marvelous soft was her hair to his weapon-man's calloused hands, and her weight on him, too, was good. The needs that rose in him were not of the sort that brooked thought or enhanced the reasoning process.

The sun chilled as it grew distant. It deepened in colour to a gold that shaded into orange and seemed to set Samaire's tresses aflame. Still the two at the very top of Samaire-heim lay together, moving but a little. Hands and mouths moved restlessly and were not satisfied. Coats of steel chain and leather were discarded with weapon belts, with neither ceremony nor sensible orderliness.

Her large eyes seemed to smoulder and yet at once to deepen into pools for the falling into. His blood was wine coursing in his veins, hot and strong. Restless womanly hands transferred their warmth and their insistence to the very core of him. They moved as his did, tracing out every line and hollow and curve of his hard body as though she were determined to commit all to memory.

God of my father, he marveled as he had before, *how at once soft and firm, slim and rounded, is this woman who calls me love!*

Though his throat was dry and there was a strong hunger for her on him, he teased, "Companions . . ."

She did not smile, but stared hungrily as she panted, and she pulled at him with hands that at once begged and demanded, the princess of the landless warrior.

Prim and discreet, the sun hid its face in a great final glow of orange and blood that hurled blotting shadows across the sky. But the shameless moon rode up to stare down at the couple so totally alone on a great seabound chunk of rock like a desert surrounded by ocean. The moon had seen such, millions of times over the eons, hundreds of millions. It took no note but remained cold of light and face. Warmthless light bathed them when they'd shared and transferred their warmth and lay still and lazy while their breathing returned to normal.

Then a shamelessly naked Samaire, her skin all snow and coal in moonlight and shadow, knelt up over the supine man. She smiled down on Cormac mac Art, and lazily he smiled in return. Fear and horror were far from his mind.

And then he saw the glint of steel in her hand, and the skin fell from her face all in an instant so that it was a ghastly apparition he stared up at, his eyes dilated and his hair striving to leave his head.

A faceless fleshless skull grinned down upon him as long bony fingers curled into a fist around the dagger's hilt, and raised it and drove it down at Cormac's bare chest, and with a wild cry of horror and soul-deep torment he moved convulsively and hurled, not Samaire, but Thulsa Doom over the cliff to hurtle down as had the other of the only two Cormac mac Art loved on the ridge of the world.

And a shuddering, madness-tinged Cormac mac Art . . . wept.

Chapter Thirteen:

To Die Twice

Cormac awoke to physical discomfort, as mental agony had tormented him for hours ere he'd sunk into sleep.

A stabbing brightness struck through his eyelids so that he saw blazing yellow without opening his eyes. Realizing that he lay on his back in the open and that the sun of morning was swinging up over him, he kept his lids fast shut until he rolled over onto his side. That brought lancing twinges of pain and a grunt, which was followed by a curse at his own stupidity.

For any person to sleep lying on his back on solid stone was stupid. For a weapon-man to do so, and in his armour with the dampness of sea-breeze on him; t   t was worse than stupid. It was a sin.

On hands and knees, near the edge of the precipice overlooking the sea, Cormac mac Art was assaulted by memory.

Oh gods and blood of the gods! Wulfhere and then Samaire—even Samaire! O gods, how—

Unworthy!

The Gael set his strength against the horror and despair that were a pall over his mind, as if they were

a binding chain on his sanity. By superior strength
and a complete exertion of a will more powerful than
sorcerous mental chains, he snapped them.

Cormac rose from hands and knees to his feet. He
ignored his stiffness of back and limbs and the complaining twinges from every area of his body—including his empty belly. Back went his mailclad shoulders. It was a weapon-man of Eirrin who stood
stalwart and proud—and angry.

The sun of early morning flashed off his coat of
linked chain as he turned all about; flashed even more
blindingly from the broad long blade of the sword he
brandished aloft. Atop the mesa that was Samaire-
heim high above the sea, he waved his sword high at
the end of a stiff-held arm. But it was not the gods to
whom Cormac mac Art issued shouted challenge.

He bellowed it forth, and his voice raced like the
wind out over the sea and the sprawling mesa.

"Thulsa Doom! Twice have ye sought my blood,
man out of time! Twice, Thulsa Doom, and in the
most cowardly possible manner!" Deliberately he repeated that fearsome name, that by shouting it out
again and again he might tear its thrumming repetition from his mind.

"As my best friend ye've come, Thulsa Doom, and
as my—as Samaire ye've come to do death on me,
Thulsa Doom—*scum of ancient Valusia!* It is as Bas
ye'll come death-seeking on me next, Thulsa Doom
who should be dead? Come *Yourself,* sea-slime, cowardly mage, in your own form, and face me direct!
Cormac *despises* you, Thulsa Doom! It's Cormac
calls you, Thulsa Doom . . COME!"

But Thulsa Doom came not, though Cormac
waited long. His only reply was a rumbling growl
from his empty stomach.

Samaire of Leinster knew fear and horror and
pain, and she knew not why.

Long had she waited for Cormac's return, and then it had come upon her where he must have gone, though for what reason she could not fathom. Then it was long and long she waited for the others to fall into sleep. At last all had done, or so she supposed, and she had crept through the dark castle of Atlantis with an unlighted torch in her hand. Not until she was in the passageway of sorcery that lurked behind a small room's wall did she pause and use her strike-a-light to ignite her torch.

With it held high in her left hand and her sword naked in her right, Samaire had trod that ever-turning passage in quest of Cormac mac Art.

She was well past the remains of the slain monster serpent when, though she felt no breath of wind, her torch made a windswept, snarling noise—and went out.

Instantly clutching cold hands fell upon her.

She fought. Back she jammed her feet and elbows, and she attempted to cut behind her at him who held her in the darkness. Yet she succeeded not in slashing him. The blows of her elbows and heels he took without letting go, and in silence. An arm came over her shoulder and across her neck, where it pressed and steadily forced up the chin she strove to clamp down in protection of her throat. Another arm enwrapped her at the waist, and a powerful hand clamped viciously.

As if her silent assailant knew her thoughts, that hand leaped away when, with care for herself, she brought her sword down to slice at it. With a jolt as of a bar of steel the hand slammed into her wrist, and clamped. She moaned. The sword fell into the dust. Then the hard-chested man behind her had inveigled his arm under her chin, and it continued to clamp.

Long she held her breath and struggled without panting to free herself. At last the air had to be expelled from her seemingly bursting lungs—and the arm across her throat prevented her drawing another breath.

She knew that she made hideous sounds. Her head grew enormous. Pain like ice grew until it owned her chest. Her ears reported a roaring that she knew was not there, and a redness seemed to grow in the darkness, and Samaire knew that she was beginning to die.

Samaire began to shiver, almost violently.

Not to be able to speak, even to cry out or know her killer or the reason for her death! She felt tears ooze from her eyes. The trickles were first warm, then cool on her cheeks. Her eyes were huge, her staring gaze like claws scratching at the dark in an effort to tear it away. Growing weaker and weaker, she writhed helplessly and strove to cry out.

She heard her own sounds; tiny hints of voice emerged from her gaping mouth, pitiful sick-chicken noises. Her skin goosefleshed.

The darkness was gone. There was only the deep glowing red that seemed to undulate and pulse like visible heat before her staring, aching eyes. She shivered again. Her intestines seemed to knot themselves.

Desperately, ridiculously, she tried to fight death from powerful hands that could not be fought.

The breathless woman felt herself go absolutely limp throughout her body; felt the tickly trickle of perspiration down the insides of her arms and her flanks; felt the oozing dampness on her forehead and between her breasts. She felt the numbness coming.

I . . . die.

The thought made her angry. She was dying, dying at the hands of a grimly silent and unknown coward who would not face even a woman, but somehow took away her light and then seized upon her in the dark, from behind, and continued strangling her thus until there was no longer any need.

More anger than fear Samaire of Leinster knew, and then she knew nothing.

Consciousness, full of throbbing pain, seeped back to her. There was an ache in her head, which felt enormously swollen, a dull throbbing that increased in tempo and volume when she moved it. She strove now to dispel the confusion within that aching head, to think. Surely this was not death. Surely pain ended with death.

He but choked me into unconsciousness, then ceased, and I began to breathe again. Another thought followed close: *How long ago? How long have I . . . slept?*

She was aware of a pressure against her forehead. She could not account for it. *Am I lying face down? No . . . no . . . I stand . . .*

Slowly, finding it an effort, she peeled open her eyes.

Before her was a wall of stone. She stood leaning against it. Her head scraped the smooth surface as she turned it to left and to right. Gone was the darkness; no less than two torches burned. The flickering flame sent dancing ghost-shadows about her, upon her. Her body ached. Her chest hurt and breathing came hard. She tried to think about that, seeking the cause with a mind that refused to work properly but oozed along the thought process like honey poured in January.

Her body was constricted. She was not lying down. Yet—an she had been unconscious, asleep, how was it that she was standing? Each limb ached and quivered. Blinking again and again, she looked at herself in the flickering yellow light of the two glims. Her cheek rubbed smooth stone as she turned her head this way and that.

Samaire saw that both her modesty and her freedom were gone.

She was both bound and naked.

Though she was hardly in possession of the full awareness and reasoning powers choked away from her, the confused captive was aware that she was still in the passageway beneath the castle. Somehow . . . yes: she was bound to the very wall itself. *How* . . . *how possible* . . . . Spikes, driven into the stone?

She had no idea. She could not see her wrists. But she was bound, and she was in worse than discomfort.

Her ribs felt crushed by the tautness of her body, stretched and flattened, the skin drawn tight over each several rib because her arms were drawn up and out and made fast. Her breasts pressed against the stone worse than uncomfortably; they were naked and vulnerable and the stone was cold. She felt her heart pounding, felt the ache in her limbs, and she felt the fluttering in her bare stomach with her laborious breathing.

Awareness increased. Pain sharpened her senses, hastened her return from near-death to full consciousness. Nevertheless, thinking remained an effort of conscious will.

She took stock of her situation, like a barely-competent steward tallying the master's holdings. And she *would* again be master of her own body and brain . . .

She was bound facing the wall, standing close against it with her arms dragged out at worse than right angles to her body, so that she formed a living Y. Almost rigid were her arms; the binding at the wrists she could not see were almost without slack. Relief came from the simple completed chore of discovering how it was she had stood while unconscious. To such had she been reduced, a heady appreciation of the simplest realization.

Samaire Ceannselaigh wondered how long ago she had been secured thus. How long had she stood sagging against the unyielding wall in a way that in-

creased the terrible strain on her arms and shoulders?
—and back, she realized, and chest, and tautened
stomach. . . .

Slim, smooth-muscled thighs quivered. Realizing
only now that they were braced wide apart and that
her knees were pressed against the cavern wall,
Samaire thought on that. No intuitive leap aided her;
she was forced to labour through the entire thinking
process.

Aye. Her wide-braced legs lowered her posture,
and thus added to the burden of her arms. She willed
aching muscles to serve her. They complained. She
winced and a little groan escaped her when she
straightened, bringing her legs together. Gods be
thanked, they were not bound!

Other sinews shrieked, for now her elbows were
able to bend, however slightly, and every long-
strained muscle in each arm hurled icy stabs of pain
along its length and into her torso. Her shoulders
burned. Both hands remained bound above the level
of her head.

And then it occurred to her, with the return of full
intelligence and ability to reason, to wonder. About
the torches, about the *who*—she wondered where *he*
was, and that thought was like a cruel hand that
clutched at her stomach from within.

Her mouth was open to call out. She reconsidered,
and compressed her lips.

Not knowing who had strangled her into unconsciousness and bound her here, or why, she held
herself in check. There was determination upon her
not to be some pleading quavery-voiced captive. She
was Samaire of Leinster, she was a weapon-woman of
Eirrin, and she did not speak until she knew she could
trust her voice and had chosen her words.

"It's awake I am. Which am I to be, raped or tortured? Or do we continue with the cowardice of you
behind me in silence?"

Her voice was hollow in the cavern, and it welled about her like a physical object. She was grateful for the sound.

No voice answered.

It was then she heard the leathery rustling sound, the little snap from well behind her, followed closely by the *fweep* noise that was as of a rushing arrow cleaving the air. Nor had she time to flinch or tense before the loud cracking sound came. It was so loud and close to her ears, taking her so by surprise that she gasped and lurched painfully against the wall.

For just an instant there was the feeling as of ice on her back.

Then sudden white-hot pain burst there. It engulfed her back in a blazing agony that misted her mind. Her eyes opened wide and stared, bulging, at nothing. Her breath exploded from her in an ugly grunt. Involuntary tears rushed hot down her cheeks in a watery cascade. She jerked violently and tried to put back her shoulderblades against the pain. She felt her knees buckle at the sudden weakness the pain imbued, but at the same time she knew there was no escape, nowhere to go, nothing she could do about the pain—and that which was to come. She knew what she'd felt, what had been done to her.

She had been struck with a whip.

Now she felt it slither down her back, catch for a moment on the shelf of her backside, and drop from her.

The agonized woman's skin rippled and tensed with sudden desperate efforts to break free. The ropes only chewed remorselessly at her wrists when she tried to jerk her way to freedom. She could not. The awful thought struck her that the raw pain and sudden warmth at her wrists meant that the ropes had bitten in, that each torn wrist was now streaming blood.

She could not tear free. She had accomplished only

the spilling of her own blood.

Again the vicious lash came, a leather serpent that dashed onto her shoulder this time, and again her eyes snapped wide and spurted tears and her body lurched from the fiery caress. It was all she could do to keep from screeching as new searing fire tore through her.

Silent and unseen, her captor struck again.

The sinews of Samaire's arms and thighs and calves knotted and bulged outward at the strain, for she could not help tugging at her bonds. Her chest ground painfully into stone and stone-hard earth. She knew that rivulets of blood streaked her arms. Constant shudders of pain and anguish twitched through the flesh of her beaten body, and she knew frustration with the pain, and then anger.

I will not be reduced.

Even with that determined vow she felt a blow of monstrous agony between her shoulders. A lancing pain began there and raced down to her heels and out to the tips of her flexing fingers. Surely she'd not have been stung so had a knife transpierced her. Again the lash hissed downwards, streaking through the air to streak her skin with scarlet.

Now the first whip-cut was a pleasant memory, a sweet caress compared with the fifth, which cut across her full calves. She *felt* the quivering of her every nerve, from scalp to toenails. The pain in her lungs seemed more severe than it had while she was strangled. Ignominy struck with the whip, for her body failed her and released the valve of her kidneys.

The rushing leathern lash struck, and struck again, and then again until the white-faced victim knew she was crossed and crisscrossed with purple-red welts that were like ugly serpents writhing across her scarified flesh.

A princess born, she had never known such pain and terrible anguish, mental and physical. She felt as if she would surely burst in the internal parts of her body.

Samaire's determination held. Not giving the unseen *him* the satisfaction of making her cry out became the sole object of her concentration, the entire purpose of her existence. When she realized on the fiery falling of the twelfth or twentieth lash that she had emitted a groaning sound, she mentally cursed its utterance. To prevent repetition, she thrust her tongue between her teeth and clamped. She held it there with no care whether she bit through.

Every stroke seemed to penetrate more deeply into her flesh, and now the filthy jackal behind her was aiming his lash so as to torment her with the most reviling violation of her body.

Samaire felt as if she had lived all the time of this life in pain and torture, and that the time when existence was painless, much less pleasurable, was but a dimly-remembered fantasy. The whip hissed and cracked.

Who and *why* no longer mattered. Nothing mattered. Relief, perhaps: death would bring that. For she knew that he was leaving bloody gashes on what had been the white flesh of her body.

Maintaining silence with an effort of sheer will and a surely ridiculous determination, she sobbed without sound at the agony in her back and shoulders, the throbbing in her wounded haunches and legs, the wounds that quivered and swelled and seethed with a liquid fury—while leaking forth the blood of life. She could feel it trickling in warm rivulets that went swiftly cold and thick.

Nameless and nigh-mindless, the victim knew that she was washed with crimson, that she would soon bleed to death. She wished sincerely that she had died before, of strangulation. Logic had left her, and Samaire's thought was only that it was not *fair* that one should be made to die twice.

The princess of Leinster knew the absolute depths of human despair as she felt her skin being flayed off by the cruel whip. From tear-dimmed eyes she stared at nothing. Shaking in constant spasms, her body moved weakly. She ground herself against the wall hewn from stone and earth as though that pain could alleviate the other. Desperately she reminded herself to keep her blood-washed thighs together.

In silence, unseen and unknown, *he* struck on.

Idiot, she thought incongruously, that stripped a woman and beat her, rather than used her!

A new, surely insane thought filled her reeling mind: She was bitterly sorry not to be able to aid Cormac in his struggle against the undying wizard Thulsa Doom, not even to be able to be with him . . . and then she broke, and Samaire of Leinster tore her body against the stone wall of the cavern while she screamed and screamed.

Chapter Fourteen:
The Undying Wizard

Cormac heard the strange little snapping sounds long before he reached their source. Pacing determinedly back along the subterrene passage from sea to castle, he wondered at those inexplicable sounds well ahead, with no idea as to what they might be.

He did not walk like a man who had been subjected to the most cruel of torments and had been reduced to quaking shudders. He had rescued himself from insanity. He had stood tall and angry and bellowed forth his challenge to his enemy. He had waited grimly, prepared for anything at all.

Thulsa Doom had not responded.

He'll not be meeting me face-on in sunlight then, Cormac mused, and he had shouted that aloud, as a new challenge and a taunt.

Mayhap then it's given up he has, and fled this isle or withdrawn into "that other dimension," whatever be the meaning of that. In which case—there are ships to be loaded and sails to be spread! And if he be here still —I'll see that no man is out of sight of all others. And if it's Cutha Atheldane comes walking among us—why then we'll be hewing him into so many pieces none will recognize so much as a toe!

And back along the corridor beneath the island

Cormac mac Art strode, a man full of mettle and un-wavering purpose.

Then the screaming began.

The shrieks that fled to him down the tunnel were those of a woman in unbearable agony, and there was but one woman on this accursed isle that wrongly bore her name, and Cormac mac Art broke into a mindless run.

His re-lit torch roared and streamed fire in his wake with his running along that dark cavern beneath the earth. He raced as though a thousand demons sent from the Norse *Hel* slavered on his trail. The corridor's squared turnings he took at the run, so that he struck the wall again and again. And he paid no mind.

Cormac ran, and the dust of centuries flew up from his feet.

He came upon the strange scene, and it brought no horror but only puzzlement—and anger. Cormac took it all in with slitted eyes—while never slowing his pace.

Against one wall of the cavern stood Samaire, pressed to the stone with her arms outstretched. Vermillion hair sprayed out over her leather coat of armour; in their tall boots of gleaming, soft black leather her legs quivered. Indeed her entire body quaked as though freezing cold, while she stood fully clothed and armoured, stretched and tense as if she were frozen in place—or bound by invisible cords or chains.

Behind her stood Osbrit the Briton of Wroxeter.

The only survivor of his crew was steadily tapping the woman's back with a folded belt. Though he was only *tapping* her leather-sheathed legs and back, not striking her, the walls echoed Samaire's constant shrill, throat-tearing cries. She squirmed and lunged against the wall as though bound to it and afflicted with awful torment.

Cormac did not pause to consider or question. With the full unthinking fury of his dash, he charged the Briton. With such force did the Gael smash into Osbrit that the bronze-haired warrior was knocked off his feet and hurled through the air.

Cormac paid the flying body no heed, but plowed to a stop ere he crashed into the cowering woman. His torch he held high; his other hand and arm slid around the seemingly agonized Samaire's waist from behind.

"Samaire . . . Samaire!"

Once more che screamed, in mortal agony. Then, "Cormac," she gasped in a weak sigh, and she sagged back against him. Yet her arms remained in place, stretched along the wall higher than her head. "Oh . . . oh Cormac . . . cut free my wrists!"

Cormac's stomach lurched and his scalp prickled. She was not bound, but thought she was . . . *Wulfhere was not there, but I thought he was* . . . she had not been whipped, but thought she had been . . . *O ye gods, he torments her too!*

"There, my love," he told her, "I have done. You're free."

On the instant, her arms dropped, falling as if her hands were leaden weights. With a groan she began sliding down, so that only his hand under her breast prevented her dropping into the dust of the cavern's floor.

No sound warned the Gael, and he was not aware of seeing aught from the edge of his eye. Nevertheless he twitched his head rightward in a weapon-man's instinct—to see Osbrit Drostan's son coming at him with naked sword. A malevolent smile of anticipated death-dealing twisted the man's mouth.

Cormac's hands were full of torch and limp woman. The one he released, pushing her sideward so that again she sagged against the tunnel wall; the other he swung before him as both defensive shield and fiery offensive weapon. Flame streamed and roared in the tunnel's fetid air.

The rush of fire gave Osbrit of Wroxeter pause, and that swiftly Cormac's sword rushed from its sheath. A ferocious delight was upon him; here was something he could fight, here was a living body to receive the frustration and vengeance-need that were like a canker in his guts.

The Gael did not strike, but advanced a foot and thrust with all his strength.

He felt the familiar jolt of glaive-point against mail, metal against metal, and the resistance, then the rushing of his extended arm as scales bent and twisted and snapped and sharp steel buried itself in flesh and blood.

Belly-stabbed, Osbrit stared at the other man.

"Treacherous snake! Was I showed ye kindness, and I alone!" Cormac snarled, and gave his wrist a twist before he yanked forth his blade.

It emerged agleam. No blood followed the emergence of steel blade from sundered flesh.

Osbrit's lips writhed in a smile. "Aye . . . so ye did . . . kindness. For it was you slew serpent and robed Norseman, and freed me from the one that I might animate the other!"

Then that smile widened, and the lips shriveled up as the skin writhed and *moved* on that tanned face, and it paled and paled while the skin left it, and once more Cormac mac Art stared into the death's head face of Thulsa Doom.

Knowing the man had shown pain when the sword went into him, Cormac stabbed again. His blade plunged into the robed body just below the ribs. This time he drove forward with knotting calves to hurl the wizard backward and to the cavern floor, impaled on two feet of steel.

Dust flew up as his foeman fell, and again when Cormac dropped beside him, to his knees. Maintaining his grip on his pommel, he ground the sword in, seeking to pin the other man, if man he was, to the cavern's floor.

"Ahgh—it *hurts*, lowborn vulture! It—hurts! It's *cold!*"

"But kills ye—not!" Cormac grunted, exerting his strength to twist the impaling blade.

The supine body lurched and writhed. "Aahhhhhh! Son . . . of a moment's dalliance . . . that is *pain-n-nn!*"

Cormac kept his eyes on the skull face, his squeezing, downpressing hand on his pommel. *"Samaire— I need you!"*

She must have turned then, and seen for the first time what he held pinned down like some unslayable writhing serpent.

"Gods of my—he has no face!"

"Nor blood, but he's a body, and it's helpless I have it, and there's cord enow on my arm to enwrap two such! Hither, love, and bind him with this rope!"

Samaire's horror at the awful apparition did not prevent her responding to Cormac's need for aid in subduing . . . the thing. Already he was changing his squatting position and leaning hard on his pommel with his right hand, while he held out his shield-arm. Samaire hurried to remove the coil of rope.

And Thulsa Doom *changed.* The gaunt but powerful weapon-man's body shivered—but the shiver was a *shimmer,* as eerie metamorphosis commenced. Flesh and bone changed. . . .

"Demon!" Cormac cried out in his surprise.

"Cormac—it's *Bas!*"

"Cor . . . mac," gasped the druid, his face stricken. His hands shook as they went to the steel blade that pinned him down, hovered there as if he only just prevented himself from seizing the sharp steel. "Why . . . ? Let me up, Cormac . . . I . . . I can exert druidic powers to heal myself . . . but . . . not if you will not let me up swiftly—"

Cormac spoke betwixt clenched teeth. And he leaned on his sword, though instinctive horror and unease at *apparently* thus pinning the druid he respected brought the sweat starting from his palm.

"No, ancient monster! It's as Wulfhere I've seen ye, and then as Samaire herself; there can be no using this trick on me again! This time ye grow desperate, Thulsa Doom! Now I know the horrors of wizardry ye be capable of, I might not be surprised to see the face of Bas become your ugly relic from a boneyard. But . . . to see *you* become *Bas?* It's not such a fool I am, skullface. I know who ye are, creature, and it's hard your sorceries have made my heart. So—writhe and wriggle, Thulsa Doom, and if ye choose to retain the face of Bas the Druid—then so be it. I am unmoved by such petty attempts!"

"Barbarian *scum!*" Bas snarled. "Nescient as a foal newly born ye are, and proud and crowing of what ye think is knowledge! I cannot be killed, barbarian! Already I have known death, and longer ago by thousands of years than your simple mind can comprehend!"

Cormac braced himself, leaned on his sword with his right hand, and again extended the left arm. "Prate on, wizard. Samaire—the rope."

The head of Bas the Druid whipped toward the woman. "Aye, fetch the rope, ignorant blowze. And note well that my *hands* are not pinned down—bend to me and I'll tear your head from your shoulders!"

Cormac's swift-flicking eyes caught Samaire's shiver, and he doubted her. But in that he erred against her.

Samaire drew the dagger that had never left her sheath whilst she had thought herself naked and beaten. "Then I shall have to be pinning your hands to the earth, one by one!"

The teeth of Bas of Tir Connail clashed in rage— and then the lips fell away from those teeth, and again there was only the fearsome skull with its teeth that seemed ever to grin. Skull-set eyes burned in a face that was bare white bones. . . .

Next instant it was changing, growing new skin, and slitted eyes, and a snouted mouth from which a long forked tongue flickered and plunged. The flattened head that was bigger than her hand lashed at Samaire, and instinct made her flinch away.

Cormac was hard put to hold down, with point of sword, what Thulsa Doom had now become: a serpent. A writhing thick cable of muscle it was that lashed and snapped its cold slender barrel of a body.

"Cormac," Samaire called, and there was a shrill pleading note to her voice that ascended toward hysteria. "I—I cannot bind a *serpent!*"

"No," the Gael said grimly. "But I can lean on this good glaive so that—"

With a sibilant hiss of waist-thick body, the serpent hurled itself halfway up the sword. As it dropped back, the scaly form twisted and wrenched wildly. These were not death-throes, but a fresh attempt at escape. Partway through its barrel form Cormac's sword sliced—and then its tail lashed. Thicker than his wrist it was, and it slammed against his shins with every bit of force Thulsa Doom could concentrate there.

Cormac fell sidewise. His hand on the sword twisted, and the blade sliced crosswise a bit more. . . .

But such was not the escape scheme of a man who had survived unbelievable centuries. With Cormac fallen on his side and striving to maintain grip on pommel to hold the impaling brand in place, the wizard resumed his own form once more.

Hands that were like steel cables and hardly less cold clamped the Gael's wrist. Hand and pommel were slicked with the sweat of both exertion and instinctive horror; no supreme effort was required to force away the fallen man's fingers.

Thulsa Doom was rising triumphantly to his feet

even as he drew the blade bloodlessly from his abdomen. Raising the sword, he turned to loom over his fallen enemy.

Both Cormac's feet struck the wizard's knees with sufficient force to cripple a normal man for life. But Thulsa Doom was neither a normal man nor alive—nor yet dead. He was hurled backward against the cavern wall, and the sword went flying—but the sorcerer did not fall.

"Damn you!" The skullface's voice was little above a whisper in its rage, and filled with the most baleful hatred. The eyes that seemed to burn in that mask of death followed Samaire's rush to snatch up the sword.

"And damn *you*, pigeon-chested *wench* . . . ye should be on your knees and babbling like the pretty-faced little girl ye are, not mindful of what you're about. *Next* time, carrot-tressed bitch, it will be no mere illusion I work to amuse myself with you—I *will* whip you till the blood flows like a mountain stream rushing after the rain!"

"Pretty faced little girl is it," she said, whirling up Cormac's sword. "Monster!" And she rushed the mocking wizard.

Thulsa Doom vanished and Samaire crashed into the wall of stone and earth.

Chapter Fifteen:
The Wizard's Challenge

"HO! Cormac old wolf—where have ye *been,* man?"
Wulfhere's cry was as that of a parent nervous over
a supposedly lost child; relief and happiness were
mingled with irritation and a touch of accusation.
Others lifted their heads or whirled about to look on
the man and woman coming along the beach toward
them. They had emerged from the defile leading to
the castle, the black-haired Gael and the Leinsterish
woman whose hair was a spray of gold and bronze
and new brass in the sunlight.

"Working up a terrible hunger and thirst," Cormac called equably, and looked about.

The ships with their furled sails and banked oars
were here, Britonish and Eirish, drawn up close on
the beach like allies. Judging from the small quantity
of litter left on the sand, the last of the booty was
being stored aboard *Quester*. Helmets and armour
were spread on the beach, while men in tunics, some
dark with sweat, handed up their loads or reached
down from the long boat to accept it. Autumn or no,
the sun was bright and warm.

Cormac and Samaire continued to stride toward
them, seeming oddly martial with him in his clinking

mailcoat and her in her leather armour. They did carry their helmets. Mac Art's eyes roamed about, bright and intent, taking in the scene and considering, planning, re-acclimating himself to reality and the mundane after . . . horror.

"Are all here?"

Wulfhere nodded and swept a brawny arm. "Aye. Osbrit works with us. It was that or be bound, and he prefers a bit of labour to bonds. The druid is yon, at the business of talking to your gods." The Dane smiled. "Odin hears too, surely!"

Cormac glanced in the direction indicated by Wulfhere's nod. There was nothing dramatic to be seen, no lean tall priest standing atop a promontory with outstretched arms and the wind flapping white robe and flowing beard. Instead, in his robe of dark olive girt with a brown-dyed cord, Bas of Tir Connail stood a little way down the beach, nor was there wind to stir his jetty hair or robe. Gazing out to sea he was, past the murderously rearing offshore rocks that were like vicious teeth ever ready to chew ship and crew. His arms were not a-gesture, or even upraised. He merely stood, gazing seaward. Cormac could not see the druid's mouth, but assumed his lips were moving.

If prayer and spelling be of value, Cormac thought, *we need all of both Bas knows!*

He came up to Wulfhere, who stood a little way from the ships, supervising—probably having convinced them a lookout was needed.

"All has been brought away from the castle?"

"This is the last of it. We've searched for ye, Cormac, as best we could! Where—"

"Has aught . . . untoward happened?"

The Dane shook his head, noting from Cormac's eyes that the question was not so casual as it might have sounded. He'd get his explanation later, and answered rather than repeated his own question. "No."

"Nothing?"

"No. Should it have done?"

"Much untoward has befallen us since last we saw ye, Wulfhere. Methought the mage had been busy enow with the two of us so that ye'd not been troubled. But—"

"Ye've seen him? *Him,* himself?"

"Aye."

"It's much we've been through," Samaire said.

Cormac nodded. "It's to be feared, and talked of." Cormac's voice was passing quiet; he spoke for Wulfhere's ears only. "The sorcerer is still here, and he cannot be slain. Not for the lack of our trying!"

"He—has no face," Samaire said, not without a bit of shudder in her voice.

"No f—" Wulfhere broke off, staring from one to the other of them.

"A skull," the Gael told him. "And more . . . . Since yester even, when last I saw ye, it's several faces I've seen him wear. A serpent's, and Samaire's, and that of Bas, and . . . yours, Wulfhere." Cormac swallowed and reached out to touch the other man's great knotty arm, as if to assure himself his old friend was indeed yet alive and unscathed.

Wulfhere clamped his jaws and his eyes blazed. He too sought reassurance; his hand rose to touch his fiery beard, then tarried there to scratch within the curling long hairs. "He . . . this ghoulish raiser of the dead imitates others? He wore *my* face?"

"*And* body, and voice," Cormac told him quietly. "And he fought as you fight."

"*Fought?*"

"Aye—" Cormac broke off and almost smiled, eyebrows curving ruefully up. He was covering; he did not care to tell Wulfhere just now that he had . . . slain the Dane, only last night. "Heard ye that?"

The Dane went all fighting man and looked about. "What?"

"I heard it," Samaire said. "Cormac's stomach!

Our bellies are angry, Wulfhere, and snarl like
gryphons. We are long without food, and have endured much."

"Ah. But ye must tell me—"

"In a little," Cormac said. He glanced down the
strand, at Bas. "Mayhap it were best to save our chatter yet awhile, till it's off this misnamed isle we are,
and asea. For now, though—an all provisions are on
the ships, it's onto the ships Samaire and I go.
Hunger's upon us Wulfhere, and we thirst." He
slapped the other man's belly, unarmoured and
tautening his tunic of faded red. *You* understand
that."

"Aye, but—" Wulfhere broke off. He bobbed his
head in a swift nod. "Feed your belly then; glut-
tonous son of a pig-farmer, an that's all ye can think
of. But it's no need of armour ye have, in this un-
seasonable sun."

Cormac glanced skyward, squinting. Though the
time of autumn was upon land and sea, Behl seemed
not to know it. Closer to Samain, the sun seemed to
celebrate Beltain. The Gael's eyes dropped to lock
onto the Dane's.

"Haven't I?"

Wanting no answer, Cormac and Samaire walked
to *Quester.*

"Missed the work ye have, Captain," Ros mac
Dairb called, grinning. More seriously he added,
"We've worried over ye."

Cormac nodded, but made no answer to the implicit question despite the hopeful, even expectant
gazes of the other men. Their hustle and bustle had
come to pause; their converse and jibing jests had
ceased.

"We've broke no fast since yester day," Cormac
said, reaching up to the ship drawn onto the sparkling sand. "Where be food stored?"

"And *water,*" Samaire said fervently, "or ale."

They had returned into the Castle of Kull to find
no one and nothing, not so much as a morsel of food
or a discarded skin with the slosh of ale remaining in
it. Nor had they tarried for the intimacy they both
wanted, perhaps needed. The skull-faced wizard was
still abroad, in addition to the hunger and thirst that
drove them to hurry from castle and through the wall
of rock to the shore.

Now, aboard *Quester*, they quaffed ale and chewed
dried meat. Cormac regarded the empty skins. Too
much space had of necessity been given over on this
voyage to water and ale, with their attendant weight.
Even so, they had expected to be aweigh again yesterday, and barren Samaire-heim offered nought to
quench the thirst that slew more swiftly than hunger
or even the fever born of one of those wounds that
swelled and sent a red line out from themselves to
bring babbling delirium upon a man.

The Gael jerked his head up and his hand actually
started toward his pommel when Osbrit fared close.
Cormac quelled the motion and Osbrit stared, having
stopped very still.

"In peace, Osbrit Drostan's son," Cormac told the
man in the feathered cap and streaky blue tunic, and
the Gael's face was pleasant enow. On the instant, he
decided to speak and end their sapping suspense.
"Has been a short time, indeed," he said in no quiet
voice, "since I fought him responsible for the deaths
of your fellows and the . . . resurrection of mine. And
he wore your face and form."

Osbrit continued to stare, and like Wulfhere he put
a hand to his own features. Cormac saw a tic come
into the Briton's face, while his raised hand was
atremble. "Ye've . . . fought a mage."

"Aye." Cormac squeezed Samaire's arm. "Both of
us."

"And ye be unscathed?"

"Our minds bear scars. Our bodies, none."

"And . . . *him?*"

Cormac bit, chewed, looked at the other man. Around them, others had stopped all motion to stare at the Gael. They listened, Cormac knew, and he thought it best to say it. In enemy country, one did not hold back knowledge of the enemy, however fearsome; all must be ever on guard.

"I killed him."

Osbrit's eyes flared, then grew less wide than before. Osbrit smiled; a cheer rose and smiles flashed on Celtic faces round about.

Cormac rose from his seat on a rowing bench, and he raised the hand that held a gnawed brisket. The noise subsided; smiles remained, as did veneration in blue eyes and grey. *It will soon die,* he mused, with a sigh.

"I slew him, aye . . . *six times.*"

Sunny smiles faded as though cloud-darkened. A deathly silence enwrapped them all. Every man stared. Lips moved; no voice rose.

Cormac spoke for all ears, now.

"A wizard has stalked us like a plotting spider. Was he dragged back the dead themselves from their rest and set them against us. Was he last night came upon me in the form of Wulfhere and sought to slay me by a treacherous swift stroke of his ax—or what *appeared* to be Wulfhere, splitter of skulls. Was he sought me again, this time monstrously in the form of Samaire that I might be even more off guard, and sought to dagger me in the night. Was he seized her yester night, and inflicted a foul illusion on her so that she thought she was being whipped to death in sheets of blood."

Cormac paused, looking around at faces gone pale even in the bright sunlight.

"His name be Thulsa Doom, and it's older than old he is. Old? It's *dead* he is; he died long ago! I slew him as Wulfhere, by a fall none could survive, though

I but defended myself for then I did not understand his evil powers. As Samaire too I saw him die, in the same way. Corpses of those two, my boon sword-comrades and friends on all the ridge of the world, lay blood-splashed on rearing rocks a dozen ship-lengths below. And both vanished in seconds, so that I knew they were the enemy."

The faces of strong fighting men turned one to the other, and they frowned and muttered. Dead long ago . . . vanished corpses . . . the likenesses of others. . . .

"I slew him later as you, Osbrit! And as Bas yonder too, and as a serpent. As his own dread self too I put death on him, for he flickered from guise to guise swift as the jagged god-spear flashes across the sky. With this steel, I slew them all—*him* all." His sword scraped out to glitter and gleam in the sun, catching every eye. "Nor have I wiped it since plunging it through his several bodies."

"Behl protect," someone whispered. "He . . . cannot be slain?"

"So it seems," Cormac told him, without apparent emotion.

"By all the gods!" Wulfhere's voice came loudly. "Then what do we *do,* Wolf?"

Cormac looked at him. "We retain our armour and arms, and we *depart* this isle of sorcery with all swiftness!" He looked at them. "And we stay all in the sight of each—"

Cormac broke off to stare down the strand at the solitary figure of Bas.

"Blood of the gods! We stay all in sight of each other—*at all times!*" he snapped, pouncing to the ship's side. "Prepare both ships for sea. Sail or oars, we depart the instant they are in readiness!"

He swung over the side of the long boat and, with mailcoat clinking, he *ran* down the sandy shore to the druid. The others stared after him, shocked into brainless immobility. Until Wulfhere shouted, in a roar.

"Ye heard him! Wind or no, it's a beautiful day for being asea! Prepare to depart this abode of Loki and fire-eyed Hel!"

"But a day since," a grim-faced Bas said, "I bade ye never interrupt me and those I serve. Ye try me sore and risk godlike anger as well, son of Art."

"To Bas and Behl and all the gods I make apology," Cormac said, bowing his head—shallowly and briefly. "But there is reason, Bas, or I'd not have done and it's thanking ye I'll be for no further chiding of me like a father to a child, druid or no. Make no answer: attend. We must leave this place, Bas, and at once."

Bas spoke with a coldness Cormac had not previously known: "So I was assured, and I was begging good seas and homeward winds, that we must not row all the way to Eirrin as we rowed nearly all the way to this . . . place."

"Bas. No man must be apart from the others. None must leave the sight of all. Best indeed that we set sail in one ship—but I'll not have one left here for *him* to use."

Bas's eyes flared and gleamed and his chin lifted attentively. "Ye've been long gone—ye've seen him?"

"Ah, Bas! I've *seen* him, aye!" And hurriedly, Cormac told of it, all of it, including that which Samaire had already related to him befell her, body and mind. Bas gave ear in silence, though his face spoke much. The druid's expression changed many times during the other man's hurried and abbreviated narrative.

At last that surprisingly strong hand came out to close on the other Gael's mailed shoulder. "It's much ye've endured, much ye've won past . . . won *through*, Cormac of Connacht. The gods have blessed ye, that ye've kept sanity through such a night! Samaire?"

"—keeps hers as well. The gods blessed us both long ago, with endurance and strength of mind."

"Umm. And . . . but . . . what ye've told me is that at this moment *you* might be Thulsa Doom."

"Or you, since I know I'm not he."

The druid's eyes went past Cormac's, to the ships. "Or . . . any man of those."

"Aye, though I think not—now. Ye see why I durst not allow ye to remain here alone, Bas."

Bas considered, and shook his head slowly. "We must talk on this, when there be more time. But . . . your view of it is a sideward one, Cormac. I standing here alone am in no danger, and represent none to others. While all others are together, he could come upon me only in his own form—"

"Cutha Atheldane's."

"It's if I were to go away from sight and then return . . . aye, *then* might I be this form-changing wizard. For it's not bodies themselves he seizes, but the *forms* of bodies he assumes."

Cormac nodded, having considered and seen and agreed ere Bas finished. "Well stated. Natheless—we leave this place, now."

"Aye. Strand the monster here, forever, and hope he cannot move by means arcane."

A frown came on the instant into Cormac's face, and he wore it through every step back up the beach to the ships. Eleven men and a woman waited—all now in their armour and with weapons buckled on.

"We are ready to sail," Wulfhere greeted him. "Or to row."

Without speaking, Cormac boarded *Quester,* though it still lay drawn up on the strand. He placed himself then so as to face them all; the Gaelic druid, the woman, the giant Dane, the Briton with his thong-held hair, and nine sons of Eirrin.

"Attend me now. The druid has said something that makes me think beyond myself—which is *all* I've

considered since Princess Samaire and I drove the
dark mage from us but a short time ago. Consider.
We are here, and we know that *he* is here. Thulsa
Doom, anciently dead and raiser of the dead; master
of illusion, enemy of humankind, servant of the
serpent-god time out of mind. We know of what he is
capable—and mayhap of what he is *not*." He half-
turned to nod at the brooding pile of rock called
Samaire-heim.

"Power he has, but it is not without limit. Somewhere there, *he is*. In the body of a slain man, a priest
or druid or whatever it is the Norse call their wise
men, though he has re-assumed his own form, his
own face—a death's head. He waits, Thulsa Doom
does . . . waits for another body, another disguise."

"Let him wait until he rots!" Wulfhere rumbled,
and there were nodded heads and sounds of "Aye."

"But will he rot?" Cormac pursued. *"Can* he? And
. . . consider. Does he wait until he rots as ye put it,
or . . . until another ship haps all unsuspecting on this
place?"

There was silence. They gazed at him, waiting.

"Is it right," Cormac asked, "that we depart this
place, knowing that someday, somewhere, even on
our own soil, before our very hearths, we may have to
face him again . . . Thulsa Doom?" He paused, shook
his head. "Nay. It is not meet. It is *I* his quarrel is
with. Ye must—"

Cormac broke off. He knew abruptly that he was
no longer heard. Every eye was wide, and every gaze
was directed past him. His stomach twisted and went
acid. His nape prickled. Heat invaded his armpits and
his heartbeat speeded.

Slowly, Cormac turned to face what held their
gazes.

He stood not on the beach but atop the grim pile of
granite rising above it. Tall and thin he was, in a
night-dark robe that broke over his insteps. Its hood

was up, so that his face was invisible in shadow, yet Cormac *felt* the predatory stare. An arm rose and a finger extended, a finger that was but skin drawn tautly over bone and knobby knuckles.

"Go then," *he* shouted, and alive or dead there was much power in that pitiless voice. "Go, all of ye . . . save . . .HIM!" The finger was pointed at the lone man in *Quester's* bow. "It's him I seek, it's with him I have quarrel older than your conception of time! Go in safety, little men, and leave—"

But one among them found voice, and she dared interrupt to shout out her challenge. "Leave Cormac for you to murder, creature of evil? Only him, you without heart? Do you not want me too, monster, whom you called *pigeon-chested blowze?* Only Cormac? O ye coward who be more at home in the slithering cold body of a crawling serpent than the hide of a man—a *dead* man!"

"Samaire!" Cormac snapped, turning only his head to look at the woman in the stern.

She lashed at him with angry eyes. "You! You were about to *tell* us that his quarrel lies only with you, weren't you? You were about to *suggest* that we remain behind, to—"

Cormac turned. "No. I was about to suggest that ye all take the Britonish ship, loaded with our gains, and leave me this one. Wulfhere brought a ship to shore alone; so can I!"

"Go your way, melon-butted slut!" Thulsa Doom roared out from the rocky promontory. "I want only him ye know as Cormac mac Art!"

None noted Bas, who had swung wide his left arm and was muttering, not for their ears. His right hand was at his throat, fingers splayed out to touch, simultaneously, the lunula and sun-disk and mistletoe he wore. His eyes stared into the sky, and his words were in the language only druids knew.

"I go nowhere without you, Cormac!" Samaire said,

so vehemently it seemed as much fierce challenge as
promise made in love.

"It be true he wants only you, Wolf?"

"Aye, Wulfhere. Only me. Now do you take the Briton craft, and—"

Wulfhere bellowed so that his voice might have raised
the heads of drowsing dogs in far Eirrin. "*I go nowhere
without Cormac mac Art!*"

A slender young man with flaxen hair brushed past
the defiant reaver, and Brian na Killevy took his
stance beside his leader. "I move not from the side of
Cormac mac Art. Come down here, wizard, that I
may show you this steel close to hand!" And he
added, waving his sword on high, "Close to HEAD!"

Standing on the high rocks, the challenged enemy
withdrew his pointing hand—and thrust back his
hood. All gasped, even Wulfhere, at sight of that
fleshlessly gleaming skull atop the long dark robe.

"*Head?*" he sneered. "Strike at this head, little
boy?" Thulsa Doom laughed, and the sound was not
pleasant.

Only Cormac's hand stayed the angry Brian from
plunging off the boat and charging up the beach at
the mage.

"Brian: already ye've spoke like a fool; be not twice
one by acting so as well!"

Another shout rose from one aboard *Quester:*
"And what if that ugly skull flies grinning in the air to
bounce on the ground, creature of a dead god?" It
was Ros mac Dairb who challenged now, and he who
shouldered forward to stand beside Cormac.

That which needed to be proved to them all was
proven then by Lugh Man-hunter, though not by de-
sign. He'd been squatting, busy with something; now
he straightened to reveal a strung bow and ready arrow. He aimed, lifted a whit in windless air, and
loosed his shaft. The arrow sped lofting above the
beach separating them from the wall of granite, and

dropped—and all heard the *chunk* sound as the dart
drove into the body of Thulsa Doom.

All saw how the wizard staggered at the impact,
saw how half the feather-tipped shaft stood out from
him, the width of two fingers above the cincture of his
robe. All saw the death's head tilt forward, dark eyes
staring down at the arrow.

But none saw him fall, or so much as stagger the
more.

And all saw him seize that slim shaft of death, and
pull it from himself, broad steely tip and all, to hold
it high above his head—unmarked with blood.

"You poor little fools will soon reduce me to begging for clothing, with the holes you put in this robe,"
he called in a triumphant and mocking voice.

The words that rose among the watching men were
quite different: "Gods preserve!" and "Behl protect
and Crom defend!" and "Fire of Life!" Many too
was the hair that strove serpent-like to depart its
mooring place on a horripilating scalp.

"Be ye impervious to arrow or no, I stay with Cormac mac Art," Lugh shouted, though in truth there
was a quaver buried deep in his voice.

"I remain!" Ruadan mac Mogcorf called out.

"I stay with Cormac!" Laig mac Senain shouted,
and the navigator stepped forward to join the others
at the prow.

Others called out the same, and who was to say
whether their cries lacked total steadiness or convic-
tion? Osbrit of Britain started forward—

And then a rumble came from the clear sunny sky.

A startled Wulfhere first glanced up, then bellowed
out his laughter.

"Odin and the Hammerer declare for mac Art!"

But the words that issued from the mouth of the
man alone at *Quester's* stern were in Cormac's language, not Wulfhere's. ". . . and cast darkness over
him," Bas said, aloud now, "and smite him with the

fire from the sky that shrivels even the oak—and turns bone into dust!"

Again the skies grumbled. Clouds, though not dark, billowed wildly in elemental madness.

"Fools, fools all!" the skull-face shouted. "BE fools then, and DIE like fools—for none of ye shall leave this island ALIVE!"

Two phenomena, at once natural and yet not natural, came together. Wulfhere would claim for the One-eyed Allfather the one, while Bas knew whose pleas to Behl had brought it. As for the other—all knew it was the work of Thulsa Doom, old before sunken Atlantis rose.

Simultaneously, wind came screaming in from seaward to send hair streaming and whipping at shocked, paling faces—and from a dark cloud that suddenly appeared above, a yellow-white bolt of lightning slashed down at Thulsa Doom.

Thulsa Doom vanished, and none knew whether before the bolt arrived or after; whether he had escaped or been riven by the god-fire that sent dust and pebbles and great shards of sundered rock tumbling down onto the beach from where the mage had stood.

Chapter Sixteen:
The Wizard's Power

Sea and sky went mad.

The wind came shrieking in from the southwest with a force to hurl sand up into swirling clouds like fine dust and to tear the sails of any so foolish as to spread them. Mighty waves rushed viciously in to shore, hissing and roaring as they tumbled over one another in spectacular spumes of spray. Foaming water struck with crashes as of solid matter against the granitic seawalls that towered on either end of the small area of sandy strand. Wind-thrust sea came racing up the beach in a hurtling foaming insanity of angry water. Beached like helpless sea-turtles, the two ships rocked and shuddered with groans of tortured timbers despite their being drawn well ashore.

In that mad melée of motion and ear-battering cacophony of noise, one sound reigned supreme over all others; the wind. The forces of nature ruled, and the wind was High-king.

The wind's howl transcended the sea's rushing hiss and roar. It was the wind that drove the sea like an unwilling stallion. The wind was god; the gale from the ocean was prime mover in this savage flaunting of nature's elemental powers. Its sustained shrieking was as if boasting its awareness of a transcendent supremacy.

Air and water pounded the earth. Behind a grey sky, the sun's fire was dimmed as though even Behl was powerless.

Farther and farther up the sand the waters made their incursion. And then the water eddied, shivered while it paused as though confused, confounded by a source of enforced movement not of itself. Its anger was more than apparent, yet was not enough. The sea that had swallowed so many lives was powerless. The wind controlled; the sea could only be driven. Now those waters hesitated in their greedy landward lunge. The water shuddered. It began moving along the strand—*sidewise*.

Westward the bubble-strewn foam moved, now. Proving its insanity or at the least its capricious whimsy, the wind had shifted through many degrees. No longer did it scream its way from the southwest. Now it was from east by southeast it emanated, still blowing in to shore that no ships might leave, and it howled the while like a thousand banshees of Eirrin come to harry the living with warnings of inexorable death.

Despite its natural, gravity-dictated inclination to slip back from the strand's upward slope, the water was forced westward by the prodigious force of the gale.

More sea came to shore, sluicing in a defiant flood up the beach, and side by side the long boats from Eirrin and Britain rocked dangerously. For the sea they had been constructed; of the sea they were, more than of man, who had made them to further his pretense of conquering the domain of Manannan mac Lyr; landbound those craft were now, but surrounded by tugging extensions of the sea like foam-shot tentacles lapping and splashing all about them.

With a creaking of stout wood and a constant shifting of cargo, the vessels seemed full striving to resume their natural abode. The wind thrust at them. The water coaxed and tugged.

The craft of Britain was of less heavy construction and more buoyant as well, owing to the fact that *Quester* alone had been laden from the inland castle's trove. Dead Bedwyr's vessel shifted. It slid slightly crabwise with the gale-driven waters that rushed around it and broke over its stern in spectacular leaping gouts of white spray. The ship of Eirrin but rocked, and groaned as though in pain or frustrated desire to join its partially floating comrade.

The gale shouted down the creaking complaints of straining wood.

Nature rampaged in chaotic motion and sound and sky-darkening anger.

But it was not Nature, nor yet again the gods, that provided catalyst and control of this demonstration of enormous elemental force.

No deity was Thulsa Doom of eighteen millenia's lifespan, nor was he natural, of Nature, the dead man who was not dead. And it was Thulsa Doom who controlled, who conjured and sent wind and challenging sea onto land. Thulsa Doom had not threatened, but promised, and the undying wizard kept his promise. None on the accursed isle of Kull's abandoned castle thought this horror of natural force with a berserker rage upon it was of else than Thulsa Doom.

It was he sent the wind; it was he held ships and crew landbound; it was by his magicking that the gale shifted so unnaturally in an arrogant show of his powers.

Drenched and miserable, the thirteen with Cormac mac Art could only huddle far up the beach against the wall of rock, and watch. The wind drove sand into their faces and whipped their hair so that it stung their cheeks. Salt spray made sodden their clothing, sluiced off their armour, and sought entry into sheaths and scabbards. Those they protected as best they could.

Thulsa Doom was cursed in thirteen voices, and one of them not male.

Three times had the wind and the sea subsided, and three times had the thirteen men and a woman sought to float their ships and depart the hellish island that Thulsa Doom was determined should hold their common weird. Each time, after long labours in shifting the ships, they had been mocked anew. The lunatic wind had arisen again to whip the sea into ally, willing or unwilling. Nor could the harried knot of humans flee amain. First they must haul their craft back up the strand and, all efforts frustrated, scurry like driven mice up the sands beyond the range of the unnatural tide. The minor tidal waves that hurtled in and up the beach were major threats to frail human bodies.

Was the ban-sidhe indeed, Samaire of Leinster had made plaint; the banshee, those ancient preternatural harridans who were wont to mock the families of Eirrin by warning them of an impending death among those they loved.

Now the darkened sky became darker still. The sun, though visible for hour after hour through the grey only as a steadily westering glow, was setting once more on the mage-damned island. The day had passed. Nor had aught been accomplished by the handful of adventurers suddenly become fugitives from the wrath of the skull-faced thrice-ancient wizard who had challenged and bested them all.

With the suddenness of a blinking eye, the wind dropped.

The sea retreated from the beach, gurgling. Several feet from *Quester* and turned partially sidewise, the Britonish craft was still.

Cormac straightened and gave his head a shake like a drenched dog. His eyes were fierce.

"It's another night we'll be spending here," he growled, thinking of a dwindling supply of food and fresh water. "Come—we'll get the ships farther up the shore, and betake ourselves to that damned castle again!"

Weary men groaned, but none demurred. Should the wind arise again during the night, with the sea already tide-swollen, their only means of departure— escape?—might well be floated away. Squelching pitifully, the woebegone company trooped back down the beach.

Bas had responded to nothing for hours, so deep in his praying or conjuring was the druid. Cormac would not interrupt the man in the sodden robe of olive green; instead he laid hold of his upper arms with both hands and paced the druid, like a fear-paralyzed child, out from the seawall. Bas took no note. His eyes remained fast shut and his lips moved; his hand was at his throat where lay the symbols of the gods of Eirrin.

Curbing a shiver, Cormac paced down to join the others. Wulfhere was frowning at him. The Dane glanced past his old reaving-companion to the stationary druid.

"Why did ye that, Wolf?"

Cormac gave him a look; swept the others with it. "None of us will be out of sight of all the others," he said grimly.

"Gods," Samaire grumbled, "yet another reminder of that skullhead!"

"We will be reminded of his presence again and again if not every moment," Cormac told her, taking up a station at *Quester's* stern, "until we find a means of dealing with him."

Wulfhere snarled obscene words in the tongue of his people.

"Think ye we *will* deal with him?" a man asked; it was Ruadan mac Mogcorf, whose ax-haft mac Art had used against the living dead.

"Aye," Cormac said shortly, and stopped further nervous comment or questions. "Now lean into it, all, and heave on the count of three."

"Lean indeed, boys," Wulfhere growled. He planted his feet, stamped, reset that foot in water-logged sand. "This wet sand will do its best to hold our ship—ye'll not be defeated by mere crushed rock, will ye?"

No, and amid groans and grunts and tremendous effort from all, the ship was forced, inch by inch, farther up the beach. Cormac and Wulfhere would not let them stop until *Quester's* prow was merely the length of a man from the towering natural wall of granite and basalt. Then all stood gasping and panting—and prideful.

Next the ship from Britain, bearing the name of *Amber Rowan* for reasons known only to him who had named it—a dead man—had to be forced and boosted farther ashore. To men already wearied from many such exertions this day, it seemed no less heavy than *Quester*. Nor did Samaire shirk. It was even she who helped up Ros when his foot found softer sand than he'd expected and he fell with a splat.

It was done. All stood heaving their chests, staring balefully at the two well-beached craft in what was now less than twilight.

"The food," Brian said.

"And ale!" Wulfhere added without necessity of thought.

"Aye, we must take both with us, and what water remains. All of it."

They stared at Cormac mac Art. "All!"

He nodded. "Lest we discover on the morrow that *he* had visited here whilst we slept . . ."

"Gods!" Wulfhere burst out, and his eyes were wide. "Aye! An he spoils our provender . . ." He broke off, nor did any wish to hear him finish.

Now Osbrit was staring with eyes wide in revelation. "And—the trove! What if he steals and secretes *that* while we sleep?"

Cormac was boosting Brian aboard *Quester*. He turned his head only partway in Osbrit's direction to make reply: "An ye care to bear it all back to the castle, Osbrit, do so. I'll not."

"I will remain and keep guard!" Brian volunteered.

"And I," Ros mac Dairb said, though with more resignation than enthusiasm.

Cormac shook his head. "No. All go to the castle. All remain in sight of all others."

"It's all this way we've come for this load of treasure," Findbar mac Lirchain said. "Are we to leave it here now, for that . . . creature to steal from us?"

Cormac turned slowly to face the man from Meath. "Aye, son of Lirchin, we are. Think, man. How many treks made all to fetch it here? It's the same number will be necessary to carry it back!"

Findbar stood gazing at his leader, and his eyes dropped before the staring challenge. "We . . . could hide it, bury it in the sand . . ."

Wulfhere looked about in the deep greyness. "And who's to say boneface be not looking on the while?"

Samaire touched Cormac's arm. "Mayhap . . . we should remain here. . . ."

"It's of no moment to me," Cormac told her, and the others as well, for they were gathered close and he raised his voice. "I and Wulfhere have spent many nights sleeping under stars, even in rain and worse, with wood or sand or stone for beds. Is that what ye'd do?"

The voice of Bas, so long absent, made all jump. "*Quester* will not be touched by Thulsa Doom," he said. "All will be here when next the sun comes. It's we who will be in danger."

All the company stared at the druid who had rejoined them as it were after being so long far distant in his mind. **None asked whence** came his certainty.

They decided to carry all provisions to the castle, and to leave the treasure aboard their ship. In darkness, led by Wulfhere and herded close by Cormac who walked last, they made their way through the narrow and winding corridor in the stone. Onto the castle's plain they emerged, and across it they marched, and once more they entered the ancient citadel of horror. Chunks of wood from old furniture provided firelight once it had been carved by sword and dagger and rent apart by strong hands. They ate lightly and drank even more sparingly, for their tyrannical leader would allow them little. His reminder that they were growing short of provisions had to be made but once.

It was on the landing above the sprawling main chamber they sat and ate, for they would not join those corpses and bones and tattered clothing below, nor cared any to remove the remains of corpse-slain Britons and the others . . . men on whom death had needs been brought twice.

Cormac rose, stretched, looked about, and gave them a wolfish grin.

"We should have seen to armour and weapons afore we fed our bellies," he said, and there were sour looks and groans. "But—hunger spoke more loudly than the weapon-man's instinct. Now, though . . . we must rub and with care, for water is no friend to steel, and salt water is worse—and in our steel rests our lives!"

"What boots steel against an enemy already dead?" Findbar grumbled.

"Leave your blades and armour as they are then, son of Lirchin," Cormac said, and he assumed the posture familiar to those who wore coats or shirts of linked steel. Once his belt was opened and removed, he hitched up the skirts of his mailcoat—and bent forward from the waist until his hands slapped the

floor. With legs braced, he wiggled his torso and
shook his shoulders—and forty pounds of steel links
slid clinking and jingling down his body and arms.
With one hand he coaxed the weighty mass at his
neck, and his mailcoat jingled off over his head to
form a smallish pile on the floor. Only fools attempted to press such weight as if removing an ordinary shirt, and then but once.

Straightening, he peeled off the padded coat beneath, and with a wrinkling of noses all knew that
soon they must endure not just that of Cormac mac
Art, but the odorous sweat of all their number.

Seating himself on the floor in wet tunic and leggings, Cormac proceeded to the examination and
rubbing of his armour. His sword scabbard was
propped against the wall upside down. The long
brand lay beside it, though it bore no trace of
seawater. He had been more than mindful of protect-
ing blade and sheath, and had reminded and warned
his companion.

The oil all weapon-men carried was rubbed into
leathern armour; steel coats were carefully rubbed
and wiped with cloth; a bale of linen had been
brought from the ship for that purpose, though it was
far too fine.

Armour, Wulfhere Hausakluifr of the Danes observed, was finer.

"Someone stinks abominably," he also observed,
without looking up from his clinking mail.

"*Some*one!"

Wulfhere grinned; Cormac chuckled. "Would that
all that bluster today had brought rain as well,"
Samaire said, aware of her own addition to the odour
in the narrow, longish defense hall.

"Rain will come," Bas said, and once again the entire company stared at him.

Cormac pursed his lips. "Tonight?"

"On the morrow, more likely," the druid said in a
careless tone.

"Ye know this?" Brian asked in a voice little above a whisper.

"Rain will come," Bas said, and seemed to vanish within himself once more. He had no armour to see to, but sat crosslegged in his woolen robe that must have weighed twenty pounds with its burden of sea water.

"Druid," Wulfhere said, rubbing and rubbing, shifting links, rubbing and rubbing. "Ye said it was your talk to Behl and Crom and whatever other gods of Eirrin brought down the sky-fire at . . . *him.* I had as much reason to believe it was Father Odin and his son the Thunderer. Now ye've said that *Quester* and all aboard it will be safe on the morrow, and too that rain will come. No such clouds I saw today—nor does this old wound in my . . . ham bespeak its coming." The Dane paused; Bas mac Miall said naught. "An all this comes to pass, Druid of Eirrin, I shall bethink myself of . . . changing my allegiances."

Far away, thunder rumbled.

Samaire smiled. "Thor heard, Wulfhere—or is it Thunor?"

"Behl," the druid said, sounding as though he spoke from a deep well, "heard."

There was silence long upon them, then, but for the clink of mail and the swish of cloth.

At last Ros mac Dairb of Dun Dalgan rose and started for the steps. Instantly Cormac challenged.

"Where go ye, Darb's son?"

Ros paused, looked back. "Nature calls." Then he remembered, catching his lip in his teeth for a moment like a child caught in the wrong. "Och! Each in sight of the others—but mayhap two or several others also have need to make a little rain of our own?"

Cormac showed them his almost-smile, nodded, and returned his attention to his mailcoat. It had been long with him, and was valuable, and had proven itself among his best friends—with sword and buckler—on many occasions. He was more methodical in its cleaning than any man he had ever known. A single rust spot could weaken a link so that a swordpoint would enter! Never had mac Art lost so much as one link to rust.

Ros and three others left, close together.

"Small value that be to *me*," Samaire muttered.

"When they return," Cormac said, "you and Wulfhere and I will go and examine the stars."

Samaire's eyes rose; so did the Dane's. "Wulfhere!"

After a moment he rumbled, "I know how to stand close, with my back turned, weapon-companion."

After another moment, Samaire and another actually managed to laugh.

And so it was accomplished, and when all had sallied forth and returned, Cormac rose, stripped his leggings to reveal what none but Wulfhere and Samaire had seen afore: very pale, hairy legs with bulging calves and thighs solid as biceps. He spread padded coat and leggings on the floor and leaned against the outer wall to gaze upon them.

He told, then, all he knew of Thulsa Doom, and when he'd done, their exclamations and questions consumed as much time as his narrative.

"It is only with me, then, that Thulsa Doom had quarrel," he said quietly, when questions had dribbled away and he had silenced them again. "To-day or on the morrow, all of you could take your leave, and most likely in safety."

"Methinks we have covered this point afore," Brian na Killevy said.

"Aye," Wulfhere said, and others nodded.

"It's foolish ye all be," Cormac told them.

"No more foolish than yourself," Wulfhere told him in an equable tone.

"Time approaches, Champion of Eirrin," Samaire said, "when ye should still your foolish tongue that we may all sleep."

Cormac appeared to take no note of either remark. "It's not giving myself up for dead I am. Ye all can take *Amber Rowan,* and the booty, and go. I shall follow, in *Quester.* I have coped with Thulsa Doom afore, and—"

"You *and* I will follow in *Quester,*" Wulfhere said.

"And I," Brian said, and they began again, until Cormac's look again brought silence.

Into that new quiet Osbrit said hopefully, "I was navigator on *Amber Rowan.* The sea I know, and—"

Ros was staring at the Briton; he interrupted. "Can ye handle her alone?"

Osbrit shook his head.

"Then ye'll not be going," Ros told him, and Brian and Wulfhere grinned.

Cormac said, "We must sleep. After this day of fruitless toil, it will not come hard. Remember: None must leave this group." He swept them with his gaze, and decided to be more graphic. "For he who does will then be prey for Thulsa Doom, and when next we see our companion he will *be* Thulsa Doom."

He looked around about at them, and he saw fear and apprehension in their faces. *Good,* Cormac mac Art thought. *Let them be fearful—let us all be fearful. Else—Thulsa Doom wins, and I am no such fool as to believe he will let any of this company live.*

Next day it did indeed rain, and they were able to catch drinking water aplenty. It was good that they did; they left not the island that day, either.

Chapter Seventeen:
The Wizard Strikes

Three more days passed, and still the will of Thulsa Doom prevailed.

At least there was the fresh water Bas had promised. As he had said too, the ship from Eirrin was found each morning untouched by the baleful wizard. They saw him no more; daily they saw evidence of his power.

Lugh contrived to gain them fresh meat. Though it was stringy, there were few complaints about the two birds he brought down with his bow—at cost of one broken arrow, three lost, and two retrieved from the bodies of the pale seafaring birds. Others of their ilk, too far distant to be reached by arrows no matter how strongly loosed and skillfully directed, the company looked upon with open envy.

The soaring, inanely screeking birds came and went as they pleased. The birds were free. The birds found what food they needed on other islands less inhospitable than Samaire-heim and, faring as they did well asea on their broad, current-catching wings, plucked forth those shining fish so careless as to cavort at the surface. The birds were free, mobile, and free too of the frustrating overwork and muscles strained for naught.

Thulsa Doom had no quarrel with birds.

Salt water fish seemed to avoid the isle, but meagre and dwindling supplies of food were supplemented by the catching of one great silver-blue denizen of Manannan's abode—upon the spearing and landing of which burly Cet mac Fergus became a hero. Two other smaller fish were merely picked unheroically up from the sands whence they had been borne and tossed by wind-swept water, and left gasping behind when the wind died and the sea receded.

Men sought shellfish among the rocks surrounding the island that had become their prison, and were un-rewarded—though punished with skinned shins and one wrenched wrist.

"It's only me right wrist," Duach said with an attempt at a shrug and a grin, for the slim but accomplished swordsman from the Slieve Cuilinn area of northern Dalriadia was left-handed. But no one laughed.

The druid had drunk little, eaten nothing at all, and spoken hardly more. Bas remained busy with his accumulation of oak and patched-together symbols and his muttering—and, ever accompanied by at least two others, his "reading" of the many pictures and glyphs on the castle walls. All knew he was working on their behalf against a wizard far more accomplished and experienced. Nevertheless that failed to prevent a growing impatience with Bas as day followed dreary day of imprisonment; the men of Eirrin fell out of infatuation with him on whom they'd set such hopes.

"He seeks to save us all, and he fasts on our behalf," Cormac told Findbar mac Lirchain, after the Meathman had snarled against Bas.

"Fasts—so do we all fast!" Findbar retorted. "And what sustenance has our enemy?"

"Ye saw his . . . face," Samaire said. "The wizard died years agone—centuries agone. He has no need of sustenance—as ye will not, an ye lean not on that hull —here comes the wind again!''

Day after day, winds that rose on the instant from nowhere drove them back—and then died as abruptly once they'd manhandled the ships well up the strand and taken what shelter they could against the island's forbidding walls of stone; there was no lee side.

Night after night they slept in the castle, all together along the upper defense hall and complaining of the snoring of Wulfhere and Cet and Lugh. Thence they repaired each even at dusk, carrying their provisions—which they returned to the ships each day in their new attempts to depart this place of Hel.

With ample opportunity to grow sick at the sight and smell and sound of each other in this constant frustration and enforced proximity, they did. Laden with the spoils of Norsemen they'd not had even to slay, they sought only to leave Samaire-heim. And daily the power of Thulsa Doom drove them back.

Cormac had still his confidence and his rope, and he plotted and murmured a secret plan. Thus, on the second night after their confrontation with the wizard they'd not seen since, the company of fourteen laboriously gained the mesa paralleling the castle's upper storey. Thence they hurried silently in the dark to the ships. In silence they forced *Quester* down to the tidewaters for a perilous attempt to ply treacherous shoreward waters by night.

The wind came, and cursing they set their shoulders to the stern of the long boat whose bow they'd just been apushing. Then the wind died . . . and on its last sighs came borne the sound of mocking laughter.

There were more frowns and angry words and curses than cooperation that third day. Returned to the castle once more, Cormac mac Art relieved himself of a lecture. Some received it with set teeth; others with sheepish looks; Findbar with a sneer he would not disguise.

Thulsa Doom must have had means of witnessing

that scene, for that night he made another direct attempt at gaining his ends. Later, the survivors of that new horror could only reconstruct what took place from imagination and supposition. Somehow the wizard must have lured Findbar from their midst while all others slept; that, or the sullen Meathman awoke to nature's call and ignored the one overweening rule. He fared from his companions, and outside, and there he found his weird. Dawn was acoming, the sky going from black to deep blue lightening to an orange-shot grey in the east, but the enemy worked swiftly.

Some faint noise awoke Wulfhere rather than Cormac, who had striven the hardest on the day previous and, his brain full of frustration and plans that came to naught even in the thinking, had lain long awake. It was Wulfhere awoke his former reaving companion, quietly.

"Half our number have left us," he whispered. "Look."

Creep-footed, Cormac moved to one of the arrow-niches from which their first approach to this isle, months agone, had been contested by the two Norsemen left as guards. He peered forth into a chill morning just greyed with dawn.

Far out across the plain, a knot of men was just on the point of entering the narrow gorge slicing through the towering wall of stone that separated plain from beach. Cormac opened his mouth to call out; closed it. He sighed.

"Let them go, Wulfhere," he murmured. "It's not they are Thulsa Doom's prey; they can escape him thus, without me."

"And if they take *Quester* rather than the Britonish ship?"

Again Cormac mac Art heaved a weary sigh. "Can we have the heart to contest them? Fight those men, my picked men, for the right to leave me—and live?"

Wulfhere frowned deeply, but said nothing, and his

friend turned from the embrasure. He glanced about at those remaining, all asleep—and then he went spear-stiff and peered close.

"Blood of the gods! Up, up all, and into your armour!"

While those sprawled lumps of shadow stirred and sat up to become human beings and then rose, Cormac's words drove sleep from them and determination into their hearts.

"All the others have departed us, but a few minutes past. Look about ye—it's *all* the water and *all* the food they've taken! It's abandoned to die we are, not from the sorcerer, but from the death that comes more swiftly than starvation—thirst!"

Chapter Eighteen:
Steel Against Sorcery

They clad themselves hurriedly in armour of leather and steel. Buckling on sheaths and scabbard belts, they settled helmets over skulls and took up their bucklers. When they left the castle of Atlantis at a trot, ax or sword was naked in every hand, including that of Bas. Solemnly, without a word, the druid had descended to the great hall and there girt up his robe with a Norseman's broad belt. He took up a Norse ax as well, after slipping the buckler of a dead Dane up his arm as though he well knew how to wear and use it.

Even so, weapon-gripping hands were few. The loyal remnant of Cormac's fourteen now consisted only of Samaire, Wulfhere, Brian, Lugh called Manhunter, and Bas. They were six; eight had left surreptitiously, apparently to abandon them with nothing to quench their thirst.

Though his blood was high and the desire to run at full speed was on him, Cormac forced them to walk, once they were in the deep-cut corridor that led through solid rock to the beach. Two reasons he had for slowing, both good.

There was no way the narrow and twisty defile

could be traversed at any gait above a speedy walk without running into or scraping the stone walls again and again, with the danger of injuring leg or arm, or falling. Too, as Cormac told his tiny company, they were far better to arrive on the strand unwinded.

Brian could not understand that Ros could have gone with the others, and said so repeatedly.

"Aye, I thought Laig and I were friends," Wulfhere said as they walked in the gloom, hurriedly, quivering the while like eager hounds held on taut leashes.

"It's *none* of them I understand," Samaire said. "Leaving, perhaps . . . but taking all ale and water—evil!" .

"Worse than evil," Wulfhere growled from behind her.

"Findbar perhaps, the constant complainer. And Osbrit I suppose—though it's not as a captive we've treated that Briton we found so prostrate in fear. But Ros, and Laig . . ." Samaire gave her leather-helmeted head a jerk. "Yet no more can I understand Ruadan's leaving us, taking all food and drink, or big Cet either . . . and Duach, and Laegair . . ."

"It is the wizard's dark work," Bas muttered. "I'm after seeing to the protection of ship and spoils, day after day, aye, and all of ye as well, whilst ye've been at fruitless toil with the ships. But while we slept . . . somehow, he struck."

"That ever-snarling Findbar may have struck a bargain even with him," Wulfhere snarled.

"But the others?" Brian's voice was plaintive, disbelieving. "Even *Ros? Why?*"

"How," Lugh said, and the others were silent; that question seemed more to the point.

"Cormac," Bas said quietly. "I'm thinking that it's *his* creatures they may well all be."

Cormac made no reply. The thought was already in

his mind. But if that were true, then—

"We may have to fight them," Wulfhere said, as if for his longtime sword-companion. Nor did the rumbly Dane sound overmuch perturbed at the possibility of such ghastly civil war among the members of a company already passing small.

Brian's tone was fraught with worry: "Might they be lying in wait? Even one Cet, mayhap. One man could hold us at bay in this narrow passageway with no room to pass him, and Cet be the biggest among us." And sadly he corrected: "Among them."

Cormac mac Art led the way. His voice came back to the others hoarse, and far from pleasant. "An such be the case, it's not long Cet mac Fergus will bar my way, for all our being comrades and his good fighting against those Picts!" Sword held ready, he went on as if there were absolutely no danger.

That proved to be the case; reaching the point at which the shadowed defile debouched onto the sunlit beach, Cormac paused.

"I will talk," he said. "Follow my lead. And make no hostile move on your own. Now—sheathe our swords." And he did, silently.

From Wulfhere, a low chuckle: "Ye'll not be minding that the druid and I keep our axes naked in hand, will you, Wolf?"

"Be not overweening anxious to bear arms against our own comrades," Cormac reminded. "But, as we move toward them, stay not too close together to . . . hamper one another."

"An we cease not this chatter and move," Wulfhere grumbled, "it's naught we'll see but *Quester's* stern and that well out to sea!"

But Cormac had already stepped forward, and out into the sunlight.

They were a hundred paces away on the beach, not asea, but the eight men were well about the business of taking leave of the island. Already the foremost reach of *Quester's* keel lay in the water, though the grunting men had not yet got it far enough out to float. Cormac could see five of them, straining the long boat down to the water's edge.

Pausing at the entrance to the sharply sliced defile so that his companions were blocked within, Cormac shouted.

"Ho, comrades—had ye but waited a little I'd have helped ye—since there's more strength in me than any of ye!"

At that affable shout all activity ceased. Five men stared at him, and then eight, for Osbrit and Duach and burly Cet Fergus's son came around from the far side *Quester*. They stared, with their faces showing them surprised and far from happy at the appearance of their leader.

"Let there be no discussion of strength," Findbar said, and he gestured at Cet mac Fergus.

Cet strutted a chest like a barrel split lengthwise from its center. But he said nothing. Indeed, confusion appeared on his jowly face, and he glanced at Findbar, for Cormac's eyes had never left that less burly Meathman.

"It's yourself had bade us leave, again and again," Findbar said. He paused, but Cormac said nothing, holding his cold blue eyes on the man who'd made so many disgruntled noises in the past few days of their adversity.

Then Cormac moved, and Findbar's eyes flickered. From behind the Gael came the others, one by one; Brian and Lugh and Samaire and then Bas, his robe girt and an ax in his hand. Wulfhere appeared last, great ax on one broad shoulder in the manner of a woodsman.

"We want no help," Findbar said.

"And none offered," Cormac said as he strolled down the strand toward Findbar's company. "It's fit enough ye all look this morning. Nay, we but followed to call to your forgetful minds two matters ye doubtless forgot in your haste."

"We've forgot nothing, Cormac mac Art!"

Cormac's eyes swerved to the speaker. "At least ye've not forgot the name of the man who spoke softly to ye when ye had the fear of a nightmarish child on ye, Osbrit of Britain, and treated ye not as an enemy!"

"Slow your steps, Wolf," Wulfhere muttered, so low of voice as not to be heard by the men about the ship. "See them squint; the sun's behind us. I'd be keeping it there."

Cormac was only ambling; aware of the warrior's wisdom of the Dane's words, he paused. "Two matters, as I said, want more than discussion ere ye sail, Findbar. The first is that it's *all* the food and drink ye've brought away." He made a boyishly reproachful face. "For shame. A serious oversight, that; we'd be dead in three or so days, and ye'd have the blood of both a druid and a royal princess on your hands."

"And a Dane not yet ready to dine in Odin's hall!" Wulfhere added, from just behind Cormac and to his left.

"And too, if ye be of no mind to sail with Lady Samaire and the Splitter of Skulls, ye must leave a goodly portion of *Quester's* cargo for them."

Cormac noted that all the men with Findbar looked both confused and stiff—save Findbar himself. And all watched Findbar. He spoke.

"The dead have no use for water or spoils," he said. "And those who remain with you, accursed mac Art, are *dead*."

"Murdered by comrades who abandon us to die of thirst?" Samaire demanded; she was between Cormac and Wulfhere, at a distance of four or more paces from each.

Ros looked stricken by her words.

"Ros!" Brian called from Cormac's right. "Sword-companion!"

Young Ros of Dun Dalgan shook his fair head in its gleaming helm and knitted his brows, as though torn by painful thought. This Findbar saw, and he spoke three words.

"Ros mac Dairb!"

The youth stiffened; trembled. Then his face lost all expression. It was as if his mind left his body.

"Behl protect," Samaire murmured.

"And Crom defend," Lugh added, with fervor.

"You will leave half the castle's trove," Cormac told Findbar, less equably now. Though he looked not at Ros, he felt his skin a-crawl from that one brief glance. "And a like amount of ale and water. Ye be but two days from an isle with a fine spring and fresh waterfall tumbling into the sea."

"Fare there in *Amber Rowan,* then," Findbar said. "We leave nothing."

"Then ye'll not be departing."

Findbar's eyes remained fixed on Cormac, but he said, "*Cet!* There stands your enemy. Ye heard him, man; he'll not suffer ye to depart this place! It's Cormac mac Art stands betwixt ye and the Eirrin ye long to be in—*kill him!*"

"No, Cet! We've sailed together, man, fought Picts together, bled together and endured the horror of Thulsa Doom together, day after day. Blood of the gods, Cet—ye and me cannot war one with the other!"

Cet paid the Gael's words no mind. He came on past Findbar with buckler high and ax low and balanced to swing, a thick man of surpassing strength who lacked only Wulfhere's height to balance him in size. Nor was he without skill at weapons, else Cormac would not have picked him as part of a carefully chosen crew.

"Cet!" Cormac called out as the big man neared.

"Cet!" Findbar echoed from behind Cet mac Fergus. "*Kill him!*"

Cet essayed to do. Cormac waited until the ax was swinging in a blur of silvered grey ere he spun away, drawing steel on the move, coming about to face Cet across the three feet of space through which the ax had whished.

"This must not *be*, Cet Son of Fergus!"

Cet spoke not, and Cormac remembered Wulfhere that day on the mesa. And like Wulfhere then, Cet and his ax now came attacking still.

Cormac contrived to twist his buckler as he swung it to meet the ax, deflecting it with a great grating *cran-n-ngg* of ax on shield of ironbound wood thick with enamel. At the same time the Gael aimed a stroke at the bigger man's head. This Cet's green-and-blue targe caught with a great noise; surprisingly, he anticipated and caught, too, Cormac's murderous backswing.

The two men circled, fighting with brain rather than with the necessity of the combat among many, or the berserker rage upon them. Each eyed the other, ever shifting their feet in the sand, flexing muscles to keep shields and weapons amove.

Cormac feinted low; Cet met point with buckler and tried a sidearm chop. That Cormac both ducked and deflected with interposed shield. The bear emblazonment of Camal Uais was long since ruined, though the buckler was undented. Steel on wood hardened to the likeness of iron boomed out. Once more the two men's arms were stilled but for a constant swaying as each sought an opening or slip on the other's part; either would lead to the one cut that was frequently all that was necessary.

Moving warily, each made small feinting movement, the other's obvious readiness for which stopped them short of full cuts or stabs.

Shaken still as Cet seemed not to be, Cormac made an error. Circling, testing each several step in the sand, he moved more to his right, until he was unable

to see the ship and the seven men before it. He had
accepted the unstated but tacit understanding that he
and Cet would duel whilst the others awaited the out-
come and the decision it brought.

He was wrong.

Findbar spoke no word; he must have gestured.
Cormac saw nothing; heard nothing until Wulfhere
shouted.

"Cormac! FALL!"

The Gael reacted instantly, as if instinctively.
Many months had passed, over a year had gone since
Cormac had heard that cry. He knew its meaning. It
told him that he was in danger from someone other
than him he faced. He was to betake himself from
that attack with all swiftness—and *down,* not merely
aside. With a feint at Cet's legs, the Gael lunged sideward and let his knees drop him to a squat. His sword
he held upward to keep Cet back; at the same time he
rolled his eyes to the side.

Cormac saw Laegair mac Gol in the act of attacking him where he'd been; he heard the rush overhead
of Wulfhere's thrown ax; he saw it smash fully into
Laegair's face. Laegair mac Gol of Tir Edgain died
on the instant of a crushed skull, far from his home in
Ailech of Eirrin.

Cormac thought, *Why?*

Then he was up, meeting a vicious whirring stroke
of Cet's ax and doing his very best to chop off the
burly Meathman's sword-arm.

Wulfhere was meanwhile taking two strides to the
side and with a swift twist, plucking the ax from the
hand of Bas the Druid.

"Your pardon, Druid, but I have more need of this
than you!" The Danish giant strode forward past
Cormac and Cet to face the other followers of
Findbar. "Stay back. These two fight. I'll not in-
terfere on Cormac's behalf. We all wait, unless any of
you is of a mind to join that treacherous weasel!" He

jerked his shield-arm at the fallen Laegair, whose face was no longer recognizable.

Findbar turned, and in a passionless voice he pronounced a sort of litany: "Ruadan mac Mogcorf . . . Ros mac Dairb . . . Laig Senain's son . . . Osbrit Drostan's son of Britain . . . Duach mac Laig of Airgialla." As men aslumber and yet afoot they stared at him. Findbar pointed at Wulfhere. "Slay the foreigner; kill the Dane!"

Every man raised weapon and shield and turned eyes on Wulfhere.

With a twinned yell, Brian and Samaire came running. Lugh was close on their heels. All three armoured attackers held shields and long swords up for combat.

It was chance set Samaire against Duach, who was also left-handed. Though willow-slim, Duach had been picked by Cormac for the expedition because of the speed and agility that made him, with some skill, a formidable swordsman. He wheeled and braced round shield against Samaire's rushing sword and sent his own forward in a blur of silver-grey steel to open her face. Her buckler whipped up; both blades clanged harmlessly on bucklers.

Brian's initial charge would have done for Laig the navigator, but Ruadan cut at the youth, and on the instant he who loved to fight gained opportunity more than enow. Brian was beset by two countrymen bent on the sight of his blood.

After a wild passing swipe at Samaire that she surprised them both by sword-blocking, young Ros of Dun Dalgan met Lugh with a new ring and skirl of clashing steel. But a little distance removed, Osbrit and Findbar harried Wulfhere like cautious but fierce dogs, while he kept the two busy ducking and fending off his swooping ax.

The sound of battle cries, challenges, and curses rose on the air to mingle in cacophony with the steely clangor of blade on helm and buckler and armour. Stamping, twisting, sliding feet churned up the sand around the twelve unevenly divided opponents. This was battle indeed, made more horrible by the fact that all were shipmates.

The broad side of Cet's ax slammed into the mailed leg of a twisting Cormac, and with a grunt of pain he was knocked off his feet. Grinning, Cet raised his ax for a killing stroke. Hastily he aborted that attack when he found himself staring at a swordpoint extended upward so as to spit him with his own movement. He rushed sideward, ax still on high; Cormac kicked himself over and rose fluidly with sand falling from his steel links. A swift lunge forced Cet to parry with buckler and back away to seek another opportunity.

Findbar, in ducking, lost his footing and sprawled backward. Wulfhere hove up his ax for the stroke of death but Osbrit interfered; his sudden rain of stabbing, hacking steel kept the Dane busy long enow for Findbar to scramble up. A bear-like stroke tore through the edge of Osbrit's shield and down so that ax-edge rang on iron boss.

As the ax caught momentarily in sheared iron and splintered wood, only Wulfhere's swiftly swung shield prevented Findbar's blade from splitting his scalemail and flesh—his shield, and the vicious hopping kick Wulfhere gave the other man's calf. The Dane's ax came free; the flurry ended. The three men moved warily, watching each other.

Duach was perhaps stronger, but Samaire was not only good with sword, she had been shown certain concepts of tactic by Cormac, who had surprisedly pronounced her an instinctive weapon . . . woman. In swiftness she and Duach were well matched. The lean man of five-and-twenty or so, with his fortnight-old orange beard, was hard pressed physically and mentally to protect himself from her unpredictability, while Samaire must guard against the man's longer reach.

Both wielded sword in the off-hand and buckler in right; both were armoured in leather, though Duach had got a round Norse helmet from the throne room of Kull's castle. His shield was new and Norse, too, blazoned with a blue dragon on a deep red facing. Samaire's long-bossed buckler was painted and enameled the blue of Leinster—though it bore the angry boar of her cousin's husband Cumal. Swiftly Duach learned of her unorthodox methods, learned of Cormac mac Art who'd learned them elsewhere than in Eirrin. Duach was not prepared for the maneuver when her shield flashed out defensively. Though he back-lunged with sufficient swiftness to prevent the stoving in of his face, her buckler's outside boss tore his cheek.

After that they fought as intelligent weapon-men fight who respect each other, not in a mad flurry of cuts and lunges but with much watchful movement that erupted from time to time into a sudden clangorous exchange.

The two hounds of Cormac were young, exuberant, and *skillful*. This Lugh learned, though it was his last knowledge gained in this life. The flashing brand of golden-haired Ros tore through mail and flesh and bone and the horrified Lugh stared down at his right arm. It flopped to the sand, spraying scarlet as did its stump. Then the archer only gurgled as Ros slashed away half his face and more.

Without so much as a pause in elation, Ros whirled, another instinctive weapon-man. It was at Wulfhere's rear he moved. Osbrit and Findbar kept the big red-beard passing busy; he was an easy target.

"STOP AND TURN!"

At that challenging roar Ros froze for an instant, in his youth. Then he spun. The youth found with a blink that he faced Bas the Druid, who had already appropriated Lugh's sword from the archer's severed hand.

"Ye'd slay from behind, *Boy;* I'd not!" And Bas attacked as though he'd borne arms all his days.

"Druid—I—" Ros blocked a fierce cut that dented his shield's iron rim and buckled the wood so that it crackled and bulged outward. The young man's pale eyes again mirrored confusion and agony, and he backed. To launch death-bringing blows at a druid. . . .

"Break it, Ros mac Dairb!" Bas bade him sharply. "Break the hold of Thulsa Doom, who is evil incarnate! Fight me not, Ros mac Dairb—it's a druid of your own people ye face with naked steel in hand!"

Perhaps Findbar heard and perhaps it was but unfortunate coincidence. Again he bellowed out the name of each of his followers, shouted after each name the single word: "Kill!"

And Ros, jerking his head as if arousing from slumber, attacked the druid of his people.

Eyes glinted with the bright madness of slaughter-lust and swords and axes flashed in the sun like silver lightning. Already the sand looked as if torn by a passing horde of galloping horses. Helmets and armour and blades, ever amove, sent back bursts of light at the fire of Behl on its ascent into the heavens. Like a carrion-eating beast the shade of death stalked grimly among the stamping slashing combatants in that horrid battle among comrades and countrymen.

The shade of death, stalked, chose. . . .

Its icy hand fell on Ruadan mac Mogcorf. With an awful cry he fell, his thigh chopped more than half through by Brian's downward-curving backstroke. Brian gave him no death-stroke but lunged away from Laig's ferocious chopping slash. Too shocked to do aught for himself, Ruadan lay shuddering while he bled to death.

Samaire was prey to a similar stroke from Duach's brand. But she had been twisting away, and his steel failed to open her leather-clad leg. She felt as if struck with a battering-ram nonetheless, and fell. A-wallow on the sand, she gritted her teeth and strained to keep her eyes open. Pain was like a dark cloud striving to fall over her brain.

At almost the same instant, a few feet away, Wulfhere's rushing ax was not even slowed by a thick Briton neck. Osbrit's head went flying twenty feet on a wake of scarlet. Spatters fell on Samaire and Duach, who was chopping down at her. She rolled with a desperate speed she could not have matched outside the superhuman stimulus of combat and life-saving desperation. Duach's sword actually scraped the boiled leather at her shoulder on its downward rush. The blade buried itself in the beach with a crunching of sand on steel.

Like an animal, Samaire was scoot-boosting herself to her feet and then running headlong to stay on them, despite her limp and the screaming of her leg. Wrenching his shining glaive from the sand, Duach rushed after her.

She turned as he made his thrusting charge. Even as her leg failed her and she tilted crazily sideways, the fugitive princess caught his rushing point on a moving shield. Wideswept, the buckler sent the swordblade and Duach's left arm with it swinging wide of his body. Immediately and desperately he covered with a crossing-over buckler—and Samaire chopped into his right side.

She fell to her knees then, watching the young man's sky-coloured eyes go enormously wide, watching him gasp and stagger, seeing the appearance of blood at the lips of an inches-deep wound at his belt line. His sword dropped and he clamped that hand to the wound, half-turning—but her following stroke was already in motion.

Grimly, teeth clenched, she chopped again from her kneeling posture. Her edge clove through leather and flesh and then bone, in almost precisely the same area in Duach's left side. Come far from Slieve Cuilinn in quest of adventure and spoils, Duach Laig's son of Airgailla became a twinned fountain of blood. He fell, dying as his life's blood rushed from him—slain by a woman of Leinster.

In horror Samaire turned her face from that former shipmate. But yesterday they had heaved side by side at the ship. . . .

She looked among the others just as Wulfhere booted Findbar so violently under the front of his tunic that both the man's feet left the ground. And a triumphant Wulfhere nearly died then, for incredibly Findbar caught his balance and seemed unharmed by what should have dropped him with his mouth wide in a soundless scream. Not only that, he slashed, and the astounded Dane had to hurl himself sidewise and full length to avoid the opening of his neck.

Samaire saw him sprawl, saw him roll and flounder away, saw him bash aside Findbar's next sally, saw the Dane rise unharmed and back a bit while he recollected his shock-scattered wits. A lunatic cry caused Samaire to jerk her eyes to stare elsewhere.

With the Pictish battle scream Cormac put his entire body behind a shield-lunge. His and Cet's bucklers were in line; the Gael struck the other's with such force that Cet's brawny arm was smashed back into his face. Blood spurted from his nose, hot on his arm. He was given no time to reflect on his destroyed nose; Cormac thrust the big Meathish ax-man through the belly and was looking about him ere he'd given his blade a twist and yanked it free.

Seeing that ugly wolfish grin contort Cormac's scarred face, Samaire followed his gaze with her own. Both Brian's blood-streaming sword and Laig's head were still in the air. For a moment Laig's body stood quivering, and then the crimson jet erupted from the stump between his shoulders. Jerking as though in some horrid dance of the dead, the body fell into its own blood.

With others stilled, Wulfhere and Findbar circling, the sound of a single encounter rose loudly now.

Brian and Samaire and Cormac looked in the direction of that constant sound of hammer and hack. They saw Bas well up the beach, backing and backing, his sword not in use as he could only defend against the incessant fierce battering of young Ros of Dun Dalgan.

A thought that was not rational and the more horrible under the circumstances jolted through Cormac mac Art's weapon-man's brain: *Och, what a beautiful young fighter he is! The magnificent berserker rage has come on him, and him not even one of mine!*

He charged after druid and youthful warrior, roaring out a new cry in hopes of disconcerting the fiercely hacking Ros.

But the other hound of Cormac was there before him.

"Ros! Friend, sword-comrade—STOP this!"

Ros turned on Brian. Aye, there was the madness in his eyes, though a deep torment seemed too to haunt them. Brian na Killevy could not believe, as Cormac could not believe Wulfhere's attack that afternoon on the "Roof of the World", and it nigh cost him his life. Only a reflexive interposing of his sword saved his entrails from Ros's blade-edge. With a screeching ear-torturing crang of steel on steel, Brian's brand went flying from his hand.

Samaire noted that Ros did not grin in triumph. Later she told the others; there was no victor's joy on the one youth's face as he moved confidently to put death on the other.

He was over-confident. A man at death's-point would either freeze, or accept, or scream and run, or adopt the role of beleaguered wolf—and weapon-man—and do all in his power to avoid doom and destroy its bringer. Brian I-love-to-fight, Cormac saw then, was not only a good man, a born weapon-man, but a wolfish Cormac as well.

Viciously and desperately his shield whipped back and forth in a blurring wall of defense that kept Ros's sword at bay. And Brian braced his left leg, and with the force of rushing adrenalin he kicked his former friend in the calf.

The leg buckled. Ros fell.

"Brian!" he gasped. Staring up, his eyes went bright as though he'd awoken. "Br—got to wake Brian! The wiz—"

Then Brian's shield-edge smashed down on his nose and drove splintered shards of bone into his brain.

Brian knelt aside the dead man with whom he had found and felt such camaraderie. In his eyes now was the same torment and confusion that had been in Ros's just before he died.

"Damn you, Ros," he choked, "you could have bested me!" The pitiful cry was an anguished accusation.

Brian and Bas missed what Cormac saw, then.

With one of those full-circle swings of his terrible ax, Wulfhere took off the head of Findbar of Meath with such perfection that Findbar might have been a stuffed dummy positioned for the stroke. The head, eyes and mouth gaping, rolled on the sand with a grating of its helmet. And . . . like a stuffed dummy . . . no blood spurted up from the headless shoulders.

Wulfhere was struck motionless in renewed shock at a foeman who fought on after a crotch-kick that should have ruined him forever, and who now bled not from the loss of his head. In those instants of the Dane's frozen staring, the arm of the headless man swung. Edge of sword met the rounded side of steel helmet with a great crashing clang. So great was the force of that blow that Wulfhere fell sidewise without a grunt.

The corpse-strewn beach was suddenly horribly silent.

A moment the headless man stood over the fallen Wulfhere Hausakliufr. Then a death's-head *appeared* on the shoulders of Findbar, and his body changed, and he stood there in a night-dark robe already rent by sword and arrow. Dark eyesockets gleamed in their depths like rubies and Findbar's sword whipped high in a fist suddenly become mere skin stretched over knobby bones.

The silence that had closed like a death-shroud over the strand so long chaotically alive with the shouts and clangor of combat was split, seconds after it fell. For the third time that bloody morning the ghastly shrieking cry of a charging Pict clove the air and ululated. The skull of Thulsa Doom jerked sidewise and up, and he was only just able to meet the mad sword-rushing charge of Cormac mac Art.

Blade rang on shield anew. But it had been long and long since Thulsa Doom had entered sword-wielding combat; long and long since he and a sorcerous sword had been able to hold off a weakening King Kull for hours.

Three violently slashing strokes bent his shield, split his shield, and then tore it from his arm. The fourth slash Cormac turned into the thrust that he favoured. The long blade of his sword drove into Thulsa Doom as it had that other time, widening the same tear in the robe.

Once again Cormac bore his sorcerous foe back and down, and held him spitted.

The impaled mage groaned, writhed—and struck with his sword. That cut Cormac met with his shield, so that its edge drove into a bony wrist. The fingers flexed open; the sword dropped. Cormac leaned on his own pommel while he shook off his buckler.

"BRIAN! I NEEEED YE!"

Behind him Wulfhere moaned; a score and more feet away Samaire got to her feet. Her face twisting in pain, she began hobbling toward him. Thulsa Doom writhed like a gaffed eel on the impaling sword. Hands cold as a serpent's hide closed on Cormac's wrists. He grunted, pressed down. The hilt of his brand ground into the mage's abdomen. The blade was buried in the beach beneath Thulsa Doom, and Cormac feared the impermanent lack of solidity of sand.

Samaire was staggering laboriously toward him, and he durst not glance back to see if Brian had recovered from his horrified, self-blaming reverie. Then there were crunching footsteps, and Bas was there.

"My buckler, Bas! Lay it there beside him, boss up!"

Bas did as he was bade, without a word. The buckler formed an overturned bowl beside Thulsa Doom, the iron boss gleaming. Cormac's flesh twitched and raised the million excrescences of horripilation as he thought on the ghastly plan he had devised.

"The blade hurts him and is cold to him," he grunted through his teeth. "Nor can he vanish or escape whilst he be—uh!—impaled thus!" The mage's hands were seeking to break his wrist, and those hands were *strong*. "I dare not let go this sword with either hand—one cannot hold against his sorcerous strength. Here, Bas—LEAN on this brand!"

Almost, while Bas and Cormac exchanged hands on the pommel, Thulsa Doom escaped, for he writhed and strove and his strength was far more than normal. But the maneuver was effected—though Bas gasped in horror when the mage's face took on the likeness of the Princess of Leinster.

"Bas! Bas! Oh Druid it *hurts . . . please . . .*"

Cormac had risen to stand over the hideous

tableau of druid kneeling over Samaire, pinning her
to the earth on the point of a sword.

"Obscene monster, we can both *see* Samaire, but
paces away!" And Cormac entered into what seemed
ghoulish madness.

Motion followed swift motion as he seized Bas by
the shoulders. By main force he tumbled the druid
backward onto the sands. The sword came partway
forth, and Samaire became Thulsa Doom once more
as the real Samaire reached them. Cormac was still in
swift action, executing his desperate plan with as
much speed as ever he'd shown in his life. He drew his
sword free; it emerged easily. Ere Thulsa Doom could
take advantage of his instant of freedom, the vengeful
Gael turned him over—on the buckler with its upstanding metal boss, fist thick, over three inches long,
and not-quite pointed.

Without pause Cormac's right fist leaped up and
rushed down like a hammer. Thulsa Doom emitted a
hideous groan and shuddered when he was struck on
the back just above the waist and the metal boss
drove into his belly.

With both hands and all his might Cormac mac
Art drove his sword into the mage's back, through his
body, and into the shield.

On her knees, Samaire faced him across the spitted
body. "Gods," she murmured, and shivered.

The writhing form of the wizard strove to break the
impaling prison. Like claws his hands tore at the
sand. Suddenly he changed again, into a whipping
lunging serpent, but still he could not break free.
Again he resumed man-shape, and put back his
hands in an attempt to tear the blade free of his back.

"My next shield," Cormac muttered, "will have a
sharpened boss!" He grunted the words with exertion;
with the flat of Wulfhere's ax he struck his sword's
upstanding pommel. The sword seemed to shorten as
its tip drove farther into the buckler. No splintering

sound came; the shield held. Again, Cormac struck.

Wulfhere sat up, touching the small trickle of blood that ran down from under the helmet that had skinned his head, even with its shaggy mop of hair, before the unnatural force of Thulsa Doom's blow.

"Odin and Thor and Woten and Thunor, my he— by all the gods! What are ye *about*, Wolf?"

"Carpentry."

Cormac stood over the wizard who was helplessly impaled, face down, betwixt sword-hilt and stout shield. Bas and Samaire, the one sitting dazedly as Wulfhere and the other on one knee, stared at the constantly moaning, twisting mage.

"Making fast one who cannot be slain," Cormac said in a sepulchral voice. "Thulsa Doom: You are my prisoner!"

Chapter Nineteen:
Doom-heim

"In times more ancient than we count," Bas said, "an exile from Atlantis found employment as weapon-man in a land called Valusia. Time came when he made challenge to the king, and brought defeat and death on him, and the Atlantean was king over Valusia. His name was Kull. Trusted counsellor to him was a man named Tu; just that: Tu. I am . . . I was Tu, as I have been others since, in the endless cycle of birth and death and rebirth. And Cormac, who has been others as well, is and was Kull."

Wulfhere Skullsplitter of the Danes gave ear in silence. This talk was alien to that which he had been taught, but others of the beliefs he'd held true had been shaken, more than once. *Father Odin . . . will I not dine and drink with you, but return once more in another body to live another life on this same Midgard?*

Brian, too, listened, and Samaire. She believed. She *knew;* certainty was upon her that she had known Cormac mac Art in a life lived out before this one. Though actual memory was not there, knowledge was. She had not been attracted instantly to him; she had *recognized* him, as did others who liked or loved at first sight. Whether she had been of Atlantis or

211

Valusia or indeed had known *of* Kull or no, she did not know. It mattered not; afore now she had known the life-force that had been Kull, and Conan, and Cormac, and others. The when of it was of no import. Now was important. This time, and the time to come. Nor did she assume there had been or would be ease; this life-force to which hers was connected throughout time was a volatile one.

Cormac was most likely Cuchulain himself, Brian mac Dairb thought, and was glad and proud.

"A great enemy and plotter against King Kull," Bas who had been Tu went on, "was Thulsa Doom. In no less than four several plots did Kull foil the wizard and put defeat on him, though in each wise Thulsa Doom prevailed for a time. On two occasions did the king like to lose his life to this unrelenting enemy. And eventually Kull and Tu and a mage on Kull's behalf won the final victory—on the isle where we're just after being."

At those reminding words all looked back to where Samaire-heim was receding behind their ship—very slowly, in the gentlest and most unsteady of little breezes.

There were but five of them, and their captive, and *Quester* was both large and well-laden. Not for them was the using of oars. Cormac and Wulfhere did give constant attention to sail and rudder. Bas had promised better winds; they had learned to listen to Bas, and to believe.

The druid spoke on.

"There Thulsa Doom was left, trapped by sorcerous bonds; the bondage of a body without hands or feet or voice. There he existed for eighteen thousand years. Then those forces that control such matters brought Thulsa Doom's ancient enemy himself to the isle, and another too; Cutha Atheldane from Norge. It fell out that Cormac himself proved the instrument of the wizard's release, for it was you slew the serpent, son of Art. Thus was liberated the wizard's life force—and in time he found a home in the body of Cutha Atheldane. With his powers he replaced it with one like his own, of old, though it's Cutha Atheldane's robe he wears yet. It was on him then to remain yet, for there was no means of leaving the island."

"Doom-heim," Wulfhere muttered, for all had been happy to rename the isle that had eaten so many men.

"He used that time of his further incarceration," Bas the Druid said, "to practice his dark arts, and raised the dead as his legion. All else we know."

"Vengeance over eighteen thousand years!" Brian said in a voice quieted by awe.

"Was all that sustained him," Bas said, with a glance at the wizard. *Though it made or kept him less than sane,* he mused, while that hideous travesty of a face clashed its lipless teeth in fury.

"And the vanishing?" Samaire asked. "Those several times he vanished whilst we laboured to place the dead aboard *Amber Rowan,* when we saw only the buckler impaled by Cormac's sword, and the mage both there and not there?"

Laden with their dead, *Amber Rowan* wallowed behind them, slowing them the more.

"Of old," Bas made reply, "Thulsa Doom effected escape into another dimension, a sort of world parallel to this and not unlike it and yet *different.* There he is invisible to eyes from this world of ours. That explains his disappearings; he sought similar escape from us. But his body holds him. Sword and shield held him fast, pinioned between them in the *only* way he can be held. Was Cormac saw the key to this, when he pinned him that morn in the corridor beneath the castle of Kull."

"He will . . . attempt again?" Brian asked.

"Yessss," Thulsa Doom hissed in rage, and he vanished from *Quester.*

"He be still here," Cormac said grimly.

"During the night he somehow gained control of Findbar," Samaire began, after their awestruck silence and Cormac's words of certainty. But Bas shook his head.

"Nay. He *was* Findbar. Rather he was not; he slew Findbar and assumed his form. Mayhap Findbar rose to fare outside for a natural reason—and such was his mental state by then he paid no mind to our one overweening rule. Or flaunted it."

"He paid," Wulfhere said in a rumble.

"Aye. Then did he return—but he was Findbar mac Lirchain no more. One by one, he gained control of the minds of the others—"

"Why not us? Brian demanded.

"Mayhap only we were too determined of purpose," the druid said.

"Too staunch," Cormac mac Art said.

"Too loyal to yourself," Samaire said, looking at him.

Cormac glanced at Brian, and he thought of Lugh, who had been loyal, and who had been of them, and who was dead for his determination and staunchness and loyalty. Brian's face had gone dour again, and none doubted but that his thoughts were again on Ros. Brian, Cormac reflected without pride or comfort, was young; he'd not experienced the loss of friends and comrades-at-arms again and again. It never became commonplace and easy; that it was now so readily bearable, Cormac thought, bespoke the existence of as many inner scars as he bore on his body.

"Bas," he said, "what have ye done? What know ye now that we must needs know?" He glanced aside; Thulsa Doom was there once more, and the eye-spots in the deeply cratered sockets glowed rage-red.

"I was able to protect us all during our waking hours. And *Quester* and all aboard, for it's of Eirrin this ship is, and my powers are strongest on our own soil and with those that were born there—human or no. And . . . there are other things. Let me keep their knowledge; the telling ye of them will avail ye naught and may weaken me—and empower *him*."

They looked at the undying wizard.

The ship wallowed slowly along, towing *Amber Rowan* seaward from the isle of horror and death. Aboard sat its pitifully tiny crew; a druid, a weapon-woman, and three weapon-men—one of them but little past his first beard-growth. The woman suffered of a thigh bearing a large and lurid bruise.

These were *Quester's* crew. *Quester* carried but one passenger.

He stood helpless where Cormac had forced and imprisoned him in ghastly impalement, for only so could Thulsa Doom be held. The picture he presented was monstrous and horrible. The owner of any eyes not cognizant of the situation or of Thulsa Doom's powers and nature would have been shocked at the seeming cruelty of his captors.

As Wulfhere had done southward from Britain, the mage stood against the thick mast. He was bound there, but not with ropes. Cords could not hold a man not alive and who could assume the form of a slithering serpent; nor could leather or chains of iron or steel. Two sword-pommels stood out from the erect body of the wizard. Thulsa Doom was held in the only way he could be held; impaled and pinned to the motionless and unmovable. The swords nailed him to the mast.

No blood flowed.

"I will tell ye of what I read on those castle walls," Bas said, and their gazes returned to him, leaving the wizard's dreadful aspect and plight with more than willingness.

"Those pictures *did* speak, then!" Wulfhere glanced at Cormac, remembering how when first they'd come here the Gael had gone to those walls as if preternaturally drawn. Cormac had stared at them long, and his eerie *remembering* had come upon him.

"Aye, the pictures and certain markings. Runes. Some of what I learned I will tell you of . . . later. But this—this I shall enjoy speaking in *his* presence, that he will know we know the means of destroying him. For it is only vengeful and hateful I feel toward ye, Thulsa Doom, who exist only in vengefulness and hate. The wall told of how ye may be slain *again*, Skull-face, and *permanently!*"

The death's-head mage snarled like an animal, and the teeth of that dread faceless skull clashed and ground in frustration and overweening hatred.

"That skull," Bas said, staring not at his companions but at Thulsa Doom, "severed and wrapped in good leather, must be put into the hands of a crowned woman. She—"

Thulsa Doom writhed and strained and gnashed his teeth with a clack and clash. The ship was suddenly amove, rocking with much noise of slapping sloshing waters. Such was the fury-heightened strength of the sorcerer from the past. Another sound came from him, a hiss—and an enormous serpent replaced him at the mast. It sought to writhe and whip and tear itself free of the impaling swords. Cormac came hurriedly to his feet, pulling steel partway out of scabbard. But the reptile was no more able to escape those bonds like gigantic nails than the man-shape. That form the mage resumed.

Again, Thulsa Doom disappeared.

"It is strange," Brian said, and there was a quaver in his voice he sought to conceal. "In such a short while have I learned to accept the impossible; I do not even gooseflesh now at his vanishing!"

The boat lurched so wildly that Samaire slid along the rowing-deck and groaned at the leap of pain in her leg. Cormac staggered. Water splashed high. The Gael looked about. There was no wind.

"He is not gone from us," Bas the Druid said.

"A crowned *woman,* though," Wulfhere said. "Of what value be that—no such exists!"

Bas made a gesture. "Perhaps such does, or will. Meanwhile, we know how to hold him against the day we find her—or until I devise another means."

"More sorcery," Brian said, little above a whisper.

Bas only looked upon him with coolly wide grey eyes. "Will ye hear the rest?"

"We will," Cormac said.

Samaire added, "Please."

"This crowned woman must then pound the skull into dust, with a hammer of iron."

"Iron?"

"Aye, so I believe the ancient picture-writing tells us. Mayhap there was no steel in the days of Atlantis."

Cormac's face was grim and hopeful. "But—a crowned *woman!* Where rules a woman?"

"Nowhere," Samaire said, with a sigh. Her face went reflective.

"Then—"

"Then," Bas began. But he gave pause at a renewed turmoil. Their craft rocked violently. When it abated, eyes were fearful and knuckles white from gripping handholds as though to keep from being hurled off the ridge of the world.

Bas began anew, "Then we must keep him our prisoner, as our duty to all humankind, for dead Thulsa Doom cannot otherwise be slain."

As they sat in tight-lipped silence, the ship on that calm sea rocked as though gale-struck. Then it was still, and Thulsa Doom reappeared, helpless at the mast.

"Dam-m-mnnnye!" he ground out.

The eyes of Bas were very bright and wide, and he looked skyward. His fingers fingered the symbols of his gods and their powers, which were those of na-

ture. The others felt that he wrestled now with Thulsa
Doom, whose powers were of else than nature.

Then Samaire was calling out. "There was a little
island—there! It—it's gone!"

Her companions looked about, and in a babble of
voices they agreed that she was right. The sea had
changed; the world had changed. Bas turned from
them, paced in his woods-green robe to the wizard.

"May ye be damned! It's again and again ye've
tried, tried amain, and it's both failure and success
ye've grasped, isn't it? Ye did break through into
your other dimension—but ye've brought us with ye,
into a different world!"

If you enjoyed THE UNDYING WIZARD, here's a small sampling from another swashbuckling tale of heroic fantasy that we think you'll like as well: THE SIGN OF THE MOONBOW by Andrew J. Offutt. THE SIGN OF THE MOONBOW is a sequel to THE UNDYING WIZARD, and is available from Ace Science Fiction.

THE SIGN OF THE MOONBOW
by Andrew J. Offutt

Prologue

A cadaverously thin man stood close against the ship's mast, his back to it. His robe flapped in the breeze that drove the one-sailed craft across the sea that lapped south and east of Britain. Night-dark was that robe; tall was its wearer. He was bound in place, though not with ropes. Cords could not hold such a one able to assume slithering forms other than his own. Nor could he be prisoned with leather, or with chains of iron or steel.

Two sword pommels stood out from his chest and abdomen. He was held fast in the only way he could be held: impaled and pinned to the mast, motionless and unmovable. The swords nailed him to the mast.

No blood flowed.

He writhed, snarling.

It was not from lips those snarls emerged, for the doubly impaled man had no lips. Nor mouth, nor face he had; there was neither cartilage nor skin nor hair on the shining, grey-white skull that was his head. Yet within the shadowed holes that had been eye sockets, red lights burned, more like hellish and ever-maleficent flames than eyes. He writhed, and snarling sounds emerged from his lipless mouth.

He saw; he felt; he complained of cold, but not of pain.

He was neither alive nor dead. Dead, he lived. Yet he could not be slain, for he was not truly alive. Undead he had been for eighteen thousand years, escaping all the means that had slain so many others, the countless deaths he had personally wrought and callously caused. He could only be held—and only by this ghastly means.

The skewered man in the dark robe rode the foremost of two ships that slid over little known seas.

Each could loft a single sail, though the gentle breeze filled only the sail of the first. Each was constructed of overlapping planking in the clinker style. Each could ship over thirty oars, though neither did. Neither had as many as twenty aboard to man her oars, nor even ten. Many men lay dead in their dual wake, all victims of the power and machinations of the baneful captive with the skull for a face.

The second ship was without crew at all. All those who had sailed her hence down from Britain were dead; all she had borne out to sea now provided food for the plants and creatures on its floor. Unmanned, bearing the name *Amber Rowan* along her blue-painted side, she wallowed along at the end of thick plaited cables of rope, doubled and tripled. Her greyed sail was furled against a sudden change in the light breeze, whether of direction or force.

The towing ship was heavy laden, though it bore six persons—and one of those was the repugnant creature nailed to her mast. Not for so few was the using of oars. Green-streaked *Quester* was no merchant vessel, but bore considerable cargo.

The fine fabrics and the gold, the silver and jewellery of precious stones, the arms and armour and wrapped personal possessions of some twenty men were not trade goods.

All had been stolen—if aught could be called stolen that had been paid for in the scarlet coin of so many lives. The cargo had been the booty of murdering

Norse reavers, all four months dead; it had been sought by three-and-twenty Britons, all dead over a fortnight. The cargo had been taken from the Norse pirates' cache, and that on a tiny isle where stood a castle raised by men dead these hundred and eighty centuries.

The undead man was of long-sunken Atlantis. The survivors and possessors of the rich plunder, his captors, were four of the Eirrin-born and one of the land they called Loch-linn, home of the Danes, Danemark.

The Dane was a giant, red of hair and bushy unkempt beard, huge of chest and broad of shoulder. His arms were the size of the thighs of other men. He lounged at the tiller, his ax, shield, and coat of scale-mail nearby. Little effort was required of him. The sun was bright, the breeze steady and not swift, the ship slowed by the similar long boat she towed. When the sun was lower, he would use the sun-stick to check their course. By day, there was no other means.

One man was speaking. Like the fell writhing captive he was robed, though in the green of nature, and girt with a length of rope. A lunula hung on his chest, a half-moon of gold that returned the sun's light in dull flashes. Above, more closely fitting, he wore the twisted necklet of the Celts, a torc. He it was who had promised fair skies and good winds. His companions had learned to believe this servant of Behl and Crom, and to believe.

"In times more ancient than we count," the green-robed druid told the others, "an exile from Atlantis found employment as weapon-man in a land called Valusia. Time came when he made challenge to the king, and brought defeat and death on him, and the Atlantean was king over Valusia. His name was Kull. Trusted counsellor to him was a man named Tu. Just that: Tu. I am . . . I was Tu, as I have been others since, in the endless cycle of birth and death and re-

birth. And you, Cormac, who have been others as
well, are and were Kull. For it is all the same, Celt
and Keltoi and the Keltii of the Romans; Kull and
Cormac, Cull and Kormak."

The others looked at the man the druid addressed
as Cormac.

Dark of hair and skin he was, like the druid, and
with the same grey eyes though the druid's held more
blue; both men were Gaels, of Eirrin. A life fraught
with hacking swords and venomously whining arrows
and rushing battle axes had left scars that, with his
narrowed deepset eyes, imparted a rather sinister
aspect to the face of the man called Cormac. Yet he
was loved by four of the six aboard, including the
woman, and hated by one—the captive.

"I . . . remember," Cormac said.

The Dane frowned, giving ear in silence. Their talk
was alien to that which he had been taught, but others among the beliefs he'd held true had been shaken
in this company, more than once. *Father Odin . . . will
I not dine and drink with you, but return once more in
another body to live another life on this same Midgard?*
The redbeard looked not happy; one-eyed Allfather
Odin made no reply.

"A great enemy and plotter against King Kull,"
the druid said who had been Tu of Valusia, "was the
mage and master of illusion, *Thulsa Doom*. In no less
than four plots did Kull foil the wizard and put defeat
on him, though in each wise Thulsa Doom prevailed
for a time. On two occasions did the king like to lose
his life to this unrelenting enemy. And eventually
Kull and Tu and a mage on Kull's behalf won the
final victory—on the isle where we're just after
being."

The others glanced back. But the isle of sorcery-
wrought dread and evil, that isle of Kull's sorcerously
preserved castle, was long since left behind and lost to
sight. Hours ago they had consigned to the sea the

comrades they had lost to death there, of the power and plottings of their captive and the iresome illusions he created.

"There Thulsa Doom was left," the druid said, "trapped by sorcerous bonds; the bondage of a body without hands or feet or voice."

"The serpent Cormac slew!" the Dane rumbled. "Four months agone that was, when he and I rescued Samaire from the Norsemen."

Redbearded Dane looked at the red-maned woman he called Samaire. She was in her second decade of life and wore strange tall boots of black leather that rose up her thighs to vanish under her folded tunic. Her long hair gleamed orange and gold in the sunlight.

"And the vanishing?" she asked, this Samaire. "Those several times Thulsa Doom vanished, Bas, whilst we laboured to load our ships, and his disappearing even when impaled?"

"And returned, still impaled," the youngest aboard said, and he glanced at the undying wizard. The youth sat on a rowing bench, near Cormac. His hair was very fair.

"Of old," Bas the Druid made reply, "Thulsa Doom effected escape into another dimension, a sort of world parallel to ours and not unlike it—and yet *different*. There he is invisible to eyes from this world of ours. Frown on; I can explain no better. This explains his disappearings. He seeks similar escape from us. But his body holds him. Sword driven through him into shield held him ashore, pinioned in the only way he can be held. Even then he took my form, and yours Samaire, and that of a serpent—and aye, he sought escape by disappearing. Was Cormac saw the key to this, holding captive even Thulsa Doom, and thus we must keep him pinned still."

"Forever, if need be," the other Gael muttered.

"He will . . . attempt again?" This from the young

man, a youthful weapon-man with flaxen hair and pale eyes.

"Yesssssss," Thulsa Doom hissed in rage, and he vanished from *Quester*.

"He be still here," Cormac son of Art said grimly.

Awestruck silence cloaked the little ship, despite Cormac's words of certainty. The vanished wizard could assume the form of any man he had seen—or woman, as Cormac had learned in a night of horror on the island they'd quitted. Too, they had learned in manner dismaying that he could gain control of the very minds of some, so that they dully carried out his will. Yet none of those now aboard *Quester* had succumbed, though they'd been forced to slay their former companions—which was why only these five survived.

And why had none of them fallen under the illusionist's mind-control, neither Bas the Druid nor Wulfhere the Dane nor Samaire Ceannselaigh nor Brian na Killevy whom Cormac called I-love-to-fight?

"Mayhap we were too determined of purpose," Bas said.

"Too staunch," Cormac suggested.

"Too loyal to yourself," Samaire said.

Young Brian nodded, for he adulated the tall and rangy Gael who had been a noble of Connacht in Eirrin, and weapon-man for the King of Leinster though not of age, and then of the King of Dal Riada in Alba when he was exiled from Eirrin's shores, and then riever or reaver: pirate, and then Champion of Eirrin welcomed home by the High-king on Tara Hill and then captain of this expedition on behalf of Samaire and her royal brother; finally it was Cormac mac Art who had somehow conquered the unconquerable, slain again the dead men raised by Thulsa Doom—and at last he had conquered the undying wizard himself.

Brian I-love-to-fight saw Cormac as the man he hoped to emulate though knew he could never equal; Cormac mac Art saw Brian as the youth he had been, before the years had laced him, body and mind, with so many scars. Brian of Killevy was glad and proud to know the man and be in his company, for surely Art's son of Connacht had been Eirrin's great hero of old, the legendary Cuchulain himself of Muirthemne.

Samaire looked asea and pensiveness was on her. Loyal, she had said, but it was more.

Though it was companion she called herself, and weapon-companion to Cormac mac Art she was, she loved the man. Too, she *knew* that the words of Bas were true. Sureness was upon her that she had known Cormac in a life or lives lived out before this one. Though actual memory was not there, certain knowledge was.

Cormac glanced up at the mast. Thulsa Doom was there once more, and the eye-spots in the deeply cratered sockets glowed rage-red. Almost, Cormac smiled. Then he directed his gaze at Bas.

"Bas—what have you done? We've seen your powers prevail over his, in the matter of the wind and clouds. What know ye now that we must needs know?"

Bas's black hair blew in the salted breeze. "I was able to protect us all during our waking hours. And *Quester* and all aboard, despite Thulsa Doom's wizardry. For it's of Eirrin this ship is, and my own powers are strongest on our own soil and with those that were born there, human or no. And . . . there are other things. Let me keep that knowledge. The telling of them will avail ye naught and may weaken me— and empower *him*."

They looked at the death's-head apparition at the mast.

He writhed, snarling.

He did not bleed.

"I will tell ye what I read on the walls of the castle of Kull," Bas the Druid said, and the gazes of his companions returned to him, leaving the wizard's dreadful aspect and plight with more than willingness.

"Those pictures *did* speak, then!" Wulfhere glanced at his longtime weapon-companion and fellow reaver, for Cormac had stared at those thrice-ancient walls as though preternaturally held fast by them. It was then the Gael's *remembering* had come upon him. From time to time, confused and fearful until Bas had made explanation, Cormac mac Art *remembered* events of long, long, incredibly long before his birth.

Before his birth this time, the huge Dane mused, for how could he disbelieve the endless cycle of return, of death and rebirth, in which the sons of Eirrin held belief? Were not they living evidence of that theory alien to the adherents of Odin/Woden and Thor/Thunor?

Aye, and Wulfhere Hausakluifr gave listen to the servant of Behl and Crom of Eirrin. With a great sigh that expanded his chest a prodigious number of inches, the Dane slid a horny fingernail up into his beard. Listening, pondering, Wulfhere scratched at the crust left by sea-breeze and salt spray.

"I read the pictures on the walls," the druid said, "and certain markings. Runes. Some of what I learned I will tell you of, later. But this—this I shall enjoy speaking in *his* presence, that *he* will know we know the means of destroying him. For it's only vengeful and hate-filled I am toward you, Thulsa Doom, who exist only in vengefulness and hate. The wall told of how ye may be slain *again*, Skullface, and permanently."

The death's-head mage snarled like a predatory beast. The teeth of that faceless, skinless skull clashed and ground in frustration and overweening hatred.

"That skull," Bas said, staring not at his companions but at Thulsa Doom, "severed and wrapped in good leather, must be put into the hands of a crowned woman. She—"

Thulsa Doom writhed and strained and gnashed his teeth with a clack and clash. The ship was suddenly amove, rocking with much noise of slapping sloshing water. Yet the wind had not risen. Such was the fury-heightened strength of the sorcerer from the past. Another sound came from him, a hiss—and an enormous serpent replaced him at the mast.

The reptile sought to writhe and whip and tear itself free of the impaling swords. Cormac came hurriedly to his feet, pulling steel partway from scabbard. But the snake was no more able to escape those bonds like gigantic nails than the man-shape. That form the mage resumed—

And again, Thulsa Doom disappeared.

"It is strange," Brian said, and there was a quaver in his voice he sought to conceal. "In such a short while have I learned to accept the impossible. I do not even gooseflesh now at his vanishing."

The boat lurched so wildly that Samaire slid along the rowing-deck and groaned at the leap of pain in one bruised leg. Cormac staggered. Water splashed high and white. The Gael looked about. The other ship was placid, stirred only by *Quester's* bucking; there was no wind and the sea lapped softly.

"He is not gone from us," Bas the Druid said.

"A crowned *woman*, though," Wulfhere said. "Of what value be that information—no such exists!"

"More sorcery," Brian said, little above a whisper.

Bas only looked upon the youth with coolly wide grey eyes. "Will ye hear the rest?"

"We will," Cormac said.

Samaire added, "Please."

"This crowned woman must then pound the skull into dust, with a hammer of iron."

"Iron?"

"Aye, so I believe the ancient picture-writings tell us. Mayhap there was no steel in the days of Atlantis."

Cormac's face was grim and not hopeful. "But—a crowned *woman!* Where rules a woman?"

"Nowhere," Samaire said, with a sigh. Her face went reflective.

"Then—"

"Then—" Bas began.

He gave pause at renewed turmoil. Their craft rocked violently. Water spumed high. The sky seemed to shimmer. When all abated, eyes were fearful and knuckles white from gripping handholds as though to keep from being hurled off the ridge of the world.

Bas commenced anew. "Then we must keep our prisoner, as our duty to all humankind, for dead Thulsa Doom cannot otherwise be slain."

And he was fixedly, madly bent on horrid vengeance against Cormac mac Art—or him he had been in the distant past.

As they sat in tight-lipped silence, the ship on that calm sea rocked as though gale-struck. Groans rose as stomachs seemed to be wrenched, seemed to somersault. Then all was still but for the gentle breeze that swept *Quester* away from Kull's isle they'd named Doom-heim, toward distant Eirrin. Thulsa Doom reappeared, helpless at the mast.

"Da-a-m-m-mnnn ye!" he ground out, and he was still.

Two ships that were in truth long boats slid across the sea in a gentle breeze, bearing history and horror.

The eyes of Bas were signally bright and wide, and he looked skyward. His hands fingered the symbols of his gods and their powers, which were those of nature, like the green of his robe. The others realized that he wrestled now with Thulsa Doom, whose powers were of darkness and illusion, rather than nature and the light.

Then Samaire was calling out. "There was a rocky little island—there! It—it's gone!"

Her companions looked about, and in a babble of voices they agreed. The exiled princess of Leinster was right. The sea had changed; the world had changed. Bas turned from them, paced in his woods-green robe to the wizard.

"May ye be damned! It's again and again ye've tried, tried amain and it's both failure and success ye've grasped, isn't it? Ye did break through into your other dimension—but ye've brought us with ye, into a different world!"

—from THE SIGN
OF THE MOONBOW
by Andrew J. Offutt

WHY WASTE
YOUR PRECIOUS
PENNIES ON GAS OR
YOUR VALUABLE
TIME ON LINE
AT THE BOOKSTORE?

We will send you, FREE, our 28 page catalogue, filled with a wide range of Ace Science Fiction paperback titles—we've got something for every reader's pleasure.

Here's your chance to add to your personal library, with all the convenience of shopping by mail. There's no need to be without a book to enjoy—request your *free* catalogue today.

 ACE SCIENCE FICTION
P.O. Box 400, Kirkwood, N.Y. 13795   A–05

ALL TWELVE TITLES AVAILABLE FROM ACE
$2.25 EACH

- ☐ 11630 **CONAN, #1**
- ☐ 11631 **CONAN OF CIMMERIA, #2**
- ☐ 11632 **CONAN THE FREEBOOTER, #3**
- ☐ 11633 **CONAN THE WANDERER, #4**
- ☐ 11634 **CONAN THE ADVENTURER, #5**
- ☐ 11635 **CONAN THE BUCCANEER, #6**
- ☐ 11636 **CONAN THE WARRIOR, #7**
- ☐ 11637 **CONAN THE USURPER, #8**
- ☐ 11638 **CONAN THE CONQUEROR, #9**
- ☐ 11639 **CONAN THE AVENGER, #10**
- ☐ 11640 **CONAN OF AQUILONIA, #11**
- ☐ 11641 **CONAN OF THE ISLES, #12**

Available wherever paperbacks are sold or use this coupon.

ACE SCIENCE FICTION
P.O. Box 400, Kirkwood, N.Y. 13795

Please send me the titles checked above. I enclose $_____.
Include $1.00 per copy for postage and handling. Send check or
money order only. New York State residents please add sales tax.

NAME_____

ADDRESS_____

CITY_____ STATE_____ ZIP_____

A-04

WITCH WORLD SERIES

☐ 89705	**WITCH WORLD**	$1.95
☐ 87875	**WEB OF THE WITCH WORLD**	$1.95
☐ 80806	**THREE AGAINST THE WITCH WORLD**	$1.95
☐ 87323	**WARLOCK OF THE WITCH WORLD**	$2.25
☐ 77556	**SORCERESS OF THE WITCH WORLD**	$2.50
☐ 94255	**YEAR OF THE UNICORN**	$2.50
☐ 82349	**TREY OF SWORDS**	$2.25
☐ 95491	**ZARSTHOR'S BANE** (Illustrated)	$2.50